ADA[illegible] INCH

A. E. COPPARD

ZINCREAD

Published by
This edition copyright © 2024 by Zinc Read
Design and setting By Zinc Read
Email- zincread@gmail.com
ISBN-978-93-6266-785-4

CONTENTS

MARCHING TO ZION

In the great days that are gone I was walking the Journey upon its easy smiling roads and came one morning of windy spring to the side of a wood. I had but just rested to eat my crusts and suck a drink from the pool when a fat woman appeared and sat down before me. I gave her the grace of the morning.

"And how many miles is it now?" I asked of her.

"What!" said she, "you're not going the journey?"

"Sure, ma'am," said I, "I'm going, and you're going, and we're all going ... aren't we?"

"Not," said she, looking at me very archly, "not while there are well-looking young fellers sitting in the woods."

"Well, deliver me!" said I, "d'ye take me for the Angel Gabriel or the duke of the world!"

"It's not anything I'm taking you to be, young man ... give me a chew of that bread."

She came and sat beside me and took it from my hands.

"Little woman ..." I began it to her; but at that she flung the crust back in my face, laughing and choking and screaming.

"Me ... that's fat as a ewe in January!"

* * *

"Fat, woman!" says I, "you're no fat at all."

But, I declare it, she'd a bosom like a bolster. I lay on my back beside her. She was a rag of a woman. I looked up through the tree branches at the end of the shaw; they were bare, spring was late that year. The sky was that blue ... there wasn't a cloud within a million miles ... but up through the boughs it looked hard and steely like a storm sky. I took my hat from her, for she had put it on her own head, and I stood on my feet.

"Fat, ma'am!" says I ... and she looked up at me, grinning like a stuffed fox.... "Oh no, ma'am, you're slim as the queen of Egypt!"

At that she called out to another man who was passing us by, and I went to walk on with him. He had a furuncle on one side of his chin; his garments were very old, both in fashion and in use; he was lean as a mountain cow.

I greeted him but he gave me glances that were surly, like a man would be grinding scissors or setting a saw—for you never met one of that kind that didn't have the woe of the world upon him.

"How many miles is it now, sir?" I asked, very respectful then. He did not heed me. He put his hand to his ear signifying deafness. I shouted and I shouted, so you could have heard me in the four kingdoms, but I might just have been blowing in a sack for all the reason I got from him.

I went on alone and in the course of the days I fell in with many persons, stupid persons, great persons, jaunty ones. An ass passes me by, its cart burdened with a few dead sprays of larch and a log for the firing. An old man toils at the side urging the ass onwards. They give me no direction and I wonder whether I am at all like the ass, or the man, or the cart, or the log for the firing. I cannot say. There was the lad McGlosky, who had the fine hound that would even catch birds; the philosopher who had two minds; the widow with one leg; Slatterby Chough, the pugfoot man, and Grafton. I passed a little time with them all, and made poems about them that they did not like, but I was ever for walking on from them. None of them could give me a direction for the thing that was urging me except that it was "away on, away on."

Walk I did, and it was full summer when I met Monk, the fat fellow as big as two men with but the clothes of a small one squeezing the joints of him together. Would you look at the hair of him—it was light as a stook of rye; or the face of him and the neck of him—the hue of a new brick. He had the mind of a grasshopper, the strength of a dray horse, the tenderness of a bush of reeds, and was light on his limbs as a deer.

"Look ye're," he said to me; he had a stiff sort of talk, and fat thumbs like a mason that he jiggled in the corners of his pockets; "look ye're, my friend, my name is Monk."

"I am Michael Fionnguisa," said I.

"Well I never struck fist with a lad like you; your conversation is agreeable to me, you have a stride on you would beat the world for greatness."

* * *

"I could beat you," said I, "even if you wore the boots of Hercules that had wings on 'em."

"It is what I like," said he, and he made a great mess of my boasting before we were through. "Look ye're, my friend, we needn't brag our little eye-blink of the world; but take my general character and you'll find I'm better than my ... inferiors. I accomplish my ridiculous destiny without any ridiculous effort. I'm the man to go a-travelling with."

He had that stiff way of his talk, like a man lecturing on a stool, but my mercy, he'd a tongue of silk that could twist a meal out of the pantry of Jews and strange hard people; fat landladies, the wives of the street, the widows in their villas, they would feed him until he groaned, loving him for his blitheness and his tales. He could not know the meaning of want though he had never a coin in the world. Yet he did not love towns; he would walk wide-eyed through them counting the seams in the pavements. He liked most to be staring at the gallant fishes in the streams, and gasping when he saw a great one.

I met him in the hills and we were gone together. And it was not a great while before he was doing and doing, for we came and saw a man committing a crime, a grave crime to be done in a bad world leave alone a good one like this, in a very lonely lovely place. So Monk rose up and slew him, and the woman ran blushing into the woods.

I looked at Mr. Monk, and the dead man on the road, and then at Mr. Monk again.

* * *

"Well," I said, "we'd ... we'd better bury this feller."

But Monk went and sat upon a bank and wiped his neck. The other lay upon his face as if he were sniffing at the road; I could see his ear was full of blood, it slipped over the lobe drip by drip as neat as a clock would tick.

And Monk, he said: "Look ye're, my friend, there are dirtier things than dirt, and I would not like to mix this with the earth of our country."

So we slung him into an old well with a stone upon his loins.

And a time after that we saw another man committing crime, a mean crime that you might do and welcome in America or some such region, but was not fitting to be done in our country.

So Monk rose up and slew him. Awful it was to see what Monk did to him. He was a great killer and fighter; Hector himself was but a bit of a page boy to Mr. Monk.

"Shall we give him an interment?" I asked him. He stood wiping his neck—he was always wiping his neck—and Monk he said:

"Look ye're, my friend, he was a beast; a man needn't live in a sty in order to become a pig, and we won't give him an interment." So we heaved him into a slag pit among rats and ravels of iron.

And would you believe it, again we saw a man committing crime, crime indeed and a very bad crime.

There was no withstanding Monk; he rose up and slew the man as dead as the poor beast he had tortured.

"God-a-mercy!" I said to him, "it's a lot of life you're taking, Mr. Monk."

And Monk he said: "Life, Michael dear, is the thing we perish by." He had the most terrible angers and yet was kind, kind; nothing could exceed the greatness of his mind or the vigour of his limbs.

Those were the three combats of Monk, but he was changed from that out. Whenever we came to any habitations now he would not call at back doors, nor go stravaiging in yards for odd pieces to eat, but he would go gallantly into an inn and offer his payment for the things we would like. I could not understand it at all, but he was a great man and a kind.

"Where did you get that treasure?" said I to him after days of it. "Has some noble person given you a gift?"

He did not answer me so I asked him over again. "Eh!"

And Monk he said, "Oh well then, there was a lot of coin in the fob of that feller we chucked in the well."

I looked very straight at Mr. Monk, very straight at that, but I could not speak the things my mind wanted me to say, and he said very artfully: "Don't distress yourself, Michael dear, over a little contest between sense and sentiment."

"But that was the dirty man," said I.

"And why not?" said he. "If his deed was dirty, his money was clean: don't be deethery, man."

"'Tis not fitting nor honourable," said I, "for men the like of us to grow fat on his filth. It's grass I'd be eating sooner."

"That's all bombazine, Michael, bombazine! I got two dollars more from the feller we chucked in the pit!"

"Mr. Monk, that was the pig!" said I.

"And why not?" said he. "If his life was bad then his end must be good; don't be deethery."

"You can't touch pitch," I said....

"Who's touching pitch?" he cried. "Amn't I entitled to the spoils of the valiant, the rewards of the conqueror...."

"Bombazine!" says I to him.

"O begod!" he says, "I never struck fist on a lad the like of you, with your bombazine O! I grant you it doesn't come affable like, but what costs you nothing can't be dear; as for compunctions, you'll see, I fatten on 'em!"

He laughed outright at me.

"Don't be deethery, Michael, there was a good purse in the last man's trousers!"

I could no more complain to him; how could I under the Lord! Dear me, it never was seen, a man with the skin of that man; he'd the mind of a grasshopper, but there was greatness in him, and Mary herself loved him for a friend.

What do I say about Mary! Ah, there was never in anything that had the aspects of a world a girl with her loveliness, I tell you, handsome as a lily, the jewel of the world; and the thing that happened between us was strange above all reckoning. We gave her the good will of the evening in a place that would be as grand as Eden itself, though the bushes had grown dim on the hills and the sod was darkening beside the white water of the streams.

"And are you going the Journey?" we asked of her.

"I am going," said she, "everybody is going, why not me too?"

"Will you go along with us?" I asked of her.

She turned her eyes upon me like two sparks out of the blowing dusk that was already upon us.

"Yes, I will go with you."

At that she rested her hand upon my arm and we turned upon the road together.

She was barefooted and bareheaded, dressed in a yellow gown that had buttons of ivory upon it.

And we asked her as we went along the streams: Had she no fear of the night time?

"When the four ends of the world drop on you like death?" says I.

"... and the fogs rise up on you like moving grief?" says he.

"... and you hear the hoofs of the half god whisking behind the hedges," says I.

"... and there are bad things like bats troubling the air!" says he.

"... or the twig of a tree comes and touches you like a finger!" says I.

"... the finger of some meditating doom!" says he.

"No, I am not," cried Mary, "but I am glad to be going with you."

* * *

Her hand was again resting upon my arm.

I lay down among the sheaves of wheat that night with no sleep coming to me, for the stars were spilling all out of the sky and it seemed the richness of heaven was flowing down upon us all.

"Michael!" Monk whispered, "she's a holy-minded girl: look, look, she's praying!"

Sure enough I could see her a little way off, standing like a saint, as still as a monument.

Fresh as a bird was our gentle comrade in the dawn and ready to be going. And we asked her as we went by the roads together: What was it made her to come the Journey alone?

"Sure there is no loneliness in the world," she said.

"Is there not?" asked Monk.

"I take my soul with me upon this Journey," said Mary.

"Your what!"

"My soul," she said gravely, "it is what keeps loneliness from me."

He mused upon that a little. "Look ye're, Mary, soul is just but the chain of eternal mortality, that is what I think it; but you speak as if it were something you pick up and carry about with you, something made of gutta-percha, like a tobacco pouch."

She smiled upon him: "It is what covers me from loneliness ... it's ... it's the little garment which sometime God will take upon him—being God."

Seven days only and seven little nights we were together and I made scores of poems about her that were different from any poems that have come into the world, but I could never sing them now. In the mornings she would go wash herself in the pools, and Monk and I would walk a little way off from her. Monk was very delicate about that, but I would turn and see the white-armed girl rolling up her dark hair, and her white feet travelling to the water as she pulled the gown from her beauty. She was made like the down of doves and the bloom of bees. It's like enough she did love me in a very frail and delicate sort of way, like a bush of lavendie might love the wind that would be snaring it from its root in the garden, but never won a petal of it, nor a bloom, only a little of its kind kind air.

We asked her as we went upon the hills: Had she no fear of getting her death?

"Not if I make a wise use of it."

"A use of your death—and how would you do that, tell me," says I.

And she told us grand things about death, in her soft wonderful voice; strange talk to be giving the likes of him and me.

"I'd give the heart out of my skin," said I, "not to be growing old—the sin and sorrow of the world, with no hope of life and despair in its conclusion."

But Monk was full of laughter at me.

"Ha! ha! better a last hope than a hopeless conclusion," says Mr. Monk; "so try hope with another lozenge, Michael, and give a free drink to despair."

"Have *you* no fear of death?" Mary asked of him.

And Monk, he said: "I have no unreasonable regard for him; I may bow before the inevitable, but I decline to grovel before it, and if I burn with the best of 'em—well, I'd rather be torrid than torpid."

"It would be well," said Mary, "to praise God for such courage."

"Is that what *you* praise him for?" we asked her.

"I praise God for Jesus," Mary said to us: strange talk to be giving the likes of him and me.

We found the finest sleeping nooks, and she could not have rested better if there had been acres of silk; Monk, God-a-mercy, spent his money like a baron. One night in the little darkness he said:

"Look ye're, Mary, tell us why you pray!"

"I pray because of a dream I had."

"A dream! That's strange, Mary; I could understand a person dreaming because of a prayer she has prayed, but not praying because of a dream she has dreamed."

"Not even supposing," I said to him, "you had dreamed you were praying prayers?"

"If I did," said he, "I might pray not to dream such dreams."

"I pray," said Mary, "that my dream may come true."

And Monk, he said, "So you build your life on a prayer and a dream!"

"I do not build my life at all," said Mary; "it's my death I am building, in a wonderful world of mountains...."

"... that can never be climbed," cried Monk.

"... and grand rivers...."

* * *

"... that stand still and do not flow," says he.

"... and bright shining fields...."

"... that will never come to the reaping," says he again.

"... and if the climbing and the flowing and the reaping are illusions here, they are real in the dreams of God."

And Monk, he said: "If God himself is the illusion, Mary, there's little enough reward for a life of that kind, or the death of it either. The recompense for living is Life—not in the future or merely in the present, but life in the past where all our intuitions had their mould, and all our joys their eternal fountain."

"Yes, yes," I added to him, "beauty walks in the track of the mortal world, and her light is behind you."

She was silent. "Mary," said I, "won't you tell me now that dream of yours?"

"I will not tell you yet, Michael," said she.

But on a day after that we came to a plain, in it a great mountain; and we went away on to the mountain and commenced to climb. Near the top it was as if part of the cone of the mountain had been blown out by the side and a sweet lake of water left winking in the scoop. We came suddenly upon it; all the cloven cliffs that hung round three sides of the lake were of white marble, blazing with a lustre that crashed upon our eyes; the floor of the lake, easy to be seen, was of white marble too, and the water was that clear you could see the big black hole in the middle where it bubbled from the abyss. There were beds of heather around us with white quoins of marble, like chapels or shrines, sunk amid them; this, and the great golden plain rolling below, far from us, on every side, almost as far away as the sky. When we came to this place Monk touched my arm; we both looked at Mary, walking beside the lake like a person who knew well the marvel that *we* were but just seeing. She was speaking strange words—we could not understand.

"Let us leave her to herself awhile," said Monk.

And we climbed round behind the white cliffs until we left each other. I went back alone and found her lying in the heather beside a stone shaped like an altar, sleeping. I knelt down beside her with a love in my heart that was greater than the mere life beating in it. She lay very still and beautiful, and I put into her hand a sprig of the red rowan which I had found. I watched the wind just hoisting the strands of her hair that was twisted in the heather.

The glister was gone from the cliffs, they were softly white like magnolia flowers; the lake water splashed its little words in the quarries. Her lips were red as the rowan buds, the balm of lilies was in the touch of them.

She opened her eyes on me kneeling beside her.

"Mary," said I, "I will tell you what I'm thinking. There is a great doubt in my mind, Mary, and I'm in fear that you'll be gone from me."

For answer she drew me down to her side until my face was resting against her heart; I could hear its little thunder in her breast. And I leaned up until I was looking deeply in her eyes.

"You are like the dreaming dawn," I said, "beautiful and silent. You're the daughter of all the dawns that ever were, and I'd perish if you'd be gone from me."

"It's beautiful to be in the world with you, Michael, and to feel your strength about me."

"It's lonely to be in the world with you, Mary, and no hope in my heart, but doubt filling it."

"I will bring you into my heaven, Michael."

"Mary, it's in a little thicket of cedar I would sit with you, hearing the wild bee's hymn; beautiful grapes I would give you, and apples rich as the moon."

We were silent for a while and then she told me what I have written here of her own fine words as I remember them. We were sitting against the white altar stone, the sun was setting; there was one great gulf of brightness in the west of the sky, and pieces of fiery cloud, little flukes of flame shaped like fishes, swimming there. In the hinder part of the sky a great bush-tailed animal had sprung into its dying fields, a purple fox.

"I dreamed," said Mary, "that I was in marriage with a carpenter. His name was Joseph and he was older than I by many years. He left me at the marriage and went away to Liverpool; there was a great strike on in that place, but what he was to do there or why he was gone I do not know. It was at Easter, and when I woke in my bed on the first morning there was bright wind blowing in the curtains, and sun upon the bed linen. Some cattle were lowing and I heard the very first cuckoo of the year. I can remember the round looking glass with a brass frame upon the table, and the queer little alabaster jar of scented oil. There was a picture of some cranes flying on the wall, and a china figure of a man called O'Connell on the shelf above the fire-place. My white veil was blown from its hook down on the floor, and it was strewed over with daffodils I had carried to my marriage.

"And at that a figure was in the room—I don't know how—he just came, dressed in strange clothes, a dark handsome young man with black long hair and smiling eyes, full of every grace, and I loved him on the moment. But he took up some of my daffodils only—and vanished. Then I remember getting up, and after breakfast I walked about the fields very happy. There was a letter at the post office from my husband: I took it home and dropped it into the fire unopened. I put the little house into its order and set the daffodils in a bowl close upon the bedroom window. And at night in the darkness, when I could not see him, the dark man came to my bed, but was gone before the morning, taking more of my daffodils with him. And this happened night upon night until all my flowers were gone, and then he came no more.

"It was a long time before my husband came home from Liverpool but he came at last and we lived very happily until Christmas when I had a little child."

"And *did* you have a child?" I asked her.

"No," she said, "this was all my dream. Michael, O Michael, you are like that lover of the darkness."

And just then Monk came back among us roaring for food.

I gave him the bag I had carried and he helped himself.

"I do not feel the need of it," said Mary.

* * *

"I do not feel the need of it," said I.

When he had told us his tales and the darkness was come we went to rest among the heather.

The wild stars were flowing over the sky, for it was the time of the year when they do fall. Three of them dropped together into the plain near the foot of the mountain, but I lay with the bride of dreams in my arms and if the lake and the mountain itself had been heaped with immortal stars I would not have stirred. Yet in the morning when I awoke I was alone. There was a new sprig of the rowan in my hand; the grand sun was warm on the rocks and the heather. I stood up and could hear a few birds in the thickets below, little showers of faint music. Mary and Monk were conversing on a ridge under the bank of the lake. I went to them, and Monk touched my arm again as if to give me a warning but I had no eyes for him, Mary was speaking and pointing.

"Do you see, Michael, that green place at the foot of the mountain?"

"I do, I see a fine green ring."

"Do you see what is in it?"

"Nothing is in it," I said, and indeed it was a bare open spot in the ring of a fence, a green slant in the stubbles.

She stared at me with strangely troubled eyes.

"It's a little green terrace, a little sacred terrace; do you not see what is on it?" she asked of Monk.

"There is nothing in it, Mary, but maybe a hare."

"O look again," she cried out quickly, "Michael, there are three golden crosses there, the crosses of Calvary, only they are empty now!"

"There are no crosses there?" I said to Monk.

"There are no crosses there," he said.

I turned to the girl; she took me in her arms and I shall feel her cold cold lips till the fall of doom.

"Michael, dear, it has been so beautiful...."

She seemed to be making a little farewell and growing vague like a ghost would be.

"O lovely lovely jewel of the world, my heart is losing you!... Monk! Monk!" I screamed, but he could not help us. She was gone in a twink, and left me and Monk very lonely in the world.

DUSKY RUTH

DUSKY RUTH

At the close of an April day, chilly and wet, the traveller came to a country town. In the Cotswolds, though the towns are small and sweet and the inns snug, the general habit of the land is bleak and bare. He had newly come upon upland roads so void of human affairs, so lonely, that they might have been made for some forgotten uses by departed men, and left to the unwitting passage of such strangers as himself. Even the unending walls, built of old rough laminated rock, that detailed the far-spreading fields, had grown very old again in their courses; there were dabs of darkness, buttons of moss, and fossils on every stone. He had passed a few neighbourhoods, sometimes at the crook of a stream, or at the cross of debouching roads, where old habitations, their gangrenated thatch riddled with bird holes, had not been so much erected as just spattered about the places. Beyond these signs an odd lark or blackbird, the ruckle of partridges, or the nifty gallop of a hare, had been the only mitigation of the living loneliness that was almost as profound by day as by night. But the traveller had a care for such times and places.

There are men who love to gaze with the mind at things that can never be seen, feel at least the throb of a beauty that will never be known, and hear over immense bleak reaches the echo of that which is not celestial music, but only their own hearts' vain cries; and though his garments clung to him like clay it was with deliberate questing step that the traveller trod the single street of the town, and at last entered the inn, shuffling his shoes in the doorway for a moment and striking the raindrops from his hat. Then he turned into a small smoking-room. Leather-lined benches, much worn, were fixed to the wall under the window and in other odd corners and nooks behind mahogany tables. One wall was furnished with all the congenial gear of a bar, but without any intervening counter. Opposite a bright fire was burning, and a neatly-dressed young woman sat before it in a Windsor chair, staring at the flames. There was no other inmate of the room, and as he entered the girl rose up and greeted him. He found that he could be accommodated for the night, and in a few moments his hat and scarf were removed and placed inside the fender, his wet overcoat was taken to the kitchen, the landlord, an old fellow, was lending him a roomy pair of slippers, and a maid was setting supper in an adjoining room.

He sat while this was doing and talked to the barmaid. She had a beautiful, but rather mournful, face as it was lit by the firelight, and when her glance was turned away from it her eyes had a piercing brightness. Friendly and well-spoken as she was, the melancholy in her aspect was noticeable—perhaps it was the dim room, or the wet day, or the long hours ministering a multitude of cocktails to thirsty gallantry.

When he went to his supper he found cheering food and drink, with pleasant garniture of silver and mahogany. There were no other visitors, he was to be alone; blinds were drawn, lamps lit, and the fire at his back was comforting. So he sat long about his meal until a white-faced maid came to clear the table, discoursing to him of country things as she busied about the room. It was a long narrow room, with a sideboard and the door at one end and the fireplace at the other. A bookshelf, almost devoid of books, contained a number of plates; the long wall that faced the windows was almost destitute of pictures, but there were hung upon it, for some inscrutable but doubtless sufficient reason, many dish-covers, solidly shaped, of the kind held in such mysterious regard and known as "willow pattern"; one was even hung upon the face of a map. Two musty prints were mixed with them, presentments of horses having a stilted, extravagant physique and bestridden by images of inhuman and incommunicable dignity, clothed in whiskers, coloured jackets, and tight white breeches.

He took down the books from the shelf, but his interest was speedily exhausted, and the almanacs, the county directory, and various guide-books were exchanged for the *Cotswold Chronicle*. With this, having drawn the deep chair to the hearth, he whiled away the time. The newspaper amused him with its advertisements of stock shows, farm auctions, travelling quacks and conjurers, and there was a lengthy account of the execution of a local felon, one Timothy Bridger, who had murdered an infant in some shameful circumstances. This dazzling crescendo proved rather trying to the traveller; he threw down the paper.

The town was all quiet as the hills, and he could hear no sounds in the house. He got up and went across the hall to the smoke-room. The door was shut, but there was light within, and he entered. The girl sat there much as he had seen her on his arrival, still alone, with feet on fender. He shut the door behind him, sat down, and crossing his legs puffed at his pipe, admired the snug little room and the pretty figure of the girl, which he could do without embarrassment as her meditative head, slightly bowed, was turned away from him. He could see something of her, too, in the mirror at the bar, which repeated also the agreeable contours of bottles of coloured wines and rich liqueurs—so entrancing in form and aspect that they seemed destined to charming histories, even in disuse—and those of familiar outline containing mere spirits or small beer, for which are reserved the harsher destinies of base oils, horse medicines, disinfectants, and cold tea. There were coloured glasses for bitter wines, white glasses for sweet, a tiny leaden sink beneath them, and the four black handles of the beer engine.

The girl wore a light blouse of silk, a short skirt of black velvet, and a pair of very thin silk stockings that showed the flesh of instep and shin so plainly that he could see they were reddened by the warmth of the fire. She had on a pair of dainty cloth shoes with high heels, but what was wonderful about her was the heap of rich black hair piled at the back of her head and shadowing the dusky neck. He sat puffing his pipe and letting the loud tick of the clock fill the quiet room. She did not stir and he could move no muscle. It was as if he had been willed to come there and wait silently. That, he felt now, had been his desire all the evening; and here, in her presence, he was more strangely stirred than by any event he could remember.

In youth he had viewed women as futile pitiable things that grew long hair, wore stays and garters, and prayed incomprehensible prayers. Viewing them in the stalls of the theatre from his vantage-point in the gallery, he always disliked the articulation of their naked shoulders. But still, there was a god in the sky, a god with flowing hair and exquisite eyes, whose one stride with an ardour grandly rendered took him across the whole round hemisphere to which his buoyant limbs were bound like spokes to the eternal rim and axle, his bright hair burning in the pity of the sunsets and tossing in the anger of the dawns.

Master traveller had indeed come into this room to be with this woman: she as surely desired him, and for all its accidental occasion it was as if he, walking the ways of the world, had suddenly come upon ... what so imaginable with all permitted reverence as, well, just a shrine; and he, admirably humble, bowed the instant head.

Were there no other people within? The clock indicated a few minutes to nine. He sat on, still as stone, and the woman might have been of wax for all the movement or sound she made. There was allurement in the air between them; he had forborne his smoking, the pipe grew cold between his teeth. He waited for a look from her, a movement to break the trance of silence. No footfall in street or house, no voice in the inn but the clock beating away as if pronouncing a doom.

Suddenly it rasped out nine large notes, a bell in the town repeated them dolefully, and a cuckoo no further than the kitchen mocked them with three times three. After that came the weak steps of the old landlord along the hall, the slam of doors, the clatter of lock and bolt, and then the silence returning unendurably upon them.

He arose and stood behind her; he touched the black hair. She made no movement or sign. He pulled out two or three combs, and dropping them into her lap let the whole mass tumble about his hands. It had a curious harsh touch in the unravelling, but was so full and shining; black as a rook's wings it was. He slid his palms through it. His fingers searched it and fought with its fine strangeness; into his mind there travelled a serious thought, stilling his wayward fancy—this was no wayward fancy, but a rite accomplishing itself! (*Run, run, silly man, y'are lost.*) But having got so far he burnt his boats, leaned over, and drew her face back to him. And at that, seizing his wrists, she gave him back ardour for ardour, pressing his hands to her bosom, while the kiss was sealed and sealed again. Then she sprang up and picking his hat and scarf from the fender said:

* * *

"I have been drying them for you, but the hat has shrunk a bit, I'm sure—I tried it on."

He took them from her and put them behind him; he leaned lightly back upon the table, holding it with both his hands behind him; he could not speak.

"Aren't you going to thank me for drying them?" she asked, picking her combs from the rug and repinning her hair.

"I wonder why we did that?" he asked, shamedly.

"It is what I'm thinking too," she said.

"You were so beautiful about ... about it, you know."

She made no rejoinder, but continued to bind her hair, looking brightly at him under her brows. When she had finished she went close to him.

"Will that do?"

"I'll take it down again."

"No, no, the old man or the old woman will be coming in."

"What of that?" he said, taking her into his arms, "tell me your name."

She shook her head, but she returned his kisses and stroked his hair and shoulders with beautifully melting gestures.

"What is your name, I want to call you by your name?" he said; "I can't keep calling you Lovely Woman, Lovely Woman."

Again she shook her head and was dumb.

"I'll call you Ruth then, Dusky Ruth, Ruth of the black, beautiful hair."

"That is a nice-sounding name—I knew a deaf and dumb girl named Ruth; she went to Nottingham and married an organ-grinder—but I should like it for my name."

"Then I give it to you."

"Mine is so ugly."

"What is it?"

Again the shaken head and the burning caress.

"Then you shall be Ruth; will you keep that name?"

"Yes, if you give me the name I will keep it for you."

Time had indeed taken them by the forelock, and they looked upon a ruddled world.

"I stake my one talent," he said jestingly, "and behold it returns me fortyfold; I feel like the boy who catches three mice with one piece of cheese."

At ten o'clock the girl said:

"I must go and see how *they* are getting on," and she went to the door.

"Are we keeping them up?"

She nodded.

"Are you tired?"

"No, I am not tired."

She looked at him doubtfully.

"We ought not to stay in here; go into the coffee-room and I'll come there in a few minutes."

"Right," he whispered gaily, "we'll sit up all night."

She stood at the door for him to pass out, and he crossed the hall to the other room. It was in darkness except for the flash of the fire. Standing at the hearth he lit a match for the lamp, but paused at the globe; then he extinguished the match.

"No, it's better to sit in the firelight."

* * *

He heard voices at the other end of the house that seemed to have a chiding note in them.

"Lord," he thought, "she is getting into a row?"

Then her steps came echoing over the stone floors of the hall; she opened the door and stood there with a lighted candle in her hand; he stood at the other end of the room, smiling.

"Good night," she said.

"Oh no, no! come along," he protested, but not moving from the hearth.

"Got to go to bed," she answered.

"Are they angry with you?"

"No."

"Well, then, come over here and sit down."

"Got to go to bed," she said again, but she had meanwhile put her candlestick upon the little sideboard and was trimming the wick with a burnt match.

"Oh, come along, just half an hour," he protested. She did not answer but went on prodding the wick of the candle.

"Ten minutes, then," he said, still not going towards her.

"Five minutes," he begged.

She shook her head, and picking up the candlestick turned to the door. He did not move, he just called her name: "Ruth!"

She came back then, put down the candlestick and tiptoed across the room until he met her. The bliss of the embrace was so poignant that he was almost glad when she stood up again and said with affected steadiness, though he heard the tremor in her voice:

* * *

"I must get you your candle."

She brought one from the hall, set it on the table in front of him, and struck the match.

"What is my number?" he asked.

"Number six room," she answered, prodding the wick vaguely with her match, while a slip of white wax dropped over the shoulder of the new candle. "Number six ... next to mine."

The match burnt out; she said abruptly "Good-night," took up her own candle and left him there.

In a few moments he ascended the stairs and went into his room. He fastened the door, removed his coat, collar, and slippers, but the rack of passion had seized him and he moved about with no inclination to sleep. He sat down, but there was no medium of distraction. He tried to read the newspaper which he had carried up with him, and without realizing a single phrase he forced himself to read again the whole account of the execution of the miscreant Bridger. When he had finished this he carefully folded the paper and stood up, listening. He went to the parting wall and tapped thereon with his finger tips. He waited half a minute, one minute, two minutes; there was no answering sign. He tapped again, more loudly, with his knuckles, but there was no response, and he tapped many times. He opened his door as noiselessly as possible; along the dark passage there were slips of light under the other doors, the one next his own, and the one beyond that. He stood in the corridor listening to the rumble of old voices in the farther room, the old man and his wife going to their rest. Holding his breath fearfully, he stepped to *her* door and tapped gently upon it. There was no answer, but he could somehow divine her awareness of him; he tapped again; she moved to the door and whispered "No, no, go away." He turned the handle, the door was locked.

"Let me in," he pleaded. He knew she was standing there an inch or two beyond him.

"Hush," she called softly. "Go away, the old woman has ears like a fox."

He stood silent for a moment.

"Unlock it," he urged; but he got no further reply, and feeling foolish and baffled he moved back to his own room, cast his clothes from him, doused the candle and crept into the bed with soul as wild as a storm-swept forest, his heart beating a vagrant summons. The room filled with strange heat, there was no composure for mind or limb, nothing but flaming visions and furious embraces.

"Morality ... what is it but agreement with your own soul?"

So he lay for two hours—the clocks chimed twelve—listening with foolish persistency for *her* step along the corridor, fancying every light sound—and the night was full of them—was her hand upon the door.

Suddenly,—and then it seemed as if his very heart would abash the house with its thunder—he could hear distinctly someone knocking on the wall. He got quickly from his bed and stood at the door, listening. Again the knocking was heard, and having half-clothed himself he crept into the passage, which was now in utter darkness, trailing his hand along the wall until he felt her door; it was standing open. He entered her room and closed the door behind him. There was not the faintest gleam of light, he could see nothing. He whispered "Ruth!" and she was standing there. She touched him, but not speaking. He put out his hands, and they met round her neck; her hair was flowing in its great wave about her; he put his lips to her face and found that her eyes were streaming with tears, salt and strange and disturbing. In the close darkness he put his arms about her with no thought but to comfort her; one hand had plunged through the long harsh tresses and the other across her hips before he realized that she was ungowned; then he was aware of the softness of her breasts and the cold naked sleekness of her shoulders. But she was crying there, crying silently with great tears, her strange sorrow stifling his desire.

"Ruth, Ruth, my beautiful dear!" he murmured soothingly. He felt for the bed with one hand, and turning back the quilt and sheets he lifted her in as easily as a mother does her child, replaced the bedding, and, in his clothes, he lay stretched beside her comforting her. They lay so, innocent as children, for an hour, when she seemed to have gone to sleep. He rose then and went silently to his room, full of weariness.

In the morning he breakfasted without seeing her, but as he had business in the world that gave him just an hour longer at the Inn before he left it for good and all, he went into the smoke-room and found her. She greeted him with curious gaze, but merrily enough, for there were other men there now, farmers, a butcher, a registrar, an old, old man. The hour passed, but not these men, and at length he donned his coat, took up his stick, and said good-bye. Her shining glances followed him to the door, and from the window as far as they could view him.

WEEP NOT MY WANTON

WEEP NOT MY WANTON

Air and light on Sack Down at summer sunset were soft as ointment and sweet as milk; at least, that is the notion the down might give to a mind that bloomed within its calm horizons, some happy victim of romance it might be, watching the silken barley moving in its lower fields with the slow movement of summer sea, reaching no harbour, having no end. The toilers had mostly given over; their ploughs and harrows were left to the abandoned fields; they had taken their wages and gone, or were going, home; but at the crown of the hill a black barn stood by the roadside, and in its yard, amid sounds of anguish, a score of young boar pigs were being gelded by two brown lads and a gipsy fellow. Not half a mile of distance here could enclose you the compass of their cries. If a man desired peace he would step fast down the hill towards Arwall with finger in ear until he came to quiet at a bank overlooking slopes of barley, and could perceive the fogs of June being born in the standing grass beyond.

Four figures, a labourer and his family, travelled slowly up the road proceeding across the hill, a sound mingling dully with their steps—the voice of the man. You could not tell if it were noise of voice or of footsteps that first came into your ear, but it could be defined on their advance as the voice of a man upbraiding his little son.

"You're a naughty, naughty—you're a vurry, *vurry* naughty boy! Oi can't think what's comen tyeh!"

The father towered above the tiny figure shuffling under his elbow, and kept his eyes stupidly fixed upon him. He saw a thin boy, a spare boy, a very shrunken boy of seven or eight years, crying quietly. He let no grief out of his lips, but his white face was streaming with dirty tears. He wore a man's cap, an unclean sailor jacket, large knickerbockers that made a mockery of his lean joints, a pair of women's button boots, and he looked straight ahead.

"The idear! To go and lose a sixpence like that then! Where d'ye think yer'll land yerself, ay? Where'd I be if I kept on losing sixpences, ay? A creature like you, ay!" and lifting his heavy hand the man struck the boy a blow behind with shock enough to disturb a heifer. They went on, the child with sobs that you could feel rather than hear. As they passed the black barn the gipsy bawled encouragingly: "S'elp me, father, that's a good 'un, wallop his trousers!"

But the man ignored him, as he ignored the yell of the pig and the voice of the lark rioting above them all; he continued his litany:

"You're a naughty, naughty *boy*, an' I dunno what's comen tyeh!"

The woman, a poor slip of a woman she was, walked behind them with a smaller child: she seemed to have no desire to shield the boy or to placate the man. She did not seem to notice them, and led the toddling babe, to whom she gabbled, some paces in the rear of the man of anger. He was a great figure with a bronzed face; his trousers were tied at the knee, his wicker bag was slung over his shoulder. With his free and massive hand he held the hand of the boy. He was slightly drunk, and walked with his legs somewhat wide, at the beginning of each stride lifting his heel higher than was required, and at the end of it placing his foot firmly but obliquely inwards. There were two bright medals on the breast of his waistcoat, presumably for valour; he was perhaps a man who would stand upon his rights and his dignities, such as they were—but then he was drunk. His language, oddly unprofane, gave a subtle and mean point to his decline from the heroic standard. He only ceased his complaining to gaze swayingly at the boy; then he struck him. The boy, crying quietly, made no effort to avoid or resist him.

"You understand me, you bad boy! As long as you're with me you got to come under collar. And wher'll you be next I *dunno,* a bad creature like you, ay! An' then to turn roun' an' answer me! *I dunno!* I dunno *what's* comen tyeh. Ye know ye lost that sixpence through glammering about. Wher' d'ye lose it, ay? Wher' d'ye lose it, ay?"

At these questions be seized the boy by the neck and shook him as a child does a bottle of water. The baby behind them was taken with little gusts of laughter at the sight, and the woman cooed back playfully at her.

"George, George!" yelled the woman.

* * *

The man turned round.

"Look after Annie!" she yelled again.

"What's up?" he called.

Her only answer was a giggle of laughter as she disappeared behind a hedge. The child toddled up to its father and took his hand, while the quiet boy took her other hand with relief. She laughed up into their faces, and the man resumed his homily.

"He's a bad, bad boy. He's a vurry *naughty* bad boy!"

By-and-by the woman came shuffling after them; the boy looked furtively around and dropped his sister's hand.

"Carm on, me beauty!" cried the man, lifting the girl to his shoulder. "He's a bad boy; you 'ave a ride on your daddy." They went on alone, and the woman joined the boy. He looked up at her with a sad face.

"O, my Christ, Johnny!" she said, putting her arms round the boy, "what's 'e bin doin' to yeh? Yer face is all blood!"

"It's only me nose, mother. Here," he whispered, "here's the tanner."

They went together down the hill towards the inn, which had already a light in its windows. The screams from the barn had ceased, and a cart passed them full of young pigs, bloody and subdued. The hill began to resume its old dominion of soft sounds. It was nearly nine o'clock, and one anxious farmer still made hay although, on this side of the down, day had declined, and with a greyness that came not from the sky, but crept up from the world. From the quiet hill, as the last skein of cocks was carted to the stack, you could hear dimly men's voices and the rattle of their gear.

PIFFINGCAP

PIFFINGCAP

Piffingcap had the cup from an old friend, a queer-minded man. He had given it to him just before he had gone out of this continent, not for the first but for the last time—a cup of lead with an inscription upon it in decent letters but strange words.

"Here, Elmer," said his old friend to the barber of Bagwood, "have this—there's the doom of half a million beards in it!"

Piffingcap laughed, but without any joy, for his heart was heavy to lose his friend.

"There is in it too," continued Grafton, offering the pot and tapping it with his forefinger, "a true test of virtue—a rare thing, as you know, in these parts. Secondly, there is in it a choice of fortunes; and thirdly, it may be, a triple calamity and—and—and very serious, you know, but there you are." He gave it into the barber's hand with a slight sigh. While his friend duly admired the dull gift the traveller picked up his walking stick and winked at himself in the mirror.

And Elmer Piffingcap, the barber of Bagwood, took his friend's cup, set it in a conspicuous place upon the shelf of his shop, and bade that friend good-bye, a little knot rolling into his lungs as they shook their two hands together.

"It is true then," said he, staring at the shining baldness of his friend who stood with hat and stick in hand—for as Piffingcap dared not look into his friend's eyes, the gleam of the skull took his gaze, as a bright thing will seize the mind of a gnat—"it is true, then, I shall see you no more?"

"No more again," said the wanderer affably, replacing his hat—disliking that pliant will-less stare of the barber's mournful eyes. This wandering man had a heart full of bravery though he could not walk with pride, for the corns and bunkles he suffered would have crippled a creature of four feet, leave alone two. But—would you believe it—he was going now to walk himself for all his days round and round the world. O, he was such a man as could put a deceit upon the slyest, with his tall hat and his jokes, living as easy as a bird in the softness and sweetness of the year.

"And if it rains, it rains," he declared to Polly, "and I squat like a hare in the hedge and keep the blessed bones of me dry and my feet warm—it's not three weeks since it happened to me; my neck as damp as the inside of an onion, and my curly locks caught in blackberry bushes—stint your laughing, Polly!—the end of my nose as cold as a piece of dead pork, and the place very inconvenient with its sharp thorns and nettles—and no dockleaf left in the whole parish. But there was young barley wagging in the field, and clover to be smelling, and rooks to be watching, and doves, and the rain heaving its long sigh in the greyness—I declare to my God it was a fine handsome day I had that day, Polly!"

In the winter he would be sleeping in decent nooks, eating his food in quiet inns, drying his coat at the forge; and so he goes now into the corners of the world—the little husky fat man, with large spectacles and fox-coloured beard and tough boots that had slits and gouts in them—gone seeking the feathers out of Priam's peacock. And let him go; we take no more concern of him or his shining skull or his tra-la-la in the highways.

The barber, who had a romantic drift of mind, went into his saloon, and taking up the two cracked china lather mugs he flung them from the open window into his back garden, putting the fear of some evil into the mind of his drowsy cat, and a great anticipation in the brains of his two dusty hens, who were lurking there for anything that could be devoured. Mr. Piffingcap placed the pot made of lead upon his convenient shelf, laid therein his brush, lit the small gas stove under the copper urn, and when Polly, the child from the dairy, arrived with her small can for the barber's large jug she found him engaged in shaving the chin of Timmy James the butcher, what time Mr. James was engaged in a somewhat stilted conversation with Gregory Barnes about the carnal women of Bagwood.

Polly was a little lean girl, eight or nine years old, with a face that was soft and rosy and fresh as the bud of gum on the black branches of the orchard. She wore a pretty dimity frock and had gay flowers in her hat. This was her last house of call, and, sitting down to watch Mr. Piffingcap, the town's one barber, shaving friends and enemies alike, she would be the butt of their agreeable chaff because of her pleasant country jargon—as rich as nutmeg in a homely cake—or her yellow scattered hair, or her sweet eyes that were soft as remembered twilight.

"Your razor is roaring, Mr. Piffingcap!"—peeping round the chair at him. "Oh, it's that Mr. James!" she would say in pretended surprise. Mr. James had a gruff beard, and the act of removing it occasioned a noise resembling that of her mother scraping the new potatoes.

"What have you got this pot for?" she chattered; "I don't like it, it's ugly."

"Don't say that now," said Mr. Piffingcap, pausing with his hand on the butcher's throttle, "it was Mr. Grafton's parting gift to me; I shall never see him again, nor will you neither; he's gone round the world for ever more this time!"

"Oh!" gurgled the child in a manner that hung between pain and delight, "has he gone to Rinjigoffer land?"

"Gone where?" roared Timothy James, lifting his large red neck from the rest.

"He's told me all about it," said the child, ignoring him.

"Well, he's not gone there," interrupted the barber.

And the child continued, "It's where the doves and the partridges are so fat that they break down the branches of the trees where they roost...."

"Garn with yer!" said Mr. James.

"... and the hares are as big as foxes...."

"God a mercy!" said Mr. James.

"... yes, and a fox was big and brown and white like a skewbald donkey—he! he! he! And oo yes," continued Polly, shrilling with excitement, "there was a king badger as would stop your eyes from winking if you met him walking in the dawn!"

"Lord, what should the man be doing telling you them lies," ejaculated Timothy, now wiping his chin on the napkin. "Did he give you that cup, Piff?"

"Yes," replied the barber, "and if what he says is true there's a power o' miracle in it."

The butcher surveyed it cautiously and read the inscription:

NE SAMBRA DIVORNAK

"That's a bit o' Roosian, I should say," he remarked as he and Gregory left the saloon.

Polly picked up her empty can and looked at Mr. P.

"Won't he come back no more?"

"No, Polly, my pigeon, he won't come back."

"Didn't he like us?" asked the child.

The barber stood dumb before her bright searching eyes.

"He was better than my father," said the child, "or me uncle, or the schoolmaster."

"He's the goodest man alive, Polly," said Mr. P.

* * *

"Didn't he like us?" again she asked; and as Mr. P. could only look vaguely about the room she went out and closed the latch of the door very softly behind her.

In the succeeding days the barber lathered and cut or sat smoking meditatively in his saloon; the doom began to work its will, and business, which for a quarter of a century had flourished like a plant, as indeed it was, of constant and assured growth, suddenly declined. On weekdays the barber cleaned up the chins of his fellow townsmen alone, but on Sunday mornings he would seek the aid of a neighbour, a youngster whom he called Charleyboy, when four men would be seated at one time upon his shaving-chairs, towel upon breast and neck bared for the sacrifice, while Charleyboy dabbed and pounded their crops into foam. Mr. Piffingcap would follow him, plying his weapon like the genius he was, while Charleyboy again in turn followed *him*, drying with linen, cooling with rhum, or soothing with splendid unguent. "Next gent, please!" he would cry out, and the last shorn man would rise and turn away, dabbing his right hand into the depths of his breeches pocket and elevating that with his left before producing the customary tribute.

But the genius of Piffingcap and the neat hand of Charley languished in distress. There was no gradual cessation, the thing completely stopped, and Piffingcap did not realize until too late, until, indeed, the truth of it was current in the little town everywhere but in his own shop, that the beards once shaven by him out of Grafton's pot grew no more in Bagwood; and there came the space of a week or so when not a soul entered the saloon but two schoolboys for the cutting of hair, and a little housemaid for a fringe net.

Then he knew, and one day, having sat in the place the whole morning like a beleaguered rat, with ruin and damnation a hands-breath only from him, he rushed from his shop across to the hardware merchant's and bought two white china mugs, delicately lined with gold and embossed with vague lumps, and took them back to the saloon.

At dinner time he put the cup of lead into his coat pocket and walked down the street in an anxious kind of way until he came to the bridge at the end of the town. It was an angular stone bridge, crossing a deep and leisurely flowing river, along whose parapet boys had dared a million times, wearing smooth, with their adventuring feet, its soft yellow stone. He stared at the water and saw the shining flank of a tench as it turned over. All beyond the bridge were meads thick with ripe unmown grass and sweet with scabious bloom. But the barber's mind was harsh with the rancour of noon heats and the misfortunes of life. He stood with one hand resting upon the hot stone and one upon the heavy evil thing in his pocket. The bridge was deserted at this hour, its little traffic having paused for the meal. He took, at length, the cup from his pocket, and whispering to himself "God forgive you, Grafton," he let it fall from his fingers into the water; then he walked sharply home to his three daughters and told them what he had done.

"You poor loon!" said Bersa.

"O man! man!" moaned Grue.

* * *

"You're the ruin of us all!" cried Mavie.

Three fine women were Grue and Mavie and Bersa, in spite of the clamour of the outlandish Piffingcap names, and their father had respect for them and admired their handsomeness. But they had for their father, all three of them, the principal filial emotion of compassion, and they showed that his action had been a foolish action, that there were other towns in the world besides Bagwood, and that thousands and millions of men would pay a good price to be quit of a beard, and be shaved from a pot that would complete the destruction of all the unwanted hairiness of the world. And they were very angry with him.

"Let us go and see to it ... what is to be done now ... bring us to the place, father!"

He took them down to the river, and when they peered over the side of the bridge they could see the pot lying half sunk in some white sand in more than a fathom of water.

"Let us instruct the waterman," they said, "he will secure it for us."

In the afternoon Grue met the waterman, who was a sly young fellow, and she instructed him, but at tea-time word was brought to Piffingcap that the young waterman was fallen into the river and drowned. Then there was grief in his mind, for he remembered the calamity which Grafton had foretold, and he was for giving up all notions of re-taking the cup; but his daughter Bersa went in a few days to a man was an angler and instructed him; and he took a crooked pole and leaned over the bridge to probe for the cup. In the afternoon word was brought to Piffingcap that the parapet had given way, and the young angler in falling through had dashed out his brains on the abutment of the bridge. And the young gaffer whom Mavie instructed was took of a sunstroke and died on the bank.

The barber was in great grief at these calamities; he had tremors of guilt in his mind, no money in his coffers, and the chins of the Bagwood men were still as smooth as children's; but it came to him one day that he need not fear any more calamities, and that a thing which had so much tricks in it should perhaps be cured by trickery.

"I will go," he said, "to the Widow Buckland and ask her to assist me."

The Widow Buckland was a wild strange woman who lived on a heath a few miles away from Bagwood; so he went over one very hot day to the Widow and found her cottage in the corner of the heath. There was a caravan beside the cottage—it was a red caravan with yellow wheels. A blackbird hung in a wicker cage at the door, and on the side of the roof board was painted

FEATS & GALIAS ATENDED
AGLAURA BUCKLAND

There was nobody in the caravan so he knocked at the cottage door; the Widow Buckland led him into her dim little parlour.

"It 'ull cost you half a James!" says she when Mr. Piffingcap had given her his requirements.

"Half a what?" cried he.

* * *

"You are *not*," said the gipsy, "a man of a mean heart, are you?" She said it very persuasively, and he felt he could not annoy her for she was a very large woman with sharp glances.

"No," said Piffingcap.

"And you'll believe what I'm telling you, won't you?"

"Yes," said Piffingcap.

"It 'ull maybe some time before my words come true, but come true they will, I can take my oath."

"Yes," again said Piffingcap.

"George!" she bawled to someone from the doorway, "wher'd yer put my box?"

There was an indistinct reply but she bawled out again, "Well, *fetch* it off the rabbit hutch."

"And a man like you," she continued, turning again to the barber, "doesn't think twice about half a sovereign, and me putting you in the way of what you want to know, *I'm* sure."

And Piffingcap mumbled dubiously "No," producing with difficulty some shillings, some coppers, and a postal order for one and threepence which a credulous customer had that morning sent him for a bottle of hairwash.

"Let's look at your 'and," she said; taking it she reflected gravely:

"You're a man that's 'ad your share o' trouble, aint you?"

Piffingcap bowed meekly.

"And you've 'ad your 'appy days, aint you?"

A nod.

* * *

"Well listen to me; you've got more fortune in store for you if you know how to pluck it ... you understand my meaning, don't you?... than any man in the town this bleedun minute. Right, George," she exclaimed, turning to a very ugly little hunchbacked fellow—truly he was a mere squint of a man, there was such a little bit of him for so much uncomeliness. The Widow Buckland took the box from the hunchback and, thrusting him out of the room, she shut fast the door and turned the key in the lock. Then she drew up a bit of a table to the window, and taking out of the box a small brass vessel and two bottles she set them before her.

"Sit down there, young feller," she said, and Piffingcap sat down at the end of the table facing the window. The Widow turned to the window, which was a small square, the only one in the room, and closed over it a shutter. The room was clapped in darkness except for a small ray in the middle of the shutter, coming through a round hole about as large as a guinea. She pulled Mr. Piffingcap's shoulder until the ray was shining on the middle of his forehead; she took up the brass vessel, and holding it in the light of the ray polished it for some time with her forefinger. All her fingers, even her thumbs, were covered with rich sinister rings, but there were no good looks in those fingers for the nails had been munched almost away, and dirty skin hid up the whites. The polished vessel was then placed on the table directly beneath the ray; drops from the two phials were poured into it, a green liquid and a black liquid; mixing together they melted into a pillar of smoke which rose and was seen only as it flowed through the beam of light, twisting and veering and spinning in strange waves.

The Widow Buckland said not a word for a time, but contemplated the twisting shapes as they poured through the ray, breathing heavily all the while or suffering a slight sigh to pass out of her breast. But shortly the smoke played the barber a trick in his nose and heaving up his chin he rent the room with a great sneeze. When he recovered himself she was speaking certain words:

"Fire and water I see and a white virgin's skin. The triple gouts of blood I see and the doom given over. Fire and water I see and a white virgin's skin."

She threw open the shutter, letting in the light; smoke had ceased to rise but it filled the parlour with a sweet smell.

"Well ..." said Mr. Piffingcap dubiously.

And the Widow Buckland spoke over to him plainly and slowly, patting his shoulder at each syllable,

"Fire and water and a white virgin's skin."

Unlatching the door she thrust him out of the house into the sunlight. He tramped away across the heath meditating her words, and coming to the end of it he sat down in the shade of a bush by the side of the road, for he felt sure he was about to capture the full meaning of her words. But just then he heard a strange voice speaking, and speaking very vigorously. He looked up and observed a man on a bicycle, riding along towards him, talking to himself in a great way.

* * *

"He is a political fellow rehearsing a speech," said Mr. Piffingcap to himself, "or perhaps he is some holy-minded person devising a sermon."

It was a very bald man and he had a long face hung with glasses; he had no coat and rode in his shirt and knickerbockers, with hot thick stockings and white shoes. The barber watched him after he had passed and noted how his knees turned angularly outwards at each upward movement, and how his saddle bag hung at the bottom of his back like some ironical label.

"Fool!" exclaimed Mr. Piffingcap, rising angrily, for the man's chatter had driven his mind clean away from the Widow Buckland's meaning. But it was only for a short while, and when he got home he called one of his daughters into the saloon.

"My child," said Piffingcap, "you know the great trouble which is come on me?" and he told Bersa his difficulty and requested her aid, that is to say: would she go down in the early morning in her skin only and recover the pot?

"Indeed no, father!" said his daughter Bersa, "it is a very evil thing and I will not do your request."

"You will not?" says he.

"No!" says she, but it was not in the fear of her getting her death that she refused him.

So he called to another of his daughters.

"My child," said he, "you know the great trouble that is come on me," and he told Mavie his desire and asked for her aid.

"Why, my father," says she, "this is a thing which a black hag has put on us all and I will get my death. I love you as I love my life, father, but I won't do this!"

"You will not?" says he.

"No!" says she, but it was not for fear of her death she refused him.

And he went to his third daughter Grue and tried her with the same thing. "My child, you know the trouble that's come on me?"

"Oh, will you let me alone!" she says, "I've a greater trouble on me than your mouldy pot." And it is true what she said of her trouble, for she was a girl of a loose habit. So the barber said no more to them and went to his bed.

Two days later, it being Saturday, he opened in the morning his saloon and sat down there. And while he read his newspaper in the empty place footsteps scampered into his doorway, and the door itself was pushed open just an inch or two.

"Come in," he said, rising.

The door opened fully.

"Zennybody here?" whispered Polly walking in very mysteriously, out of breath, and dressed in a long mackintosh.

"What is the matter, my little one?" he asked, putting his arm around her shoulders, for he had a fondness for her. "Ach, your hair's all wet, what's the matter?"

The little girl put her hand under the macintosh and drew out the leaden pot, handing it to the barber and smiling at him with inarticulate but intense happiness. She said not a word as he stared his surprise and joy.

"Why Polly, my *dear*, how *did* you get it?"

"I dived in and got it."

"You never ... you princess ... you!"

"I just bin and come straight here with it."

She opened and shut the mackintosh quickly, displaying for a brief glance her little white naked figure with the slightest tremulous crook at the sharp knees.

"Ah, my darling," exclaimed the enraptured barber, "and you're shivering with not a rag on you but them shoes ... run away home, Polly, and get some things on, Polly ... and ... Polly, Polly!" as she darted away, "come back quick, won't you?"

She nodded brightly back at him as she sprang through the doorway. He went to the entrance and watched her taking her twinkling leaps, as bonny as a young foal, along the pavement.

And there came into the barber's mind the notion that this was all again a piece of fancy tricks; but there was the dark pot, and he examined it. Thoughtfully he took it into his backyard and busied himself there for a while, not telling his daughters of its recovery. When, later, Polly joined him in the garden he had already raised a big fire in an old iron brazier which had lain there.

"Ah, Polly my dear, I'm overjoyed to get it back, but I dasn't keep it ... it's a bad thing. Take it in your fingers now, my dear little girl, and just chuck it in that fire. Ah, we must melt the wickedness out of it," he said, observing her disappointment, "it's been the death of three men and we dasn't keep it."

They watched it among the coals until it had begun to perish drop by drop through the grating of the brazier.

Later in the day Mr. Piffingcap drove Polly in a little trap to a neighbouring town to see a circus, and the pair of them had a roaring dinner at the Green Dragon. Next morning when Polly brought the milk to the saloon there were Timmy James and Gregory Barnes being shaved, for beards had grown again in Bagwood.

THE KING OF THE WORLD

THE KING OF THE WORLD

Once upon a time, yes, in the days of King Sennacherib, a young Assyrian captain, valiant and desirable, but more hapless than either, fleeing in that strange rout of the armies against Judah, was driven into the desert. Daily his company perished from him until he alone, astride a camel, was left searching desperately through a boundless desert for the loved plains of Shinar, sweet with flocks and rich with glittering cities. The desolation of ironic horizons that he could never live to pierce hung hopelessly in remote unattainable distances, endless as the blue sky. The fate of his comrades had left upon him a small pack of figs and wine, but in that uncharted wilderness it was but a pitiable parrying of death's last keen stroke. There was no balm or succour in that empty sky; blue it was as sapphires, but savage with rays that scourged like flaming brass. Earth itself was not less empty, and the loneliness of his days was an increasing bitterness. He was so deeply forgotten of men, and so removed from the savour of life, from his lost country, the men he knew, the women he loved, their temples, their markets and their homes, that it seemed the gods had drawn that sweet and easy world away from his entangled feet.

But at last upon a day he was astonished and cheered by the sight of a black butterfly flickering in the air before him, and towards evening he espied a giant mound lying lonely in the east. He drove his camel to it, but found only a hill of sand whirled up by strange winds of the desert. He cast himself from the camel's back and lay miserably in the dust. His grief was extreme, but in time he tended his tired beast and camped in the shadow of the hill. When he gave himself up to sleep the night covering them was very calm and beautiful, the sky soft and streaming with stars; it seemed to his saddened mind that the desert and the deep earth were indeed dead, and life and love only in that calm enduring sky. But at midnight a storm arose with quickening furies that smote the desert to its unseen limits, and the ten thousand stars were flung into oblivion; winds flashed upon him with a passion more bitter than a million waves, a terror greater than hosts of immediate enemies. They grasped and plunged him into gulfs of darkness, heaped mountains upon him, lashed him with thongs of snakes and scattered him with scimitars of unspeakable fear. His soul was tossed in the void like a crushed star and his body beaten into the dust with no breath left him to bemoan his fate. Nevertheless by a miracle his soul and body lived on.

It was again day when he recovered, day in the likeness of yesterday, the horizons still infinitely far. Long past noon, the sun had turned in the sky; he was alone. The camel was doubtless buried in the fathoms he himself had escaped, but a surprising wonder greeted his half-blinded eyes; the hill of sand was gone, utterly, blown into the eternal waste of the desert, and in its track stood a strange thing—a shrine. There was a great unroofed pavement of onyx and blue jasper, large enough for the floor of a temple, with many life-size figures, both men and women, standing upon it all carved in rock and facing, at the sacred end, a giant pillared in black basalt, seven times the height of a man. The sad captain divined at once that this was the lost shrine of Namu-Sarkkon, the dead god of whom tradition spoke in the ancient litanies of his country. He heaved himself painfully from the grave of sand in which he had lain half-buried, and staggering to the pavement leaned in the shade of one of those figures fronting the dead god. In a little time he recovered and ate some figs which he carried in a leather bag at his hip, and plucked the sand from his eyes and ears and loosened his sandals and gear. Then he bowed himself for a moment before the black immobile idol, knowing that he would tarry here now until he died.

Namu-Sarkkon, the priestless god, had been praised of old time above all for his gifts of joy. Worshippers had gathered from the cities of Assyria at this his only shrine, offering their souls for a gift to him who, in his time and wisdom, granted their desires. But Namu-Sarkkon, like other gods, was a jealous god, and, because the hearts of mankind are vain and destined to betrayal, he turned the bodies of his devotees into rock and kept them pinioned in stone for a hundred years, or for a thousand years, according to the nature of their desires. Then if the consummation were worthy and just, the rock became a living fire, the blood of eternity quickened the limbs, and the god released the body full of youth and joy. But what god lives for ever? Not Namu-Sarkkon. He grew old and forgetful; his oracle was defamed. Stronger gods supplanted him and at last all power departed save only from one of his eyes. That eye possessed the favour of eternity, but only so faintly that the worshipper when released from his trap of stone lived at the longest but a day, some said even but an hour. None could then be found to exchange the endurances of the world for so brief a happiness. His worship ceased, Namu-Sarkkon was dead, and the remote shrine being lost to man's heart was lost to man's eyes. Even the tradition of its time and place had become a mere fantasy, but the whirlwinds of uncounted years sowing their sands about the shrine had left it blameless and unperishable, if impotent.

Recollecting this, the soldier gazed long at the dead idol. Its smooth huge bulk, carved wonderfully, was still without blemish and utterly cleansed of the sand. The strange squat body with the benign face stood on stout legs, one advanced as if about to stride forward to the worshipper, and one arm outstretched offered the sacred symbol. Then in a moment the Assyrian's heart leaped within him; he had been staring at the mild eyes of the god—surely there was a movement in one of the eyes! He stood erect, trembling, then flung himself prostrate before Namu-Sarkkon, the living god! He lay long, waiting for his doom to eclipse him, the flaming swords of the sun scathing his weary limbs, the sweat from his temples dripping in tiny pools beside his eyes. At last he moved, he knelt up, and shielding his stricken eyes with one arm he gazed at the god, and saw now quite clearly a black butterfly resting on the lid of one of Sarkkon's eyes, inflecting its wings. He gave a grunt of comprehension and relief. He got up and went among the other figures. Close at hand they seemed fashioned of soft material, like camphor or wax, that was slowly dissolving, leaving them little more than stooks of clay, rough clod-like shapes of people, all but one figure which seemed fixed in coloured marble, a woman of beauty so wondrous to behold that the Assyrian bent his head in praise before her, though but an image of stone. When he looked again at it the black butterfly from the eyelid of the god fluttered between them and settled upon the girl's delicately carved lips for a moment, and then away. Amazedly watching it travel back to the idol he heard a movement and a sigh behind him. He leaped away, with his muscles distended, his fingers outstretched, and fear bursting in his eyes. The beautiful figure had moved a step towards him, holding out a caressing hand, calling him by his name, his name!

"Talakku! Talakku!"

She stood thus almost as if again turned to stone, until his fear left him and he saw only her beauty, and knew only her living loveliness in a tunic of the sacred purple fringed with tinkling discs, that was clipped to her waist with a zone of gold and veiled, even in the stone, her secret hips and knees. The slender feet were guarded with pantoffles of crimson hide. Green agates in strings of silver hung beside her brows, depending from a fillet of gems that crowned and confined the black locks tightly curled. Buds of amber and coral were bound to her dusky wrists with threads of copper, and between the delicacy of her brown breasts an amulet of beryl, like a blue and gentle star, hung from a necklace made of balls of opal linked with amethysts.

"Wonder of god! who are you?" whispered the warrior; but while he was speaking she ran past him sweetly as an antelope to the dark god. He heard the clicking of her beads and gems as she bent in reverence kissing the huge stone feet of Sarkkon. He did not dare to approach her although her presence filled him with rapture; he watched her obeisant at the shrine and saw that one of her crimson shoes had slipped from the clinging heel. What was she—girl or goddess, phantom or spirit of the stone, or just some lunatic of the desert? But whatever she was it was marvellous, and the marvel of it shocked him; time seemed to seethe in every channel of his blood. He heard her again call out his name as if from very far away.

"Talakku!"

He hastened to lift her from the pavement, and conquering his tremors he grasped and lifted her roughly, as a victor might hale a captive.

"Pretty antelope, who are you?"

She turned her eyes slowly upon his—this was no captive, no phantom—his intrepid arms fell back weakly to his sides.

"You will not know me, O brave Assyrian captain," said the girl gravely. "I was a weaver in the city of Eridu...."

"Eridu!" It was an ancient city heard of only in the old poems of his country, as fabulous as snow in Canaan.

"Ai ... it is long since riven into dust. I was a slave in Eridu, not ... not a slave in spirit...."

"Beauty so rare is nobility enough," he said shyly.

"I worshipped god Namu-Sarkkon—behold his shrine. Who loves Namu-Sarkkon becomes what he wishes to become, gains what he wishes to gain."

"I have heard of these things," exclaimed the Assyrian. "What did you gain, what did you wish to become?"

"I worshipped here desiring in my heart to be loved by the King of the World."

"Who is he?"

She dropped her proud glances to the earth before him.

"Who was this King of the World?"

Still she made no reply nor lifted her eyes.

"Who are these figures that stand with us here?" he asked.

* * *

"Dead, all dead," she sighed, "their destinies have closed. Only I renew the destiny."

She took his hand and led him among the wasting images.

"Merchants and poets, dead; princesses and slaves, dead; soldiers and kings, they look on us with eyes of dust, dead, all dead. I alone of Sarkkon's worshippers live on enduringly; I desired only love. I feed my spirit with new desire. I am the beam of his eye."

"Come," said the Assyrian suddenly, "I will carry you to Shinar; set but my foot to that lost track ... will you?"

She shook her head gravely; "All roads lead to Sarkkon."

"Why do we tarry here? Come."

"Talakku, there is no way hence, no way for you, no way for me. We have wandered into the boundless. What star returns from the sky, what drop from the deep?"

Talakku looked at her with wonder, until the longing in his heart lightened the shadow of his doom.

"Tell me what I must do," he said.

She turned her eyes towards the dark god. "He knows," she cried, seizing his hands and drawing him towards the idol, "Come, Talakku."

"No, no!" he said in awe, "I cannot worship there. Who can deny the gods of his home and escape vengeance? In Shinar, beloved land, goes not one bee unhived nor a bird without a bower. Shall I slip my allegiance at every gust of the desert?"

* * *

For a moment a look of anguish appeared in her eyes.

"But if you will not leave this place," he continued gently, "suffer me to stay."

"Talakku, in a while I must sink again into the stone."

"By all the gods I will keep you till I die," he said. "One day at least I will walk in Paradise."

"Talakku, not a day, not an hour; moments, moments, there are but moments now."

"Then, I am but dead," he cried, "for in that stone your sleeping heart will never dream of me."

"O, you whip me with rods of lilies. Quick, Talakku." He knew in her urgent voice the divining hope with which she wooed him. Alas for the Assyrian, he was but a man whose dying lips are slaked with wise honey. He embraced her as in a dream under the knees of towering Sarkkon. Her kisses, wrapt in the delicate veils of love, not the harsh brief glister of passion, were more lulling than a thousand songs of lost Shinar, but the time's sweet swiftness pursued them. Her momentary life had flown like a rushing star, swift and delighting but doomed. From the heel of the god a beetle of green lustre began to creep towards them.

"Farewell, Talakku," cried the girl. She stood again in her place before Namu-Sarkkon. "Have no fear, Talakku, prince of my heart. I will lock up in your breast all my soft unsundering years. Like the bird of fire they will surely spring again."

He waited, dumb, beside her, and suddenly her limbs compacted into stone once more. At the touch of his awed fingers her breast burned with the heat of the sun instead of the wooing blood. Then the vast silence of the world returned upon him; he looked in trembling loneliness at the stark sky, the unending desert, at the black god whose eye seemed to flicker balefully at him. Talakku turned to the lovely girl, but once more amazement gathered in all his veins. No longer stood her figure there—in its place he beheld only a stone image of himself.

"This is the hour, O beauteous one!" murmured the Assyrian, and, turning again towards the giant, he knelt in humility. His body wavered, faltered, suddenly stiffened, and then dissolved into a little heap of sand.

The same wind that unsealed Namu-Sarkkon and his shrine returning again at eve covered anew the idol and its figures, and the dust of the Assyrian captain became part of the desert for evermore.

ADAM AND EVE AND PINCH ME

ADAM AND EVE AND PINCH ME

... and in the whole of his days, vividly at the end of the afternoon—he repeated it again and again to himself—the kind country spaces had *never* absorbed *quite* so rich a glamour of light, so miraculous a bloom of clarity. He could feel streaming in his own mind, in his bones, the same crystalline brightness that lay upon the land. Thoughts and images went flowing through him as easily and amiably as fish swim in their pools; and as idly, too, for one of his speculations took up the theme of his family name. There was such an agreeable oddness about it, just as there was about all the luminous sky today, that it touched him as just a little remarkable.

What *did* such a name connote, signify, or symbolize?

It was a rann of a name, but it had euphony! Then again, like the fish, his ambulating fancy flashed into other shallows, and he giggled as he paused, peering at the buds in the brake. Turning back towards his house again he could see, beyond its roofs, the spire of the Church tinctured richly as the vane: all round him was a new grandeur upon the grass of the fields, and the spare trees had shadows below that seemed to support them in the manner of a plinth, more real than themselves, and the dykes and any chance heave of the level fields were underlined, as if for special emphasis, with long shades of mysterious blackness.

With a little drift of emotion that had at other times assailed him in the wonder and ecstasy of pure light, Jaffa Codling pushed through the slit in the back hedge and stood within his own garden. The gardener was at work. He could hear the voices of the children about the lawn at the other side of the house. He was very happy, and the place was beautiful, a fine white many-windowed house rising from a lawn bowered with plots of mould, turretted with shrubs, and overset with a vast walnut tree. This house had deep clean eaves, a roof of faint coloured slates that, after rain, glowed dully, like onyx or jade, under the red chimneys, and half-way up at one end was a balcony set with black balusters. He went to a French window that stood open and stepped into the dining room. There was no-one within, and, on that lonely instant, a strange feeling of emptiness dropped upon him. The clock ticked almost as if it had been caught in some indecent act; the air was dim and troubled after that glory outside. Well, now, he would go up at once to his study and write down for his new book the ideas and images he had accumulated—beautiful rich thoughts they were—during that wonderful afternoon. He went to mount the stairs and he was passed by one of the maids; humming a silly song she brushed past him rudely, but he was an easy-going man—maids were unteachably tiresome—and reaching the landing he sauntered towards his room. The door stood slightly open and he could hear voices within. He put his hand upon the door ... it would not open any further.

What the devil ... he pushed—like the bear in the tale—and he pushed, and he pushed—was there something against it on the other side? He put his shoulder to it ... some wedge must be there, and *that* was extraordinary.

Then his whole apprehension was swept up and whirled as by an avalanche—Mildred, his wife, was in there; he could hear her speaking to a man in fair soft tones and the rich phrases that could be used only by a woman yielding a deep affection to him. Codling kept still. Her words burned on his mind and thrilled him as if spoken to himself. There was a movement in the room, then utter silence. He again thrust savagely at the partly open door, but he could not stir it. The silence within continued.

He beat upon the door with his fists, crying; "Mildred, Mildred!" There was no response, but he could hear the rocking arm chair commence to swing to and fro.

Pushing his hand round the edge of the door he tried to thrust his head between the opening. There was not space for this, but he could just peer into the corner of a mirror hung near, and this is what he saw: the chair at one end of its swing, a man sitting in it, and upon one arm of it Mildred, the beloved woman, with her lips upon the man's face, caressing him with her hands. Codling made another effort to get into the room—as vain as it was violent. "Do you hear me, Mildred?" he shouted. Apparently neither of them heard him; they rocked to and fro while he gazed stupefied. What, in the name of God, ... What this ... was she bewitched ... were there such things after all as magic, devilry!

He drew back and held himself quite steadily. The chair stopped swaying, and the room grew awfully still. The sharp ticking of the clock in the hall rose upon the house like the tongue of some perfunctory mocker. Couldn't they hear the clock? ... Couldn't they hear his heart? He had to put his hand upon his heart, for, surely, in that great silence inside there, they would hear its beat, growing so loud now that it seemed almost to stun him! Then in a queer way he found himself reflecting, observing, analysing his own actions and intentions. He found some of them to be just a little spurious, counterfeit. He felt it would be easy, so perfectly easy to flash in one blast of anger and annihilate the two. He would do nothing of the kind.

There was no occasion for it. People didn't really do that sort of thing, or, at least, not with a genuine passion.

There was no need for anger. His curiosity was satisfied, quite satisfied, he was certain, he had not the remotest interest in the man. A welter of unexpected thoughts swept upon his mind as he stood there. As a writer of books he was often stimulated by the emotions and impulses of other people, and now his own surprise was beginning to intrigue him, leaving him, O, quite unstirred emotionally, but interesting him profoundly.

He heard the maid come stepping up the stairway again, humming her silly song. He did not want a scene, or to be caught eavesdropping, and so turned quickly to another door. It was locked. He sprang to one beyond it; the handle would not turn. "Bah!

what's *up* with 'em?" But the girl was now upon him, carrying a tray of coffee things. "O, Mary!" he exclaimed casually, "I...." To his astonishment the girl stepped past him as if she did not hear or see him, tapped upon the door of his study, entered, and closed the door behind her. Jaffa Codling then got really angry. "Hell! were the blasted servants in it!" He dashed to the door again and tore at the handle. It would not even turn, and, though he wrenched with fury at it, the room was utterly sealed against him.

He went away for a chair with which to smash the effrontery of that door. No, he wasn't angry, either with his wife or this fellow—Gilbert, she had called him—who had a strangely familiar aspect as far as he had been able to take it in; but when one's servants ... faugh!

The door opened and Mary came forth smiling demurely.

He was a few yards further along the corridor at that moment. "Mary!" he shouted, "leave the door open!" Mary carefully closed it and turned her back on him. He sprang after her with bad words bursting from him as she went towards the stairs and flitted lightly down, humming all the way as if in derision. He leaped downwards after her three steps at a time, but she trotted with amazing swiftness into the kitchen and slammed the door in his face. Codling stood, but kept his hands carefully away from the door, kept them behind him. "No, no," he whispered cunningly, "there's something fiendish about door handles today, I'll go and get a bar, or a butt of timber," and, jumping out into the garden for some such thing, the miracle happened to him. For it was nothing else than a miracle, the unbelievable, the impossible, simple and laughable if you will, but having as much validity as any miracle can ever invoke. It was simple and laughable because by all the known physical laws he should have collided with his gardener, who happened to pass the window with his wheelbarrow as Codling jumped out on to the path. And it was unbelievable that they should not, and impossible that they *did* not collide; and it was miraculous, because Codling stood for a brief moment in the garden path and the wheelbarrow of Bond, its contents, and Bond himself passed apparently through the figure of Codling as if he were so much air, as if he were not a living breathing man but just a common ghost. There was no impact, just a momentary breathlessness. Codling stood and looked at the retreating figure going on utterly unaware of him. It is interesting to record that Codling's first feelings were mirthful. He giggled.

He was jocular. He ran along in front of the gardener, and let him pass through him once more; then after him again; he scrambled into the man's barrow, and was wheeled about by this incomprehensible thick-headed gardener who was dead to all his master's efforts to engage his attention. Presently he dropped the wheelbarrow and went away, leaving Codling to cogitate upon the occurrence. There was no room for doubt, some essential part of him had become detached from the obviously not less vital part. He felt he was essential because he was responding to the experience, he was re-acting in the normal way to normal stimuli, although he happened for the time being to be invisible to his fellows and unable to communicate with them. How had it come about—this

queer thing? How could he discover what part of him had cut loose, as it were? There was no question of this being death; death wasn't funny, it wasn't a joke; he had still all his human instincts.

You didn't get angry with a faithless wife or joke with a fool of a gardener if you were dead, certainly not! He had realized enough of himself to know he was the usual man of instincts, desires, and prohibitions, complex and contradictory; his family history for a million or two years would have denoted that, not explicitly—obviously impossible—but suggestively. He had found himself doing things he had no desire to do, doing things he had a desire not to do, thinking thoughts that had no contiguous meanings, no meanings that could be related to his general experience. At odd times he had been chilled—aye, and even agreeably surprised—at the immense potential evil in himself. But still, this was no mere Jekyl and Hyde affair, that a man and his own ghost should separately inhabit the same world was a horse of quite another colour. The other part of him was alive and active somewhere ... as alive ... as alive ... yes, as *he* was, but dashed if he knew where! What a lark when they got back to each other and compared notes!

In his tales he had brooded over so many imagined personalities, followed in the track of so many psychological enigmas that he *had* felt at times a stranger to himself. What if, after all, that brooding had given him the faculty of projecting this figment of himself into the world of men.

Or was he some unrealized latent element of being without its natural integument, doomed now to drift over the ridge of the world for ever. Was it his personality, his spirit? Then how was the dashed thing working? Here was he with the most wonderful happening in human experience, and he couldn't differentiate or disinter things. He was like a new Adam flung into some old Eden.

There was Bond tinkering about with some plants a dozen yards in front of him. Suddenly his three children came round from the other side of the house, the youngest boy leading them, carrying in his hand a small sword which was made, not of steel, but of some more brightly shining material; indeed it seemed at one moment to be of gold, and then again of flame, transmuting everything in its neighbourhood into the likeness of flame, the hair of the little girl Eve, a part of Adam's tunic; and the fingers of the boy Gabriel as he held the sword were like pale tongues of fire. Gabriel, the youngest boy, went up to the gardener and gave the sword into his hands, saying: "Bond, is this sword any good?" Codling saw the gardener take the weapon and examine it with a careful sort of smile; his great gnarled hands became immediately transparent, the blood could be seen moving diligently about the veins. Codling was so interested in the sight that he did not gather in the gardener's reply. The little boy was dissatisfied and repeated his question, "No, but Bond, *is* this sword any good?" Codling rose, and stood by invisible. The three beautiful children were grouped about the great angular figure of the gardener in his soiled clothes, looking up now into his face, and now at the sword, with anxiety in all their puckered eyes. "Well, Marse Gabriel," Codling could hear him reply, "as far as a sword goes, it may be a good un, or it may be a bad un, but, good as it is, it can never be anything but a bad thing." He then gave it back to them; the boy Adam held the haft of it, and the girl Eve rubbed the blade with curious fingers.

The younger boy stood looking up at the gardener with unsatisfied gaze. "But, Bond, *can't* you say if this sword's any *good*?" Bond turned to his spade and trowels.

"Mebbe the shape of it's wrong, Marse Gabriel, though it seems a pretty handy size." Saying this he moved off across the lawn. Gabriel turned to his brother and sister and took the sword from them; they all followed after the gardener and once more Gabriel made enquiry: "Bond, is this sword any *good*?" The gardener again took it and made a few passes in the air like a valiant soldier at exercise. Turning then, he lifted a bright curl from the head of Eve and cut it off with a sweep of the weapon. He held it up to look at it critically and then let it fall to the ground. Codling sneaked behind him and, picking it up, stood stupidly looking at it. "Mebbe, Marse Gabriel," the gardener was saying, "it ud be better made of steel, but it has a smartish edge on it." He went to pick up the barrow but Gabriel seized it with a spasm of anger, and cried out: "No, no, Bond, will you say, just yes or no, Bond, is this sword any *good*?" The gardener stood still, and looked down at the little boy, who repeated his question—"just yes or no, Bond!" "No, Marse Gabriel!" "Thank you, Bond!" replied the child with dignity, "that's all we wanted to know," and, calling to his mates to follow him, he ran away to the other side of the house.

Codling stared again at the beautiful lock of hair in his hand, and felt himself grow so angry that he picked up a strange looking flower pot at his feet and hurled it at the retreating gardener. It struck Bond in the middle of the back and, passing clean through him, broke on the wheel of his barrow, but Bond seemed to be quite unaware of this catastrophe. Codling rushed after, and, taking the gardener by the throat, he yelled, "Damn you, will you tell me what all this means?" But Bond proceeded calmly about his work un-noticing, carrying his master about as if he were a clinging vapour, or a scarf hung upon his neck. In a few moments, Codling dropped exhausted to the ground. "What.... O Hell ... what, what am I to do?" he groaned, "What has happened to me? What shall I *do*? What *can* I do?" He looked at the broken flowerpot. "Did I invent that?"

He pulled out his watch. "That's a real watch, I hear it ticking, and it's six o'clock." Was he dead or disembodied or mad? What was this infernal lapse of

identity? And who the devil, yes, who was it upstairs with Mildred? He jumped to his feet and hurried to the window; it was shut; to the door, it was fastened; he was powerless to open either. Well! well! this was experimental psychology with a vengeance, and he began to chuckle again. He'd have to write to McDougall about it. Then he turned and saw Bond wheeling across the lawn towards him again.

"*Why* is that fellow always shoving that infernal green barrow around?" he asked, and, the fit of fury seizing him again, he rushed towards Bond, but, before he reached him, the three children danced into the garden again, crying, with great excitement, "Bond, O, Bond!" The gardener stopped and set down the terrifying barrow; the children crowded about him, and Gabriel held out another shining thing, asking: "Bond, is this box any *good*?" The gardener took the box and at once his eyes lit up with interest and delight. "O, Marse Gabriel, where'd ye get it?

Where'd ye get it?" "Bond," said the boy impatiently, "Is the box any *good*?" "Any good?" echoed the man, "Why, Marse Gabriel, Marse Adam, Miss Eve, look yere!" Holding it down in front of them, he lifted the lid from the box and a bright coloured bird flashed out and flew round and round above their heads. "O," screamed Gabriel with delight, "It's a kingfisher!" "That's what it is," said Bond, "a kingfisher!"

"Where?" asked Adam. "Where?" asked

Eve. "There it flies—round the fountain—see it? see it!" "No," said Adam. "No," said Eve.

"O, do, do, see it," cried Gabriel, "here it comes, it's coming!" and, holding his hands on high, and standing on his toes, the child cried out as happy as the bird which Codling saw flying above them.

"I can't see it," said Adam.

* * *

"Where is it, Gaby?" asked Eve.

"O, you stupids," cried the boy, "*There* it goes.

There it goes ... there ... it's gone!"

He stood looking brightly at Bond, who replaced the lid.

"What shall we do now?" he exclaimed eagerly.

For reply, the gardener gave the box into his hand, and walked off with the barrow. Gabriel took the box over to the fountain. Codling, unseen, went after him, almost as excited as the boy; Eve and her brother followed. They sat upon the stone tank that held the falling water. It was difficult for the child to unfasten the lid; Codling attempted to help him, but he was powerless. Gabriel looked up into his father's face and smiled. Then he stood up and said to the others:

"Now, *do* watch it this time."

They all knelt carefully beside the water. He lifted the lid and, behold, a fish like a gold carp, but made wholly of fire, leaped from the box into the fountain.

The man saw it dart down into the water, he saw the water bubble up behind it, he heard the hiss that the junction of fire and water produces, and saw a little track of steam follow the bubbles about the tank until the figure of the fish was consumed and disappeared.

Gabriel, in ecstasies, turned to his sister with blazing happy eyes, exclaiming:

"There! Evey!"

"What was it?" asked Eve, nonchalantly, "I didn't see anything."

"More didn't I," said Adam.

* * *

"Didn't you see that lovely fish?"

"No," said Adam.

"No," said Eve.

"O, stupids," cried Gabriel, "it went right past the bottom of the water."

"Let's get a fishin' hook," said Adam.

"No, no, no," said Gabriel, replacing the lid of the box. "O no."

Jaffa Codling had remained on his knees staring at the water so long that, when he looked around him again, the children had gone away. He got up and went to the door, and that was closed; the windows, fastened. He went moodily to a garden bench and sat on it with folded arms. Dusk had begun to fall into the shrubs and trees, the grass to grow dull, the air chill, the sky to muster its gloom. Bond had overturned his barrow, stalled his tools in the lodge, and gone to his home in the village. A curious cat came round the house and surveyed the man who sat chained to his seven-horned dilemma. It grew dark and fearfully silent. Was the world empty now? Some small thing, a snail perhaps, crept among the dead leaves in the hedge, with a sharp, irritating noise. A strange flood of mixed thoughts poured through his mind until at last one idea disentangled itself, and he began thinking with tremendous fixity of little Gabriel. He wondered if he could brood or meditate, or "will" with sufficient power to bring him into the garden again.

The child had just vaguely recognized him for a moment at the waterside. He'd try that dodge, telepathy was a mild kind of a trick after so much of the miraculous. If he'd lost his blessed body, at least the part that ate and smoked and talked to Mildred....

He stopped as his mind stumbled on a strange recognition....

What a joke, of course ... idiot ...

not to have seen *that*. He stood up in the garden with joy ... of course, *he* was upstairs with Mildred, it was himself, the other bit of him, that Mildred had been talking to. What a howling fool he'd been.

He found himself concentrating his mind on the purpose of getting the child Gabriel into the garden once more, but it was with a curious mood that he endeavoured to establish this relationship. He could not fix his will into any calm intensity of power, or fixity of purpose, or pleasurable mental ecstasy. The utmost force seemed to come with a malicious threatening splenetic "entreaty." That damned snail in the hedge broke the thread of his meditation; a dog began to bark sturdily from a distant farm; the faculties of his mind became joggled up like a child's picture puzzle, and he brooded unintelligibly upon such things as skating and steam engines, and Elizabethan drama so lapped about with themes like jealousy and chastity. Really now, Shakespeare's Isabella was the most consummate snob in.... He looked up quickly to his wife's room and saw Gabriel step from the window to the balcony as if he were fearful of being seen. The boy lifted up his hands and placed the bright box on the rail of the balcony. He looked up at the faint stars for a moment or two, and then carefully released the lid of the box. What came out of it and rose into the air appeared to Codling to be just a piece of floating light, but as it soared above the roof he saw it grow to be a little ancient ship, with its hull and fully set sails and its three masts all of faint primrose flame colour. It cleaved through the air, rolling slightly as a ship through the wave, in widening circles above the house, making a curving ascent until it lost the shape of a vessel and became only a moving light hurrying to some sidereal shrine. Codling glanced at the boy on the balcony, but in that brief instant something had happened, the ship had burst like a rocket and released three coloured drops of fire which came falling slowly, leaving beautiful grey furrows of smoke in their track. Gabriel leaned over the rail with outstretched palms, and, catching the green star and the blue one as they drifted down to him, he ran with a rill of laughter back into the house. Codling sprang forward just in time to catch the red star; it lay vividly blasting his own palm for a monstrous second, and then, slipping through, was gone. He stared at the ground, at the balcony, the sky, and then heard an exclamation ... his wife stood at his side.

"Gilbert! How you frightened me!" she cried, "I thought you were in your room; come along in to dinner." She took his arm and they walked up the steps into the dining room together. "Just a moment,"

said her husband, turning to the door of the room.

His hand was upon the handle, which turned easily in his grasp, and he ran upstairs to his own room. He opened the door. The light was on, the fire was burning brightly, a smell of cigarette smoke about, pen and paper upon his desk, the Japanese book-knife, the gilt matchbox, everything all right, no one there.

He picked up a book from his desk.... *Monna Vanna.* His bookplate was in it—*Ex Libris—Gilbert Cannister*. He put it down beside the green dish; two yellow oranges were in the green dish, and two most deliberately green Canadian apples rested by their side. He went to the door and swung it backwards and forwards quite easily. He sat on his desk trying to piece the thing together, glaring at the print and the book-knife and the smart matchbox, until his wife came up behind him exclaiming: "Come along, Gilbert!"

"Where are the kids, old man?" he asked her, and, before she replied, he had gone along to the nursery.

He saw the two cots, his boy in one, his girl in the other. He turned whimsically to Mildred, saying, "There *are* only two, *are* there?" Such a question did not call for reply, but he confronted her as if expecting some assuring answer. She was staring at him with her bright beautiful eyes.

"Are there?" he repeated.

"How strange you should ask me that now!" she said.... "If you're a very good man ... perhaps...."

"Mildred!"

She nodded brightly.

He sat down in the rocking chair, but got up again saying to her gently—"We'll call him Gabriel."

"But, suppose—"

"No, no," he said, stopping her lovely lips, "I know all about him." And he told her a pleasant little tale.

THE PRINCESS OF KINGDOM GONE

THE PRINCESS OF KINGDOM GONE

Long ago a princess ruled over a very tiny kingdom, too small, indeed, for ambition. Had it been larger she might have been a queen, and had it been seven times larger, so people said, she would certainly have been an empress. As it was, the barbarians referred to her country as "that field!" or put other indignities upon it which, as she was highminded, the princess did not heed, or, if she did heed, had too much pride to acknowledge.

In other realms her mansion, her beautiful mansion, would have been called a castle, or even a palace, so high was the wall, crowned with pink tiles, that enclosed and protected it from evil. The common gaze was warded from the door by a grove of thorns and trees, through which an avenue curved a long way round from the house to the big gate. The gate was of knotted oak, but it had been painted and grained most cleverly to represent some other fabulous wood. There was this inscription upon it: NO HAWKERS, NO CIRCULARS, NO GRATUITIES. Everybody knew the princess had not got any of these things, but it was because they also knew the mansion had no throne in it that people sneered, really—but how unreasonable; you might just as well grumble at a chime that hadn't got a clock! As the princess herself remarked—"What *is* a throne without highmindedness!"—hinting, of course, at certain people whom I dare not name. Behind the mansion lay a wondrous garden, like the princess herself above everything in beauty. A very private bower was in the midst of it, guarded with corridors of shaven yew and a half-circle hedge of arbutus and holly. A slim river flowed, not by dispensation, but by accident, through the bower, and the bed and bank of it, screened by cypresses, had been lined, not by accident but by design—so strange are the workings of destiny—with tiles and elegant steps for a bathing pool. Here the princess, when the blazon of the sun was enticing, used to take off her robes of silk and her garments of linen and walk about the turf of the bower around the squinancy tree before slipping into the dark velvet water.

One day when she stepped out from the pool she discovered a lot of crimson flower petals clinging to her white skin. "How beautiful they are," she cried, picking up her mirror, "and where do they come from?" As soon as convenient she enquired upon this matter of her Lord

Chancellor, a man named Smith who had got on very well in life but was a bit of a smudge.

"Crimson petals in the bath!"

"Yes, they have floated down with the stream."

"How disgusting! Very! I'll make instant enquiries!"

He searched and he searched—he was very thorough was Smith—but though his researches took no end of time, and he issued a bulky dossier commanding all and sundry to attach the defiant person of the miscreant or miscreants who had defiled the princess's bath stream or pool with refuse detritus or scum, offering, too, rewards for information leading to his, her or their detection, conviction, and ultimate damnation, they availed him not. The princess continued to bathe and to emerge joyfully from the stream covered with petals and looking as wonderful as a crimson leopard. She caught some of the petals with a silver net; she dried them upon the sunlight and hid them in the lining of her bed, for they were full of acrid but pleasing odours. So she herself early one morning walked abroad, early indeed, and passed along the river until she came to the field adjoining the mansion. Very sweet and strange the world seemed in the quiet after dawn. She stopped beside a half-used rick to look about her; there was a rush of surprised wings behind the stack and a thousand starlings fled up into the air. She heard their wings beating the air until they had crossed the river and dropped gradually into an elm tree like a black shower. Then she perceived a tall tree shining with crimson blooms and long dark boughs bending low upon the river. Near it a tiny red cottage stood in the field like a painted box, surrounded by green triangular bushes. It was a respectable looking cottage, named *River View*. On her approach the door suddenly opened, and a youth with a towel, just that and nothing more, emerged. He took flying rejoicing leaps towards the flaming tree, sprung upon its lowest limb and flung himself into the stream. He glided there like a rod of ivory, but a crimson shower fell from the quivering tree and veiled the pleasing boy until he climbed out upon the opposite bank and stood covered, like a leopard, with splendid crimson scars. The princess dared peer no longer; she retraced her steps, musing homewards to breakfast, and was rude to Smith because he was such a fool not to have discovered the young man who lived next door under the mysterious tree.

At the earliest opportunity she left a card at *River View*. Narcissus was the subject's name, and in due time he came to dinner, and they had green grapes and black figs, nuts like sweet wax and wine like melted amethysts. The princess loved him so much that he visited her very often and stayed very late. He was only a poet and she a princess, so she could not possibly marry him although this was what she very quickly longed to do; but as she was only a princess, and he a poet clinking his golden spurs, he did not want to be married to her. He had thick curling locks of hair red as copper, the mild eyes of a child, and a voice that could outsing a thousand delightful birds. When she heard his soft laughter in the dim delaying eve he grew strange and alluring to the princess. She knew it was because he was so beautiful that everybody loved him and wanted to win and keep him, but he had no inclination for anything but his art—which was to express himself. That was very sad for the princess; to be able to retain nothing of him but his poems, his fading images, while he himself eluded her as the wind eludes all detaining arms, forest and feather, briar and down of a bird. He did not seem to be a man at all but just a fairy image that slipped from her arms, gone, like brief music in the moonlight, before she was aware.

When he fell sick she watched by his bed.

"Tell me," she murmured, her wooing palms caressing his flaming hair, "tell me you love me."

All he would answer was: "I dream of loving you, and I love dreaming of you, but how can I tell if I love you?"

Very tremulous but arrogant she demanded of him: "Shall I not know if you love me at all?"

"Ask the fox in your brake, the hart upon your mountain. I can never know if you love *me*."

"I have given you my deepest vows, Narcissus; love like this is wider than the world."

"The same wind blows in desert as in grove."

"You do not love at all."

"Words are vain, princess, but when I die, put these white hands like flowers about my heart; if I dream the unsleeping dream I will tell you there."

"My beloved," she said, "if you die I will put upon your grave a shrine of silver, and in it an ark of gold jewelled with green garnets and pink sapphires. My spirit should dwell in it alone and wait for you; until you came back again I could not live."

The poet died.

The princess was wild with grief, but she commanded her Lord Chancellor and he arranged magnificent obsequies. The shrine of silver and the ark of jewelled gold were ordered, a grave dug in a new planted garden more wonderful than the princess's bower, and a *To Let* bill appeared in the window of *River View*. At last Narcissus, with great pomp, was buried, the shrine and the ark of gold were clapped down upon him, and the princess in blackest robes was led away weeping on the arm of Smith—Smith was wonderful.

The sun that evening did not set—it mildly died out of the sky. Darkness came into the meadows, the fogs came out of them and hovered over the river and the familiar night sounds began. The princess sat in the mansion with a lonely heart from which all hopes were receding; no, not receding, she could see only the emptiness from which all her hopes had gone.

At midnight the spirit of Narcissus in its cerecloth rose up out of the grave, frail as a reed; rose out of its grave and stood in the cloudy moonlight beside the shrine and the glittering ark. He tapped upon the jewels with his fingers but there was no sound came from it, no fire, no voice. "O holy love," sighed the ghost, "it is true what I feared, it is true, alas, it is true!" And lifting again his vague arm he crossed out the inscription on his tomb and wrote there instead with a grey and crumbling finger his last poem:

Pride and grief in your heart,
Love and grief in mine.

Then he crept away until he came to the bower in the princess's garden. It was all silent and cold; the moon was touching with brief beam the paps of the plaster Diana. The ghost laid himself down to rest for ever beneath the squinancy tree, to rest and to wait; he wanted to forestall time's inscrutable awards. He sank slowly into the earth as a knot of foam slips through the beach of the seashore. Deep down he rested and waited.

Day after day, month after month, the constant princess went to her new grove of lamentation. The grave garden was magnificent with holy flowers, the shrine polished and glistening, the inscription crisp and clear—the ghost's erasure being vain for mortal eyes. In the ark she knew her spirit brooded and yearned, she fancied she could see its tiny flame behind the garnets and sapphires, and in a way this gave her happiness. Meanwhile her own once happy bower was left to neglect. The bolt rusted in its gate, the shrubs rioted, tree trunks were crusted with oozy fungus, their boughs cracked to decay, the rose fell rotten, and toads and vermin lurked in the desolation of the glades. 'Twas pitiful; 'twas as if the heart of the princess had left its pleasant bower and had indeed gone to live in her costly shrine.

In the course of time she was forced to go away on business of state and travelled for many months; on her return the face of the Lord Chancellor was gloomy with misery. The golden ark had been stolen. Alarm and chagrin filled the princess. She went to the grave. It too had now grown weedy and looked forlorn. It was as if her own heart had been stolen away from her. "Oh," she moaned, "what does it matter!" and, turning away, went home to her bower. There, among that sad sight, she saw a strange new tree almost in bloom. She gave orders for the pool to be cleansed and the bower restored to its former beauty. This was done, and on a bright day when the blazon of the sun was kind she went into the bower again, flung her black robes from her, and slipped like a rod of ivory into the velvet water. There were no blooms to gather now, though she searched with her silver net, but as she walked from the pool her long hair caught in the boughs of the strange tall squinancy tree, and in the disentangling it showered upon her beautiful crimson blooms that as they fell lingered upon her hips, her sweet shoulders, and kissed her shining knees.

COMMUNION

THE PRINCESS OF KINGDOM GONE

Long ago a princess ruled over a very tiny kingdom, too small, indeed, for ambition. Had it been larger she might have been a queen, and had it been seven times larger, so people said, she would certainly have been an empress. As it was, the barbarians referred to her country as "that field!" or put other indignities upon it which, as she was highminded, the princess did not heed, or, if she did heed, had too much pride to acknowledge.

In other realms her mansion, her beautiful mansion, would have been called a castle, or even a palace, so high was the wall, crowned with pink tiles, that enclosed and protected it from evil. The common gaze was warded from the door by a grove of thorns and trees, through which an avenue curved a long way round from the house to the big gate. The gate was of knotted oak, but it had been painted and grained most cleverly to represent some other fabulous wood. There was this inscription upon it: NO HAWKERS, NO CIRCULARS, NO GRATUITIES. Everybody knew the princess had not got any of these things, but it was because they also knew the mansion had no throne in it that people sneered, really—but how unreasonable; you might just as well grumble at a chime that hadn't got a clock! As the princess herself remarked—"What *is* a throne without highmindedness!"—hinting, of course, at certain people whom I dare not name. Behind the mansion lay a wondrous garden, like the princess herself above everything in beauty. A very private bower was in the midst of it, guarded with corridors of shaven yew and a half-circle hedge of arbutus and holly. A slim river flowed, not by dispensation, but by accident, through the bower, and the bed and bank of it, screened by cypresses, had been lined, not by accident but by design—so strange are the workings of destiny—with tiles and elegant steps for a bathing pool. Here the princess, when the blazon of the sun was enticing, used to take off her robes of silk and her garments of linen and walk about the turf of the bower around the squinancy tree before slipping into the dark velvet water.

One day when she stepped out from the pool she discovered a lot of crimson flower petals clinging to her white skin. "How beautiful they are," she cried, picking up her mirror, "and where do they come from?" As soon as convenient she enquired upon this matter of her Lord

Chancellor, a man named Smith who had got on very well in life but was a bit of a smudge.

"Crimson petals in the bath!"

"Yes, they have floated down with the stream."

"How disgusting! Very! I'll make instant enquiries!"

He searched and he searched—he was very thorough was Smith—but though his researches took no end of time, and he issued a bulky dossier commanding all and sundry to attach the defiant person of the miscreant or miscreants who had defiled the princess's bath stream or pool with refuse detritus or scum, offering, too, rewards for information leading to his, her or their detection, conviction, and ultimate damnation, they availed him not. The princess continued to bathe and to emerge joyfully from the stream covered with petals and looking as wonderful as a crimson leopard. She caught some of the petals with a silver net; she dried them upon the sunlight and hid them in the lining of her bed, for they were full of acrid but pleasing odours. So she herself early one morning walked abroad, early indeed, and passed along the river until she came to the field adjoining the mansion. Very sweet and strange the world seemed in the quiet after dawn. She stopped beside a half-used rick to look about her; there was a rush of surprised wings behind the stack and a thousand starlings fled up into the air. She heard their wings beating the air until they had crossed the river and dropped gradually into an elm tree like a black shower. Then she perceived a tall tree shining with crimson blooms and long dark boughs bending low upon the river. Near it a tiny red cottage stood in the field like a painted box, surrounded by green triangular bushes. It was a respectable looking cottage, named *River View*. On her approach the door suddenly opened, and a youth with a towel, just that and nothing more, emerged. He took flying rejoicing leaps towards the flaming tree, sprung upon its lowest limb and flung himself into the stream. He glided there like a rod of ivory, but a crimson shower fell from the quivering tree and veiled the pleasing boy until he climbed out upon the opposite bank and stood covered, like a leopard, with splendid crimson scars. The princess dared peer no longer; she retraced her steps, musing homewards to breakfast, and was rude to Smith because he was such a fool not to have discovered the young man who lived next door under the mysterious tree.

At the earliest opportunity she left a card at *River View*. Narcissus was the subject's name, and in due time he came to dinner, and they had green grapes and black figs, nuts like sweet wax and wine like melted amethysts. The princess loved him so much that he visited her very often and stayed very late. He was only a poet and she a princess, so she could not possibly marry him although this was what she very quickly longed to do; but as she was only a princess, and he a poet clinking his golden spurs, he did not want to be married to her. He had thick curling locks of hair red as copper, the mild eyes of a child, and a voice that could outsing a thousand delightful birds. When she heard his soft laughter in the dim delaying eve he grew strange and alluring to the princess. She knew it was because he was so beautiful that everybody loved him and wanted to win and keep him, but he had no inclination for anything but his art—which was to express himself. That was very sad for the princess; to be able to retain nothing of him but his poems, his fading images, while he himself eluded her as the wind eludes all detaining arms, forest and feather, briar and down of a bird. He did not seem to be a man at all but just a fairy image that slipped from her arms, gone, like brief music in the moonlight, before she was aware.

When he fell sick she watched by his bed.

"Tell me," she murmured, her wooing palms caressing his flaming hair, "tell me you love me."

All he would answer was: "I dream of loving you, and I love dreaming of you, but how can I tell if I love you?"

Very tremulous but arrogant she demanded of him: "Shall I not know if you love me at all?"

"Ask the fox in your brake, the hart upon your mountain. I can never know if you love *me*."

"I have given you my deepest vows, Narcissus; love like this is wider than the world."

"The same wind blows in desert as in grove."

"You do not love at all."

"Words are vain, princess, but when I die, put these white hands like flowers about my heart; if I dream the unsleeping dream I will tell you there."

"My beloved," she said, "if you die I will put upon your grave a shrine of silver, and in it an ark of gold jewelled with green garnets and pink sapphires. My spirit should dwell in it alone and wait for you; until you came back again I could not live."

The poet died.

The princess was wild with grief, but she commanded her Lord Chancellor and he arranged magnificent obsequies. The shrine of silver and the ark of jewelled gold were ordered, a grave dug in a new planted garden more wonderful than the princess's bower, and a *To Let* bill appeared in the window of *River View*. At last Narcissus, with great pomp, was buried, the shrine and the ark of gold were clapped down upon him, and the princess in blackest robes was led away weeping on the arm of Smith—Smith was wonderful.

The sun that evening did not set—it mildly died out of the sky. Darkness came into the meadows, the fogs came out of them and hovered over the river and the familiar night sounds began. The princess sat in the mansion with a lonely heart from which all hopes were receding; no, not receding, she could see only the emptiness from which all her hopes had gone.

At midnight the spirit of Narcissus in its cerecloth rose up out of the grave, frail as a reed; rose out of its grave and stood in the cloudy moonlight beside the shrine and the glittering ark. He tapped upon the jewels with his fingers but there was no sound came from it, no fire, no voice. "O holy love," sighed the ghost, "it is true what I feared, it is true, alas, it is true!" And lifting again his vague arm he crossed out the inscription on his tomb and wrote there instead with a grey and crumbling finger his last poem:

Pride and grief in your heart,
Love and grief in mine.

Then he crept away until he came to the bower in the princess's garden. It was all silent and cold; the moon was touching with brief beam the paps of the plaster Diana. The ghost laid himself down to rest for ever beneath the squinancy tree, to rest and to wait; he wanted to forestall time's inscrutable awards. He sank slowly into the earth as a knot of foam slips through the beach of the seashore. Deep down he rested and waited.

Day after day, month after month, the constant princess went to her new grove of lamentation. The grave garden was magnificent with holy flowers, the shrine polished and glistening, the inscription crisp and clear—the ghost's erasure being vain for mortal eyes. In the ark she knew her spirit brooded and yearned, she fancied she could see its tiny flame behind the garnets and sapphires, and in a way this gave her happiness. Meanwhile her own once happy bower was left to neglect. The bolt rusted in its gate, the shrubs rioted, tree trunks were crusted with oozy fungus, their boughs cracked to decay, the rose fell rotten, and toads and vermin lurked in the desolation of the glades. 'Twas pitiful; 'twas as if the heart of the princess had left its pleasant bower and had indeed gone to live in her costly shrine.

In the course of time she was forced to go away on business of state and travelled for many months; on her return the face of the Lord Chancellor was gloomy with misery. The golden ark had been stolen. Alarm and chagrin filled the princess. She went to the grave. It too had now grown weedy and looked forlorn. It was as if her own heart had been stolen away from her. "Oh," she moaned, "what does it matter!" and, turning away, went home to her bower. There, among that sad sight, she saw a strange new tree almost in bloom. She gave orders for the pool to be cleansed and the bower restored to its former beauty. This was done, and on a bright day when the blazon of the sun was kind she went into the bower again, flung her black robes from her, and slipped like a rod of ivory into the velvet water. There were no blooms to gather now, though she searched with her silver net, but as she walked from the pool her long hair caught in the boughs of the strange tall squinancy tree, and in the disentangling it showered upon her beautiful crimson blooms that as they fell lingered upon her hips, her sweet shoulders, and kissed her shining knees.

COMMUNION

COMMUNION

He was of years calendared in unreflecting minds as tender years, and he was clothed in tough corduroy knickerbockers, once the habiliments of a huger being, reaching to the tops of some boots shod with tremendous nails and fastened by bits of fugitive string. His jacket was certainly the jacket of a child—possibly some dead one, for it was not his own—and in lieu of a collar behold a twist of uncoloured, unclean flannel. Pink face, pink hands, yellow hair, a quite unredeemable dampness about his small nose—altogether he was a country boy.

"What are you doing there, Tom Prowse?" asked Grainger, the sexton, entering to him suddenly one Saturday afternoon. The boy was sitting on a bench in the empty nave, hands on knees, looking towards the altar. He rose to his feet and went timidly through the doorway under the stern glance of that tall tall man, whose height enabled him to look around out of a grave when it was completely dug. "You pop on out of 'ere," said Grainger, threateningly, but to himself, when the boy had gone.

Walking into the vestry Grainger emptied his pockets of a number of small discarded bottles and pots of various shapes and uses—ink bottles, bottles for gum and meat extract, fish-paste pots, and tins which had contained candy. He left them there. The boy, after he had watched him go away, came back and resumed his seat behind one of the round piers.

A lady dressed in black entered and, walking to the front stall under the pulpit, knelt down. The boy stared at the motionless figure for a long time until his eyes ached and the intense silence made him cough a little. He was surprised at the booming hollow echo and coughed again. The lady continued bowed in her place; he could hear her lips whispering sibilantly: the wind came into the porch with sudden gust and lifted the arras at the door. Turning he knocked his clumsy boots against the bench. After that the intense silence came back again, humming in his ears and almost stopping his breath, until he heard footsteps on the gravel path. The vicar's maid entered and went towards the vestry. She wished to walk softly when she observed the kneeling lady but her left shoe squeaked stubbornly as she moved, and both heels and soles echoed in sharp tones along the tiles of the chancel. The boy heard the rattle of a bucket handle and saw the maid place the bucket beside the altar and fetch flowers and bottles and pots from the vestry. Some she stood upon the table of the altar; others, tied by pieces of string, she hung in unique positions upon the front and sides, filling them with water from the pail as she did so; and because the string was white, and the altar was white, and the ugly bottles were hidden in nooks of moss, it looked as if the very cloth of the altar sprouted with casual bloom.

* * *

Not until the maid had departed did the lady who had been bowed so long lift up her head adoringly towards the brass cross; the boy overheard her deep sigh; then she, too, went away, and in a few moments more the boy followed and walked clumsily, thoughtfully, to his home.

His father was the village cobbler. He was a widower, and he was a freethinker too; no mere passive rejector of creeds, but an active opponent with a creed of his own, which if less violent was not less bigoted than those he so witheringly decried. The child Tom had never been allowed to attend church; until today, thus furtively, he had never even entered one, and in the day school religious instruction had been forbidden by his atheistic father. But while faith goes on working its miracles the whirligigs of unfaith bring on revenges. The boy now began to pay many secret visits to the church. He would walk under the western tower and slip his enclosing palms up and down the woolly rope handles, listen to the slow beat of the clock, and rub with his wristband the mouldings of the brass lectern with the ugly bird on a ball and the three singular chubby animals at the foot, half ox, half dog, displaying monstrous teeth. He scrutinized the florid Georgian memorial fixed up the wall, recording the virtues, which he could not read, of a departed Rodney Giles; made of marble, there were two naked fat little boys with wings; they pointed each with one hand towards the name, and with the other held a handkerchief each to one tearful eye. This was very agreeable to young Prowse, but most he loved to sit beside one of the pillars—the stone posties, he called them—and look at the window above the altar where for ever half a dozen angels postured rhythmically upon the ladder of Jacob.

One midsummer evening, after evensong, he entered for his usual meditation. He had no liking for any service or ritual; he had no apprehension of the spiritual symbols embodied in the building; he only liked to sit there in the quiet, gazing at things in a dumb sort of way, taking, as it were, a bath of holiness. He sat a long time; indeed, so still was he, he might have been dozing as the legions of dead parishioners had dozed during interminable dead sermons. When he went to the door—the light having grown dim—he found it was locked. He was not at all alarmed at his situation: he went and sat down again. In ten minutes or so he again approached the door ... it was still locked. Then he walked up the aisle to the chancel steps and crossed the choir for the first time. Choristers' robes were in the vestry, and soon, arrayed in cassock and surplice, he was walking with a singular little dignity to his old seat by one of the pillars. He sat there with folded hands, the church growing gloomier now; he climbed into the pulpit and turned over the leaves of the holy book; he sat in the choir stalls, pretended to play the organ, and at last went before the altar and, kneeling at the rails, clasped his orthodox hands and murmured, as he had heard others murmuring there, a rigmarole of his scholastic hours:

* * *

Thirty days hath September,
April, June and November.
All the rest have thirty-one,
Excepting February alone,
And leap year coming once in four,
February then has one day more.

Re-entering the vestry, he observed on a shelf in a niche a small loaf wrapped in a piece of linen. He felt hungry and commenced to devour the bread, and from a goblet there he drank a little sip of sweet tasting wine. He liked the wine very much, and drank more and more of it.

There was nothing else to be done now in the darkness, so he went on to the soft carpet within the altar rails, and, piling up a few of the praying mats from the choir—little red cushions they were, stamped with black fleur-de-lys, which he admired much in the daylight—he fell asleep.

And he slept long and deeply until out of some wonderful place he began to hear the word "Ruffian, Ruffian," shouted with anger and harshness. He was pulled roughly to his feet, and apprehension was shaken into his abominable little head.

The morning sunlight was coming through the altar window, and the vicar's appearance was many-coloured as a wheelwright's door; he had a green face, and his surplice was scaled with pink and purple gouts like a rash from some dreadful rainbow. And dreadful indeed was the vicar as he thrust the boy down the altar steps into the vestry, hissing as he did, "Take off those things!" and darting back to throw the cushions into proper places to support the knees of the expected devotees.

"Now, how did you get in here?" he demanded, angrily.

The boy hung up the cassock: "Someone locked me in last night, Sir."

"Who was it?"

"I dunno, Sir, they locked me in all night."

His interrogator glared at him for a moment in silence, and the boy could not forbear a yawn. Thereat the vicar seized him by the ear and, pulling it with such animation as to contort his own features as well as the child's, dragged him to the vestry door, gurgling with uncontrolled vexation, "Get out of this. Get out ... you ... you beast!"

As the boy went blinking down the nave the tenor bell began to ring; the stone posties looked serene and imperturbable in new clean sunlight, and that old blackbird was chirping sweetly in the lilac at the porch.

THE QUIET WOMAN

THE QUIET WOMAN

It was the loneliest place in the world, Hardross said. A little cogitation and much experience had given him the fancy that the ark of the kingdom of solitude was lodged in a lift, any lift, carrying a charter of mute passengers from the pavement to any sort of Parnassus. Nothing ever disturbs its velveteen progression; no one ever speaks to the lift man (unless it happens to be a lift girl). At Hardross's place of abode it happened to be a lift boy, sharp and white-faced, whose tough hair was swept backwards in a stiff lock from his brow, while his pert nose seemed inclined to pursue it. His name was Brown. His absences from duty were often coincident with the arrivals and departures of Mr. Hardross. His hands were brown enough if the beholder carried some charity in his bosom, but the aspect of his collar or his shoes engendered a deal of vulgar suspicion, and his conduct was at once inscrutable and unscrupulous. It may have been for this reason that Hardross had lately begun walking the whole downward journey from his high chamber, but it must have been something less capricious that caused him always to essay the corresponding upward flight. A fancy for exercise perhaps, for he was a robust musician, unmarried, and of course, at thirty-three or thirty-four, had come to the years of those indiscretions which he could with impunity and without reprobation indulge.

On the second floor, outside the principal door of one set of chambers, there always stood a small console table; it was just off the landing, in an alcove that covered two other doors, a little dark angular-limbed piece of furniture bearing a green lacquer dish of void visiting cards, a heap that seemed neither to increase nor dwindle but lay there as if soliciting, so naïvely, some further contributions. Two maiden ladies, the Misses Pilcher, who kept these rooms, had gone to France for a summer holiday, but though the flat had for the time being some new occupants the console table still kept its place, the dish of cards of course languishing rather unhopefully. The new tenants were also two ladies, but they were clearly not sisters and just as clearly not Pilcherly old maids. One of them, Hardross declared, was the loveliest creature he had ever seen. She was dark, almost tall, about as tall as Hardross though a little less robust and rather more graceful. Her mature scarlet lips and charming mature eyes seemed always to be wanting to speak to him. But she did not speak to him, even when he modestly tried to overcome, well, not her reserve—no one with such sparkling eyes could possibly be reserved—but her silence. He often passed her on the landing but he did not hear her voice, or music, or speech, or any kind of intercourse within the room. He called her The Quiet Woman. The other lady, much older, was seldom seen; she was of great dignity. The younger one walked like a woman conscious and proud of the beauty underneath her beautiful clothes; the soft slippers she wore seemed charged with that silent atmosphere. Even the charwoman who visited them daily and rattled and swept about was sealed of the conspiracy of silence; at least he never caught—though it must be confessed that he guiltily tried—the passage of a single word. What was the mystery of the obstinately silent ménage? Did the elder lady suffer from sorrow or nerves; was she under a vow; was she a genius writing a sublime book?

The voiceless character of the intercourse did not prevent Hardross becoming deeply enamoured and at the same time deeply baffled. Morning and evening as he went to the great city church of which he was organist he would often catch a glimpse of his quiet woman on the stairs. At favourable junctures he had lifted his hat and said Good-morning or Good-evening, but she had turned away as if overcome by confusion or an excess of propriety.

"I am a coward," he would think; "shyness and diffidence rule me, they curse me, they ruin my life; but she, good heavens! is extraordinarily retiring. Why, I am just a satyr, a rampant raging satyr, a satyr!" And he would liken her to Diana, always darting with such fawnlike modesty from the alcove whenever he approached. He did not even know her name. He wanted to enquire of the lift boy Brown or the porter, but there again he lacked the casual touch to bring off the information. The boy was too young, too cute, too vulgar, and the porter too taciturn, as difficult for Hardross to approach as an archbishop would have been. But Miss Barker now, that milliner, down below on the ground floor! She would know; she knew everybody and everything about the chambers including, quite familiarly, Hardross himself—she would be sure to know. But even she would have to be approached with discrimination.

"Evening, Miss Barker!" he cried. The good-looking spinster peered up from a half-trimmed bonnet. "When do *you* go for a holiday, then?"

"Holidays," she sighed, though the corner of her mouth was packed with pins, "I cannot afford holidays."

"Ho-ho, you can't afford!"

Their common fund of repartee lay in his confident assumption that she was rolling in surplus income and her counter assertion that she was stricken in poverty; that people—the pigs—would not pay her prices, or that those who did not flinch at her prices would not pay her bills.

"Astonishing, deplorable, this Mammon-worship!" he declared, leaning genially upon her table; "you know, it breaks my heart to see you a slave to it, a woman of a thousand, ten thousand in fact. Give it up, O,"—he beat the table with his hand—"give it up before it is too late!"

"Too late for what?" she asked.

"Why, all the delightful things a woman like you could do."

"As what?"

* * *

"O ... travel, glories of nature, you know, friendship, men ... love itself."

"Give me all the money I want,"—she was brusque about it, and began to dab the unwanted pins back into their cushion—"and I'll buy, yes *buy*, a sweetheart for each day in the week."

"Heavens now!" He was chilled by this implication of an experience that may have been dull, that must have been bitter, but he floundered on: "What now would you give for me?"

"For you!" She contemplated him with gravity: "To be sure I had not thought of you, not in that way."

"O but please *do* think of me, dear lady, put me in your deepest regard."

The ghost of a knowing grin brushed her features. Really a charming woman, in parts. A little stout, perhaps, and she had fat red hands, but her heart was a good substantial organ, it was in the right place, and her features seemed the best for wear.

"You are one of those surprising ladies"—he plunged gaily—"who've a long stocking somewhere, with trunks full of shares and scrip, stocks at the bank and mortgages at your solicitor's. O yes, yes," he cried out against her protestation, "and you will make a strange will leaving it all to me!"

She shook her head hopelessly, bending again over the bonnet whose desperate skeleton she had clothed with a flounce of crimson velvet. She was very quiet.

* * *

"Have I been rude?" he hazarded. "Forgive me."

"Well, it's not true," she insisted.

"Forgive me—I have hurt you—of course it's not true."

Apparently she forgave him; he was soon asking if there were any rooms to let in the building. "Furnished, I mean." He gave rein to his naïve strategy: "I have friends who want to come here and stay with me for a short holiday. I thought you might know of some."

"In these flats?" She shook her head, but he persisted and played his artful card:

"The Miss Pilchers, on the second floor, haven't they gone away?"

She did not know—why not ask the porter.

"Yes, I must ask the porter, but I can never catch the porter, he is so fugitive, he is always cutting his lucky. I hate that man, don't you?"

And there, temporarily, he had to leave it.

So many days passed now without a glimpse of his lovely one that he had almost brought himself to the point of tapping at the door and enquiring after her welfare, only the mysterious air of the apartment—how strange, how soundless it was—forbade any such crudeness. One morning he recklessly took a cigarette from his case and laid it upon the console table as he passed. When he returned later the cigarette was gone; it had been replaced by a chocolate cream, just one, a big one. He snatched it away and rapturously ate it. Later in the day he was blessed by a deep friendly gaze, as she flitted into her room. Hardross rejoiced; in the morning he left another cigarette and was again rewarded.

"But O God help me," he thought, "I can't go on like this!"

So he bought a whole box of bonbons, but his courage deserted him as he approached their door; he left the package upon the console table and slunk guiltily away. The next morning he observed a whole box of cigarettes, a well-known exquisite brand, laid temptingly there. He stretched his eager hand towards it, but paused. Could that be a gift for him? Heavens above! What were the miraculous gods about to shower upon him? Was this their delicate symbol? He could not believe it, no, he could not, he left the box lying there. And it lay there for hours indeed until he crept down and seized it. Afterwards he walked trembling into the brighter air and went for a long ride on the top of an omnibus. There had been no letter, but he fancied that he had got hold of a clue. "Be very careful, Hardross my boy, this is too too splendid to spoil."

An afternoon or so later he met her coming into the hall, a delicious figure with gay parasol and wide white hat. He delayed her:

"Let me thank you, may I, for those perfect cigarettes?"

The lovely creature did not reply. She just smiled her recognition of him; she did not speak nor move away, she stood there quite silent and timid.

"I wonder," he began again, "if I might"—it sounded dreadfully silly to him, but having begun he went on—"if I might invite you to my church this evening, a rather special choral service, very jolly, you know. I'm the organist; would you come?"

No answer.

"Would you care to come?"

She lifted both her hands and touching her lips and ears with significant gestures shook her head ever so hopelessly at him.

"Deaf and dumb!" he exclaimed. Perhaps the shock of the revelation showed too painfully in his face for she turned now sadly away. But the hall was divinely empty. He caught one of the exquisite hands and pressed it to his lips.

Thereafter Hardross walked about as if he too were deaf and dumb, except for a vast effusion of sighs. He could praise that delicacy of the rarest whereby she had forborne to lure him, as she could so easily have done, into a relation so shrouded and so vague. But that did not solve his problem, it only solidified it. He wanted and awaited the inspiration of a gesture she could admire, something that would propitiate her delicacy and alarms. He did not want to destroy by clumsy persistencies the frail net of her regard for him; he was quite clear about that, the visible fineness of her quality so quelled him. Applying himself to the task he took lessons in the alphabet language, that inductile response of fingers and thumbs.

Meanwhile she had marked her sense of the complication by hiding like a hurt bird, and although the mystery of the quiet rooms was now exposed she herself remained unseen. He composed a graceful note and left it upon the console table. The note disappeared but no reply came: she made no sign and he regretted his ardour.

Such a deadlock of course could not exist for ever, and one evening he met her walking up the stairs. She stopped mutually with him. He was carrying his music. He made a vain attempt to communicate with her by means of his finger alphabet, but she did not understand him although she delightedly made a reply on her fingers which he was too recently initiated to interpret. They were again at a standstill: he could think of nothing to do except to open his book of organ music and show her the title page. She looked it over very intelligently as he tried by signs to convey his desire to her, but he was certain she was blank about it all. He searched his pockets for a pencil—and swore at his non-success. There he stood like a fool, staring at her smiling face until to his amazement she took his arm and they descended the stairs, they were in the street together. He walked to the church on something vastly less substantial than air, and vastly superior.

Hardross's church was square and ugly, with large round-headed windows. Its entrance was up some steps between four Corinthian pillars upon the bases of which cabmen snoozed when it was warm or coughed and puffed in the winter cold. There was a pump on the kerb and a stand for hackney cabs. A jungle of evergreens squatted in a railed corner under the tower, with a file of iris plants that never flowered. Upon the plinth of the columns a ribald boy had chalked:

REMOVE THIS OBSTACLE

Eternally at the porch tired cabhorses drooped and meditated, while the drivers cut hunches of bread and meat or cheese or onion and swallowed from their tin bottles the cold tea or other aliment associated with tin bottles. There was always a smell of dung at the entrance, and an aroma of shag tobacco from the cabmen's pipes curled into the nave whenever the door opened for worshippers. Inside the church Hardross ushered his friend to a seat that he could watch from his organ loft. There were few people present. He borrowed a lead pencil from a choir boy, and while the lesson was being perfunctorily intoned, sounding like some great voice baffled by its infinitely little mind, he scribbled on a sheet of paper the questions he was so eager to ask; what was her name and things like that:

How can we communicate? May I write to you? Will you to me? Excuse the catechism and scribble but I want so much to know you and grab at this opportunity.

Yours devotedly
John Hardross

When he looked up her place was empty; she had gone away in the middle of the service. He hurried home at last very perturbed and much abashed, for it was not so much the perplexities of intercourse, the torment of his dilemma, that possessed him now as a sense of felicities forbidden and amenities declined.

* * *

But his fickle intelligence received a sharp admonitory nudge on the following evening when he espied her sitting in the same place at church for all the world as if she had not deserted it on the evening before. Then he remembered that of course she couldn't hear a thing—idiot he was to have invited her. Again she left the church before the close of the service.

This for several days, the tantalized lover beholding her figure always hurrying from his grasp.

He pursued the practice of the deaf and dumb alphabet with such assiduity that he became almost apt in its use; the amount of affection and devotion that he could transcribe on finger and thumb was prodigious, he yearned to put it to the test. When at last he met her again in the hall he at once began spelling out things, absurd things, like: "May I beg the honour of your acquaintance?" She watched this with interest, with excitement even, but a shadow of doubt crept into her lovely eyes. She moved her own fingers before him, but in vain; he could not interpret a single word, not one. He was a dense fool; O how dense, how dense! he groaned. But then he searched his pockets and brought out the note he had scribbled in church. It was a little the worse for wear but he smoothed it, and standing close by her side held it for her perusal. Again his hopes were dashed. She shook her head, not at all conclusively but in a vague uncomprehending way. She even with a smile indicated her need of a pencil, which he promptly supplied. To his amazement what she scribbled upon the page were some meaningless hieroglyphs, not letters, though they were grouped as in words, but some strange abracadabra. He looked so dismally at her that she smiled again, folding the paper carefully ere she passed on up the stairs.

Hardross was now more confounded than ever. A fearful suspicion seized him: was she an idiot, was it a mild insanity, were those marks just the notation of a poor diseased mind? He wished he had kept that letter. God, what a tragedy! But as he walked into the town his doubts about her intellect were dispelled. Poof! only an imbecile himself could doubt that beautiful staring intelligence. That was not it; it was some jugglery, something to do with those rooms. Nothing was solved yet, nothing at all; how uncanny it was becoming!

He returned in the afternoon full of determination. Behold, like a favourable augury, the door by the console table stood open, wide open. It did occur to him that an open door might be a trap for unwary men but he rapped the brass knocker courageously. Of course there was no response—how could there be—and he stepped inside the room. His glance had but just time to take in the small black piano, the dark carpet, the waxed margins of the floor, the floral dinginess of the walls brightened by mirrors and softened by gilt and crimson furniture, when the quiet woman, his Diana, came to him joyfully holding out both her hands. Well, there was no mystery here after all, nothing at all, although the elder lady was out and they were apparently alone. Hardross held her hands for some moments, the intensity of which was as deeply projected in her own eyes as in the tightness of his clasp. And there was tea for him! She was at her brightest, in a frock of figured muslin, and sitting before her he marvelled at the quickness of her understanding, the vividness of her gestures, the gentleness with which she touched his sleeve. That criminal suspicion of her sanity crowned him with infamy. Such communication was deliciously intimate; there came a moment when Hardross in a wild impulsive ecstasy flung himself before her, bowing his head in her lap. The quiet woman was giving him back his embraces, her own ardour was drooping beautifully upon him, when he heard a strange voice exclaim in the room: "God is my help! Well then!" A rattle of strange words followed which he could not comprehend. He turned to confront the elder woman, who surveyed them with grim amusement. The other stood up, smiling, and the two women spoke in finger language. The newcomer began to remove her gloves, saying:

"It is Mr. Hardross then. I am glad to meet. There is a lot of things to be spoken, eh?"

She was not at all the invalid he had half expected to find. She removed her hat and came back a competent-looking woman of about fifty, who had really an overwhelming stream of conversation. She took tea and, ignoring the girl as if she were a block of uncomprehending ornament, addressed herself to the interloper.

"You do not know me, Mr. Hardross?"

"It is a pleasure I have but looked forward to," he replied, in the formal manner that at times irresistibly seized him, "with the keenest possible anticipation and...."

"No, I am Madame Peshkov. We are from Odessa, do you know it? We go back to our Russia tomorrow; yes, it is true."

His organs of comprehension began to crackle in his skull, but he went on stirring his fresh cup of tea and continued to do so for quite a long time.

"No, you ... are ... Russian! I did not know." Amid his musing astonishment that fact alone was portentous; it explained so much, everything in fact, but how he could ever contrive to learn such a language was the question that agitated him, so fearfully difficult a language, and on his fingers too! Then that other thunderclap began to reverberate: they were going, when was it? Tomorrow! All this while Madame Peshkov ran on with extravagant volubility. She had the habit of picking one of the hairpins from her hair and gently rubbing her scalp with the rounded end of it; she would replace the pin with a stylish tap of her fingers. It was a long time before Hardross extracted the pith from her remarks, and then only when the hypnotism induced by the stirring of his tea suddenly lapsed; he became aware of the dumb girl's gaze fixed piercingly upon him, while his own was drawn away by the force of the other's revelations. What he had already taken in was sad and strange. Her name was Julia Krasinsky. She was not at all related to Madame Peshkov, she was an orphan. Madame's own daughter had been deaf and dumb, too, and the girls had been inseparable companions until two years ago, when Natalia Peshkov had died—O, an unspeakable grief still. He gathered that Madame was a widow, and that since Natalia's death the two women had lived and travelled together. Madame talked on; it was tremendously exciting to Hardross crouching in his chair, but all that echoed in his mind were the words Julia Krasinsky, Julia Krasinsky, until she suddenly asked him:

"Do you love her?"

He was startled by this appalling directness; he stammered a little but he finally brought out:

"I adore her. Beyond everything I deeply deeply love her." He then added: "I feel shameful enough now. I rage inwardly. All these many weeks I have dallied like a boy, I did not understand the situation. I have wasted our chances, our time, and now you are going."

"You can't waste time"; retorted the abrupt lady. "Time deals with you no matter how you use his hours."

"I suppose so," he agreed quite helplessly, "but we might have been extraordinary friends."

"O, but you are, eh! She is bewitched, you cannot speak to her, she cannot speak to you, but yet you love. O, she is vairy vairy fond of you, Mr. Hardross. Why not? She has the best opinions of you."

"Ah, she will change her opinion now. A fool like me?"

"No one ever changes an opinion. Your opinions govern and guide and change you. If they don't they are not worth holding. And most of them are not, eh, do you see, we are such fools but God is our help."

She talked confidently, intimately and quickly, but Hardross wished she would not do so, or use her hairpins in that absurd distracting way. He himself had no confidence; he was reserved by nature, irrevocably, and the mask of deliberation was necessary to him.

"Madame Peshkov, I shall take her out for a walk in the town, now, at once!" he cried.

"Ah, so?" Madame nodded her head vigorously, even approvingly. He had sprung up and approached the quiet woman. All her gentle nearness overcame him and he took her audaciously into his arms. Not less eagerly she slid to his breast and clung there like a bird to the shelter of its tree. Julia turned to Madame Peshkov with a smiling apologetic shrug, as much as to say: "What can one do with such a fellow, so strong he is, you see!" Madame bade him bring Julia later on to the café where they always dined.

His happiness was profound. He had never had an experience so moving as the adorable dumb woman by his side: yet so unsurprising, as if its possibility had always lain goldenly in his mind like an undreamed dream, or like music, half-remembered music. There was nothing, of course, just nothing they could talk about. They could look into shop windows together rather intimately, and they were a long time in a shady arcade of the park, full of lime-browsing bees, where they sat watching a peacock picking the gnats off the shrubs. It was the pleasantest possible defeat of time. Then there was the handsome girl crossing the yard of a weaving mill as they passed. She was carrying a great bale of bright blue wool and had glanced at them with a friendly smile. Her bare white arms encircled the wool: she had big gilt rings in her ears, and her fine shining chestnut-coloured hair was disarrayed and tumbled upon the bale. Julia had pressed his arm with joy. Yes, she delighted in the things he delighted in; and she felt too that sense of sorrow that hung in the air about them.

Her appearance in the café stirred everybody like a wave of sweet air. Hardross was filled with pride. He felt that it was just so that she would enrich the world wherever she wandered, that things would respond to her appearance in astonishing mysterious ways. Why, even the empty wine glasses seemed to behave like large flowers made miraculously out of water, a marvel of crystal petals blooming but for her; certainly the glasses on other tables didn't look at all like these. He drank four glasses of wine and after dinner they all sat together in the flat until the half darkness was come. And now Madame Peshkov too was very silent; she sat smoking or scratching her head with her pins. It was nine o'clock, but there remained a preposterous glare in the west that threw lateral beams against the tops of tall buildings, although the pavements were already dim. It made the fronts of the plastered houses over the way look like cream cheese. Six scarlet chimney pots stood stolidly at attention—the torsos of six guardsmen from whom head and limbs had been unkindly smitten; the roof seemed to be rushing away from them. Beyond was an echo of the sunset, faint in the northern sky. How sweet, how sad, to sit so silently in this tremulous gloom. It was only at the last when they parted at her door that the shadow of their division became omnipresent. Then it overwhelmed them.

Hardross crept upstairs to his own rooms. In such plights the mind, careless of time present and time past, full of an anguish that quenches and refills like a sponge, writhes beyond hope with those strange lesions of demeanour that confound the chronicler. Tra-la-la, sang the distracted man, snapping his sweating fingers in time with a ribald leering ditty, Tra-la-la. He dropped plumb to Atlantean depths of grief, only to emerge like a spouting whale with the maddening Tra-la-la tugging him, a hook in his body, from despair to dementia. He was roused from this vertiginous exercise by a knocking at his door. The door was thrust open, and Madame Peshkov asked if he was there. He rose up and switched on a light.

"What is to be done now?" cried the lady. If her silence below had been complete, as complete as poor Julia's, she was now fully audible and not a little agitated. "What is to be done? I cannot believe it of her but it is true, as true as God!"

Hardross beheld her sink, stricken with some trouble, into an armchair, beating her hands together.

"I have no influence, gone it is, no power over her, none whatever. What is to be done? Assist us please. She has been so.... O, for days, and now it comes, it comes...."

"What has come?" he interrupted sharply.

* * *

"I cannot believe it of her, but it is true ... as God. She is like a vast ... cold ... stone, a mountain."

"Is this about Julia?"

"She will not go. Of course she will not go! She declines, she will not come back to Odessa. She says she will not come. I have to tell you this, Mr. Hardross, I cannot move her. She is like a vast ... cold ... stone. What then?"

Madame's appeal seemed pregnant with a significance that he but dimly savoured. He asked: "What is she going to do then?"

"To stop in this England, here, in this very place! But our passages are booked, tomorrow it is—pooh, it does not matter!—I am to leave her here in this place, here she will stay, in a foreign land, without speech or understanding. But what is to be done, I ask of you?"

He was delirious himself; he kept whispering Julia, Julia, but he managed to ask with a lugubrious covering of propriety:

"What? I don't know. Shall I go to her?"

"But can you not see? Do you comprehend, you Hardross? O, it is a madness, I want to explain it to you but it is all so gross, so swift, like a vulture. You see it is impossible for me to remain an hour longer, an hour in England impossible absolutely; there are reasons, lives perhaps, depending on my return. Yes, it is true; we live in Russia, do you see, and in Russia ... ah, you understand! But how shall I leave this woman here?"

* * *

Madame stared at him with curious inquisitiveness, beating her hands upon the arm of the chair as if she expected an answer, a prompt one:

"Of course she will not go away from you now, of course, of course, she has never had a lover before—how could she, poor thing. I understand it, she is not a child. And you Mr. Hardross you are a generous man, you have courage, a good man, a man of his honour, O yes, it is true, I see it, I feel it, and so she will not be torn away from you now. I understand that, she is no longer a child."

Madame rose and took him by the arm. "Marry her, my friend! Do not you see? I can leave her to you. Marry her at once, marry her!" She stood as if it were something that could be done on the spot, as easy as giving one a cup of tea. But he did not hesitate.

"Why, I would give my soul to do it!" he cried, and rushed away down the stairs to Julia.

And surely she was as wise as she was beautiful, and as rich as she was wise.

THE TRUMPETERS

THE TRUMPETERS

They were crossing the Irish Sea. It was night, blowing a moderate gale, but the moon, aloft on the port bow with a wind, was chock full of such astounding brightness that the turmoil of the dark waves was easy and beautiful to see. The boat was crowded with soldiers on leave; the few civilian passengers—mechanics, labourers, and a miner going to his home in Wexford, who had got drunk at the harbour inn before coming aboard—were congregated in the angles on the lee-side of the saloon bunks and trying to sleep amid the chill seething, roaring, and thudding. The miner, young, powerful, and very much at his ease, sprawled among them intoxicated. He sang, and continued to sing at intervals, a song about "The hat that my father wore," swaying, with large dreamy gestures, to and fro, round and about, up and down upon the unfortunate men sitting to right and left of him. Close at hand sat another young man, but smaller, who carried a big brass trumpet.

"Throw him in the sea, why not, now!" the trumpeter shouted to the drunken man's weary supporters. "Begad I would do it if he put his pig's face on e'er a shoulder of me!" He was a small, emphatic young man: "Give him a crack now, and lay on him, or by the tears of God we'll get no repose at all!"

His advice was tendered as constantly and as insistently as the miner's song about his parent's headgear, and he would encourage these incitements to vicarious violence by putting the brass trumpet to his lips and blowing some bitter and not very accurate staves. So bitter and so inaccurate that at length even the drunken miner paused in his song and directed the trumpeter to "shut up." The little man sprang to his feet in fury, and approaching the other he poured a succession of trumpet calls close into his face. This threw the miner into a deep sleep, a result so unexpected that the enraged trumpeter slung his instrument under his arm and pranced belligerently upon the deck.

"Come out o' that, ye drunken matchbox, and by the Queen of Heaven I'll teach ye! Come now!"

The miner momentarily raised himself and recommenced his song: "'Tis the Hat that me Father wore!" At this the trumpeter fetched him a mighty slap across the face.

"Ah, go away," groaned the miner, "or I'll be sick on ye."

"Try it, ye rotten gossoon! ye filthy matchbox! Where's yer khar*kee*?"

The miner could display no khaki; indeed, he was sleeping deeply again.

"I'm a man o' me principles, ye rotten matchbox!" yelled the trumpeter. "In the Munsters I was ... seven years ... where's your khar*kee*?"

* * *

He seized the miner by the collar and shook that part of the steamer into a new commotion until he was collared by the sailors and kicked up on to the foredeck.

Nothing up there, not even his futile trumpeting, could disturb the chill rejoicing beauty of the night. The wind increased, but the moonlight was bland and reassuring. Often the cope of some tall wave would plunge dully over the bows, filling the deck with water that floundered foaming with the ship's movement or dribbled back through the scuppers into the sea. Yet there was no menace in the dark wandering water; each wave tossed back from its neck a wreath of foam that slewed like milk across the breast of its follower.

The trumpeter sat upon a heap of ropes beside a big soldier.

"The rotten matchbox, did ye ever see the like o' that? I'll kill him against the first thing we step ashore, like ye would a flea!"

"Be aisy," said the soldier; "why are ye making trouble at all? Have ye hurt your little finger?"

"Trouble, is it? What way would I be making trouble in this world?" exclaimed the trumpeter. "Isn't it the world itself as puts trouble on ye, so it is, like a wild cat sitting under a tub of unction! O, very pleasant it is, O ay! No, no, my little sojee, that is not it at all. You can't let the flaming world rush beyant ye like that...."

"Well, it's a quiet life I'm seeking," interjected the soldier, wrapping his great coat comfortingly across his breast, "and by this and by that, a quiet night too."

* * *

"Is that so? Quiet, is it? But I say, my little sojee, you'll not get it at all and the whole flaming world whickering at ye like a mad cracker itself. Would ye sleep on that wid yer quiet life and all? It's to tame life you'd be doing, like it was a tiger. And it's no drunken boozer can tame me as was with the Munsters in the East ... for seven holy years."

"Ah, go off wid you, you've hurt your little finger."

"Me little finger, is it?" cried the trumpeter, holding his thin hands up for inspection in the moonlight, "I have not then."

"You surprise me," the soldier said, gazing at him with sleepy amused tolerance. "Did you never hear of Tobin the smith and Mary of Cappoquin?"

"I did not then," snapped the other. "Who was they?"

"He was a roaring, fatal feller, a holy terror, a giant. He lived in the mountains but he went over the country killing things—a tiger or two at an odd time, I'm thinking—and destroying the neat condition of the world. And he had a nasty little bit of a bugle...."

"Was it the like o' that?" demanded the other, holding out the trumpet and tapping it with his fingers.

"'A bugle,' I said," replied the soldier sternly, "and every time he puffed in its tubes the noise of it was so severe the hens in the town fell dead...."

"The hens!"

"Yes, and the ducks on the ponds were overcome with emotion and sank to the bottom. One day he was in his forge driving a few nails into the shoe of an ass when he hit his little finger such a blow, a terrible blow, that it bled for a day. Then he seared the wound with his searing iron, but it was no better, and it bled for a night. I will go—says he—to the physician of Cappoquin and be sewn up with some golden wire. So he drove into Cappoquin, but when he was in it the physician was gone to a christening; there was only his daughter Mary left to attend to him, a bright good girl entirely, and when she saw the finger she said to Tobin: 'I declare on my soul if I don't chop it off it's not long till you have your death.' 'Chop it off, then,' says Tobin, and she did so. He came back the next day and this is how it was; the physician was gone to a wake. 'What's your need?' asked Mary. He showed her his hand and it dripping with blood. 'I declare to my God,' said Mary, 'if I don't chop it off it's short till you have your death.' 'Chop it off,' says Tobin, and she struck off the hand. The day after that he drove in again, but the physician was gone to an inquest about a little matter concerning some remains that had been found. 'What is it today, Tobin?' and he showed her his arm bleeding in great drops. 'I declare by the saints,' says she, 'that unless I chop it off you'll die in five minutes.' 'Chop it off,' says Tobin, and she struck off his arm. The next day he was back again with the stump of his arm worse than before. 'Oh, I see what it is,' said Mary, and going behind him she struck off his head with one blow of her father's sharp knife and gave it to the cat."

"That is a neat tale," said the trumpeter. "Did you hear the story of the dirty soldier and the drummer?"

"No—" The soldier hesitated reflectively. "No, I never heard it."

"Well, this is how it was...."

But just then the steamer began to approach the harbour, and in the hurry and scurry of preparations to land the two friends were separated and the tale was never told.

At the disembarkation passengers and soldiers crowded on the pier awaiting the boat train. The harbour was full of lights; the moon was still high in the heavens, but her glory faded as the sun began to rise. The thick densities of the night sky quivered into frail blues, violet and silver were mingled in the sea, the buildings on the wharf looked strange; icily, bitterly grey. The trumpeter ran about in the bleak air seeking the "rotten matchbox," but he could not find him. He comforted himself by executing some castigating blares upon his instrument. The hollow wharves and the pier staging echoed with acrid sound that pleased his simple heart. He blew and blew and blew until he was surrounded by people watching him strain his determined eyes and inflate his pale cheeks—all of them secretly hoping that the ones might fall out or the others might crack. Suddenly he caught sight of the now-sobered miner, quite close to him, almost touching him! The call he was blowing faded with a stupid squeak. The world began to flame again ... when an officer burst into the circle, demanding to know who he was, where from, and what in all the realm of blasphemous things he meant by tootling in that infernal manner on that infernal thing.

The trumpeter drew himself proudly to attention and saluted.

"Discharged I am, sir, it's with the Munsters I was, seven years, sir, with the Munsters, in the east."

"You disgrace the Army! If I hear another tootle on that thing, I ... I'll have you clapped in irons—I will! And ... and transported ... damn me if I don't! You understand?"

The trumpeter meekly saluted as the captain swaggered away. At that moment the miner laid his hand upon his arm.

"What, my little man," said he, "have you lost your teeth? Give it me now!"

And putting the trumpet to his own lips he blew a brilliant and mocking reveille, whose echoes hurtled far over the harbour and into the neighbouring hills.

"God save us!" cried the trumpeter with a furtive eye on the captain at the end of the platform, who did not appear to have heard that miraculous salvo, "it's a great grand breath you've got, sir."

THE ANGEL AND THE SWEEP

THE ANGEL AND THE SWEEP

I'd been sitting in the *Axe & Cleaver* along of Mrs. Pellegrini for an hour at least; I hadn't seen her in five years since she was doing the roads near Pontypool. An hour at least, for isn't the *Axe & Cleaver* the pleasant kind of place? Talking or not talking you can always hear the water lashing from the outfall above Hinney Lock, the sound of it making you feel drowsy and kind. And isn't the old bridge there a thing to be looking at indeed?

Mrs. Pellegrini had a family of pikeys who traded in horses, willow-wattles, and rocksalt; she was as cunning as a jacksnipe, and if she *had* a deep voice like a man she was full of wisdom. A grand great woman was Rosa Pellegrini, with a face silky-brown like a beechnut, and eyes and hair the equal of a rook for darkness. The abundance of jewellery hooked and threaded upon her was something to be looking at too. Old man and young Isaac kept going out to look at the horses, or they'd be coming in to upbraid her for delaying, but she could drink a sconce of beer without the least sparkle of hilarity, as if it were a tribute she owed her whole magnificent constitution, or at least a reward for some part of it. So she kept doing it, while her son and her husband could do no other and did it with nothing of her inevitable air.

Well, I was sitting in the *Axe & Cleaver* along of Mrs. Pellegrini when who should rove in but Larry McCall, good-looking Larry, bringing a friend with him, a soft kind of fellow who'd a harsh voice and a whining voice that we didn't like the noise of tho' he had good money in his purse. Larry gave me the grace of the day directly he entered the door, and then, letting a cry of joy out of him, he'd kissed Mrs. Pellegrini many times before she knew what was happening to her. She got up and punished him with a welt on his chin that would have bruised an oak-tree, and bade him behave himself. He sat down soothingly beside her and behaved very well. His companion stood very shy and nervous, like a kitten might be watching a cockfight.

"Who is this young man?" Mrs. Pellegrini asks.

"That's Arthur," said Larry: "I forget what Arthur knocks a living out of—I've known him but these three bits of an hour since we were walking in the one direction."

"My dad," said Arthur slowly and raspingly, "is an undertaker, and he lets me help him in his business: we bury people."

"Oh come, young man," said Mrs. Pellegrini, "that's no sort of a trade at all—d'ye think it, Mr. McCall?"

"No, I do not," replied Larry, "but Arthur does. It don't seem to be a trade with very much humour in it. Life ain't a sad solid chunk."

* * *

"Now that's just where you're wrong," drawled Arthur.

"'Tain't a life at all," Rosa interrupted severely, "it's only sniffing, having a bad cold! No sort of a life at all—d'ye think it, Mr. McCall?"

"No, I do not," said Larry with a chuckle, "but Arthur does!"

"Oh, I know what you're a deluding on," commenced the young man again, "but...."

"Strike me dead if I can see any fun in funerals!" Mrs. Pellegrini said with finality, taking up her mug. "But if you *will* have your grief, young man," she added, pausing in one of her gulps to gaze at Arthur until he quivered, "you must have it, and may fortune fall in love with what we like. Fill up that cup now!"

The young man in agitation obeyed, and while this was doing we all heard someone come over the bridge singing a song, and that was Jerry Ogwin, who could tell the neatest tales and sing the littlest songs. Well, there were great salutations, for we all knew Jerry and loved Jerry, and he loved some of us. But he was the fiercest looking, fieriest gipsy man you ever saw, and he had all the gullible prescience of a cockney.

"My fortune! Where are you from, you cunning little man?"

"I bin doing a bit o' road down Kent and London way. D'ye know Lewisham?" commenced Jerry.

"No," said Larry, grinning at me, "but Arthur does!"

"No, I don't; I never been there," chanted Arthur.

* * *

"Now what's the good of talking like that!" said McCall sternly, and letting a wink at me.

"More I ain't," asserted Arthur.

"Then I was at Deptford and Greenwich—know Greenwich?" continued Jerry.

"No," replied Larry, then adding nonchalantly, "Arthur does."

"No, I don't, I don't," said Arthur wormily, for Jerry was glaring at him, and that fighting scar all down his nose, where his wife Katey once hit him with the spout of a kettle, was very disturbing.

"What's the good of that?" urged the devilish-minded Larry. "Why don't you talk to the gentleman, you don't want to vex him, do you?"

"You ain't blooming silly, are you?" queried Jerry.

Without waiting for reply he drifted off again.

"Me and my mate was doing a bit o' road with oranges and things, you know—three for a 'eaver—down Mary's Cray; d'ye know Mary's Cray?"

But this time Arthur was looking avidly out of the window.

"Well, we was 'avin' a bit of grub one night, just about dark it was, you know, with a little fire, we'd bin cookin' something, when a blooming sweep come along. I'll tell it to you; it was just inside a bit of a wood and we was sleeping rough. My mate was a bit nervous, you know, 'e kept looking round as if 'e could see something, but it was that dark you might be looking in a sack. I says to Timmy: what's up with you? I dunno, 'e says, something going on, and just as 'e says that this blooming sweep 'oofs in from nowhere and falls over our beer. I says to Timmy, 'e's knocked over our beer; are you going to fight 'im or shall I? And Timmy shouts: look at 'im, 'e's laying on the fire! And s'elp me God so 'e was, 'is legs was in the sticks and 'is trousers was a-burning. Come out of it, we says, but 'e didn't move. No, my oath, 'e layed there like a dead sheep. Well, we pulled 'im off it, but 'e was like a silly bloke. 'E couldn't stand up and 'e couldn't say anything. 'E got a lot of froth round 'is mouth like a 'orse that's going wicked. And 'e wasn't drunk, neither, but, *you* know, 'e was just frightened out of 'is life about something. We sit 'im down with 'is back against a tree and made the fire up again. What's the matter with you, we says; you got a fit, we says; what d'ye want coming 'ere, we says? But we couldn't get no answer from 'im. 'Is face was that dam white 'cept where it was smudged with soot, and there was this froth dribbling on 'im, and what d'yer think, 'e'd got a red rose stuck in 'is button-'ole. 'E was a horrible sight; we couldn't bear 'im, so we picks 'im up, and Timmy give 'im a clout in the ear and shoves 'im out among some bushes where we couldn't see 'im. Sw'elp me if 'e didn't come crawling back on 'is hands and knees where we was sitting round the fire. Oh, 'e was horrible. Timmy went nearly daft and I thought 'e was going to give 'im one good kick in the mouth and finish 'im. 'Stead of that we picks 'im up again and runs 'im further down the wood and heaves 'im into some blackberry bushes and tells 'im what we'd do to 'im if 'e come again. That was no good; in five minutes 'e crawled back. Timmy was shaking like a dog, and fell on 'im as if 'e was going to strangle 'im, but we had to let 'im stay, and old Timmy was blacker than the sweep when 'e'd done with 'im. But the bloke *wouldn't* say nothing or open 'is eyes, *you* know, he *wouldn't* open his eyes, 'e was like something what had been murdered and wouldn't die, if you know what I mean. Blast 'im, I could kill 'im, Timmy says. That's no good of, says I, and at last we left 'im 'side the fire, and we went off somewhere just outside the wood and packed up in a clump of ur-grass. I went to sleep, but I don't believe old Timmy did, well, I know 'e didn't. Now we hadn't 'eard nothing all night, nothing at all, but when I wakes up in the morning the blooming sweep was gone and not a chink of 'im left anywhere. But," said Jerry impressively to Arthur, who eyed him with horror, "we found something else!" There was silence while Jerry's face was connected to his mug of beer. Nobody spoke. We eyed him with eager interest. He vanquished his thirst and smacked his lips but held the mug in readiness for further libation.

"Not twenty chain away a woman was laying down. Timmy touches me frightened like and says, Look, what's that? My eyes was nearly skinned out of me. I couldn't speak. We walked quietly up to 'er like two sick men. She lay there just as if she'd dropped out of the sky, naked as an angel, not a shift nor a stocking, not a button on 'er." There was again silence until Larry struck a match loudly on a jar, his pipe, hooked tightly in his forefinger, having gone out. Mrs. Pellegrini stared, and breathed audibly. "And," said Jerry impressively, "she was the grandest creature what ever you see. I touched 'er with them two fingers and she was cold as iron, stiff, gone a bit dull like pearls look, but the fine build of that lady was the world's wonder. There was not a scratch or a wound on 'er or the sign of 'er death anywhere. One of 'er legs was cocked up at the knee like she'd lay in bed. 'Er two eyes was just looking at the ground and there was a kind of funny smile on 'er face. Fine long hair she had, black as a cat's back and long as the tail of a horse. And in it there was a red rose, and in one of 'er hands she was holding a white lily. There was a little bird's dropping on 'er stomach. I wiped it off. I says to Timmy: That sweep! And 'e says to me, Jerry Ogwin, we're 'aving a share out. What about that sweep I says to 'im, but all 'e says was: we're 'aving a share out. 'E was afraid of getting pulled for this job, *you* know. I never seen a man so frightened afore, and 'e was not a chap as renagged ever, not Timmy."

"That 'e wasn't," said Mrs. Pellegrini, "I seen 'im once half murder two sojers for beating a deaf and dumb man."

"Well," continued Jerry, "I says all right Timmy, and so we 'as a share out and gits on different roads. My share was a clothes basket and a pair of spectacles cost tuppence ha'penny, *you* know, and I walked all that day as 'ard as ever I could. Then I bushes for the night, and when I woke up nex' morning I 'eard some talking going on. I looks under the 'edge and found I was side a strawberry field, *you* know, a lot of strawberries. So I 'ops in and sells my basket to the strawberry pickers for a shilling. They give me a shilling for it, so that was all right. 'Ad a shilling and a pair of spectacles for my share out. I goes on a bit and then I comes across a beanfeast party, and I showed 'em my pair o' gold spectacles—I'd just found 'em—*you* know!"

Larry burst into a peal of laughter that seemed to surprise Jerry and he said:

"Ain't you ever met a feller what's found a pair of gold spectacles?"

Larry couldn't reply and Jerry continued:

"No, ain't you really? God, what a laugh! Yes, I sells 'em to a fly young party for two and fo' pence and off I goes. Never 'eard no more of Timmy. Never 'eard no more of anything. I dunno if they found the girl. I dunno if they found that sweep. They didn't find *me*."

He paused for a moment.

"They didn't find *me*," he repeated.

There was silence at last; the room was getting dim with evening. Mrs. Pellegrini spoke:

"And you wiped it off her stomach, did you, Jerry?"

"I did," said he.

Mrs. Pellegrini turned to Arthur and said in a sharp voice:

"Fill that pot for the gentleman!"

The young man in terror obeyed, he exceedingly obeyed.

When the last pot was emptied Jerry and Larry and the wretched mute went off along the road together. Rosa Pellegrini said "So long" to me and drove off with her cavalcade. The inn was empty and quiet again so you could hear the water at the outfall.

I walked along the bank of the old river until I came to the lock where the water roaring windily from the lasher streamed like an old man's beard; a pair of swans moved in the slack water of the pool. Away there was a fine lea of timothy grass looking as soft as wool. And at the end of the lea there was a low long hill covered with trees full of the arriving darkness; a train that you could not hear the noise of shot through a grove and poured a long spool of white fume upon the trees quietly, a thing to be looking at, it was so white and soft. But I was thinking ... thinking ... thinking of the grand white slim woman who did not seem dead at all to me, lying with a lily in her hand, a red rose in her hair. And I could not think it to be true at all; I believe Jerry was only telling us one of his tales.

ARABESQUE

ARABESQUE: THE MOUSE

In the main street amongst tall establishments of mart and worship was a high narrow house pressed between a coffee factory and a bootmaker's. It had four flights of long dim echoing stairs, and at the top, in a room that was full of the smell of dried apples and mice, a man in the middle age of life had sat reading Russian novels until he thought he was mad. Late was the hour, the night outside black and freezing, the pavements below empty and undistinguishable when he closed his book and sat motionless in front of the glowing but flameless fire. He felt he was very tired yet he could not rest. He stared at a picture on the wall until he wanted to cry; it was a colour print by Utamaro of a suckling child caressing its mother's breasts as she sits in front of a blackbound mirror. Very chaste and decorative it was, in spite of its curious anatomy. The man gazed, empty of sight though not of mind, until the sighing of the gas jet maddened him. He got up, put out the light, and sat down again in the darkness trying to compose his mind before the comfort of the fire. And he was just about to begin a conversation with himself when a mouse crept from a hole in the skirting near the fireplace and scurried into the fender. The man had the crude dislike for such sly nocturnal things, but this mouse was so small and bright, its antics so pretty, that he drew his feet carefully from the fender and sat watching it almost with amusement. The mouse moved along the shadows of the fender, out upon the hearth, and sat before the glow, rubbing its head, ears, and tiny belly with its paws as if it were bathing itself with the warmth, until, sharp and sudden, the fire sank, an ember fell, and the mouse flashed into its hole.

The man reached forward to the mantelpiece and put his hand upon a pocket lamp. Turning on the beam, he opened the door of a cupboard beside the fireplace. Upon one of the shelves there was a small trap baited with cheese, a trap made with a wire spring, one of those that smashed down to break the back of ingenuous and unwary mice.

"Mean—so mean," he mused, "to appeal to the hunger of any living thing just in order to destroy it."

He picked up the empty trap as if to throw it in the fire.

"I suppose I had better leave it though—the place swarms with them." He still hesitated. "I hope that little beastie won't go and do anything foolish." He put the trap back quite carefully, closed the door of the cupboard, sat down again and extinguished the lamp.

Was there any one else in the world so squeamish and foolish about such things! Even his mother, mother so bright and beautiful, even she had laughed at his childish horrors. He recalled how once in his childhood, not long after his sister Yosine was born, a friendly neighbour had sent him home with a bundle of dead larks tied by the feet "for supper." The pitiful inanimity of the birds had brought a gush of tears; he had run weeping home and into the kitchen, and there he had found the strange thing doing. It was dusk; mother was kneeling before the fire. He dropped the larks.

"Mother!" he exclaimed softly. She looked at his tearful face.

"What's the matter, Filip?" she asked, smiling too at his astonishment.

"Mother! What you doing?"

Her bodice was open and she was squeezing her breasts; long thin streams of milk spurted into the fire with a plunging noise.

"Weaning your little sister," laughed mother. She took his inquisitive face and pressed it against the delicate warmth of her bosom, and he forgot the dead birds behind him.

"Let me do it, mother," he cried, and doing so he discovered the throb of the heart in his mother's breast. Wonderful it was for him to experience it, although she could not explain it to him.

"Why does it do that?"

"If it did not beat, little son, I should die and the Holy Father would take me from you."

"God?"

She nodded. He put his hand upon his own breast. "Oh feel it, Mother!" he cried. Mother unbuttoned his little coat and felt the gentle *tick tick* with her warm palm.

* * *

"Beautiful!" she said.

"Is it a good one?"

She kissed his upsmiling lips. "It is good if it beats truly. Let it always beat truly, Filip, let it always beat truly."

There was the echo of a sigh in her voice, and he had divined some grief, for he was very wise. He kissed her bosom in his tiny ecstasy and whispered soothingly: "Little mother! little mother!" In such joys he forgot his horror of the dead larks; indeed he helped mother to pluck them and spit them for supper.

It was a black day that succeeded, and full of tragedy for the child. A great bay horse with a tawny mane had knocked down his mother in the lane, and a heavy cart had passed over her, crushing both her hands. She was borne away moaning with anguish to the surgeon who cut off the two hands. She died in the night. For years the child's dreams were filled with the horror of the stumps of arms, bleeding unendingly. Yet he had never seen them, for he was sleeping when she died.

While this old woe was come vividly before him he again became aware of the mouse. His nerves stretched upon him in repulsion, but he soon relaxed to a tolerant interest, for it was really a most engaging little mouse. It moved with curious staccato scurries, stopping to rub its head or flicker with its ears; they seemed almost transparent ears. It spied a red cinder and skipped innocently up to it ... sniffing ... sniffing ... until it jumped back scorched. It would crouch as a cat does, blinking in the warmth, or scamper madly as if dancing, and then roll upon its side rubbing its head with those pliant paws. The melancholy man watched it until it came at last to rest and squatted meditatively upon its haunches, hunched up, looking curiously wise, a pennyworth of philosophy; then once more the coals sank with a rattle and again the mouse was gone.

The man sat on before the fire and his mind filled again with unaccountable sadness. He had grown into manhood with a burning generosity of spirit and rifts of rebellion in him that proved too exacting for his fellows and seemed mere wantonness to men of casual rectitudes. "Justice and Sin," he would cry, "Property and Virtue—incompatibilities! There can be no sin in a world of justice, no property in a world of virtue!" With an engaging extravagance and a certain clear-eyed honesty of mind he had put his two and two together and seemed then to rejoice, as in some topsy-turvy dream, in having rendered unto Cæsar, as you might say, the things that were due to Napoleon! But this kind of thing could not pass unexpiated in a world of men having an infinite regard for Property and a pride in their traditions of Virtue and Justice. They could indeed forgive him his sins but they could not forgive him his compassions. So he had to go seek for more melodious-minded men and fair unambiguous women. But rebuffs can deal more deadly blows than daggers; he became timid—a timidity not of fear but of pride—and grew with the years into misanthropy, susceptible to trivial griefs and despairs, a vessel of emotion that emptied as easily as it filled, until he came at last to know that his griefs were half deliberate, his despairs half unreal, and to live but for beauty—which is tranquillity—to put her wooing hand upon him.

Now, while the mouse hunts in the cupboard, one fair recollection stirs in the man's mind—of Cassia and the harmony of their only meeting, Cassia who had such rich red hair, and eyes, yes, her eyes were full of starry enquiry like the eyes of mice. It was so long ago that he had forgotten how he came to be in it, that unaccustomed orbit of vain vivid things—a village festival, all oranges and houp-là. He could not remember how he came to be there, but at night, in the court hall, he had danced with Cassia—fair and unambiguous indeed!—who had come like the wind from among the roses and swept into his heart.

"It is easy to guess," he had said to her, "what you like most in the world."

She laughed; "To dance? Yes, and you...?"

"To find a friend."

"I know, I know," she cried, caressing him with recognitions. "Ah, at times I quite love my friends—until I begin to wonder how much they hate me!"

He had loved at once that cool pale face, the abundance of her strange hair as light as the autumn's clustered bronze, her lilac dress and all the sweetness about her like a bush of lilies. How they had laughed at the two old peasants whom they had overheard gabbling of trifles like sickness and appetite!

"There's a lot of nature in a parsnip," said one, a fat person of the kind that swells grossly when stung by a bee, "a lot of nature when it's young, but when it's old it's like everything else."

"True it is."

"And I'm very fond of vegetables, yes, and I'm very fond of bread."

"Come out with me," whispered Cassia to Filip, and they walked out in the blackness of midnight into what must have been a garden.

"Cool it is here," she said, "and quiet, but too dark even to see your face—can you see mine?"

"The moon will not rise until after dawn," said he, "it will be white in the sky when the starlings whistle in your chimney."

They walked silently and warily about until they felt the chill of the air. A dull echo of the music came to them through the walls, then stopped, and they heard the bark of a fox away in the woods.

"You are cold," he whispered, touching her bare neck with timid fingers. "Quite, quite cold," drawing his hand tenderly over the curves of her chin and face. "Let us go in," he said, moving with discretion from the rapture he desired. "We will come out again," said Cassia.

But within the room the ball was just at an end, the musicians were packing up their instruments and the dancers were flocking out and homewards, or to the buffet which was on a platform at one end of the room. The two old peasants were there, munching hugely.

"I tell you," said one of them, "there's nothing in the world for it but the grease of an owl's liver. That's it, that's it! Take something on your stomach now, just to offset the chill of the dawn!"

Filip and Cassia were beside them, but there were so many people crowding the platform that Filip had to jump down. He stood then looking up adoringly at Cassia, who had pulled a purple cloak around her.

"For Filip, Filip, Filip," she said, pushing the last bite of her sandwich into his mouth, and pressing upon him her glass of Loupiac. Quickly he drank it with a great gesture, and, flinging the glass to the wall, took Cassia into his arms, shouting: "I'll carry you home, the whole way home, yes, I'll carry you!"

"Put me down!" she cried, beating his head and pulling his ears, as they passed among the departing dancers. "Put me down, you wild thing!"

Dark, dark was the lane outside, and the night an obsidian net, into which he walked carrying the girl. But her arms were looped around him, she discovered paths for him, clinging more tightly as he staggered against a wall, stumbled upon a gulley, or when her sweet hair was caught in the boughs of a little lime tree.

"Do not loose me, Filip, will you, do not loose me," Cassia said, putting her lips against his temple.

His brain seemed bursting, his heart rocked within him, but he adored the rich grace of her limbs against his breast. "Here it is," she murmured, and he carried her into a path that led to her home in a little lawned garden where the smell of ripe apples upon the branches and the heavy lustre of roses stole upon the air. Roses and apples! Roses and apples! He carried her right into the porch before she slid down and stood close to him with her hands still upon his shoulders. He could breathe happily at the release, standing silent and looking round at the sky sprayed with wondrous stars but without a moon.

"You are stronger than I thought you, stronger than you look, you are really very strong," she whispered, nodding her head to him. Opening the buttons of his coat she put her palm against his breast.

"Oh how your heart does beat: does it beat truly—and for whom?"

He had seized her wrists in a little fury of love, crying: "Little mother, little mother!"

"What are you saying?" asked the girl, but before he could continue there came a footstep sounding behind the door, and the clack of a bolt....

What was that? Was that really a bolt or was it ... was it ... the snap of the trap? The man sat up in his room intently listening, with nerves quivering again, waiting for the trap to kill the little philosopher. When he felt it was all over he reached guardedly in the darkness for the lantern, turned on the beam, and opened the door of the cupboard. Focussing the light upon the trap he was amazed to see the mouse sitting on its haunches before it, uncaught. Its head was bowed, but its bead-like eyes were full of brightness, and it sat blinking, it did not flee.

"Shoosh!" said the man, but the mouse did not move. "Why doesn't it go? Shoosh!" he said again, and suddenly the reason of the mouse's strange behaviour was made clear. The trap had not caught it completely, but it had broken off both its forefeet, and the thing crouched there holding out its two bleeding stumps humanly, too stricken to stir.

Horror flooded the man, and conquering his repugnance he plucked the mouse up quickly by the neck. Immediately the little thing fastened its teeth in his finger; the touch was no more than the slight prick of a pin. The man's impulse then exhausted itself. What should he do with it? He put his hand behind him, he dared not look, but there was nothing to be done except kill it at once, quickly, quickly. Oh, how should he do it? He bent towards the fire as if to drop the mouse into its quenching glow; but he paused and shuddered, he would hear its cries, he would have to listen. Should he crush it with finger and thumb? A glance towards the window decided him. He opened the sash with one hand and flung the wounded mouse far into the dark street. Closing the window with a crash he sank into a chair, limp with pity too deep for tears.

So he sat for two minutes, five minutes, ten minutes. Anxiety and shame filled him with heat. He opened the window again, and the freezing air poured in and cooled him. Seizing his lantern he ran down the echoing stairs, into the dark empty street, searching long and vainly for the little philosopher until he had to desist and return to his room, shivering, frozen to his very bones.

When he had recovered some warmth he took the trap from its shelf. The two feet dropped into his hand; he cast them into the fire.

Then he once more set the trap and put it back carefully into the cupboard.

FELIX TINCLER

FELIX TINCLER

The child was to have a birthday tomorrow and was therefore not uneasy about being late home from school this afternoon. He had lost his pencil case; a hollow long round thing it was, like a rolling-pin, only it had green and yellow rings painted upon it. He kept his marbles in it and so he was often in a trouble about his pencils. He had not tried very much to find the pencil case because the boys "deludered" him—that's what his father always said. He had asked Heber Gleed if he had seen it—he had strange suspicions of that boy—but Heber Gleed had sworn so earnestly that the greengrocer opposite the school had picked it up, he had even "saw him do it," that Felix Tincler went into Mr. Gobbit's shop, and when the greengrocer lady appeared in answer to the ring of the door bell he enquired politely for his pencil case. She was tall and terrible with a squint and, what was worse, a large velvety mole with hairs sprouting from it. She immediately and with inexplicable fury desired him to flee from her greengrocer shop, with a threat of alternative castigation in which a flatiron and a red-hot pick-axe were to figure with unusual and unpleasant prominence. Well he had run out of Mr. Gobbit's shop, and there was Heber Gleed standing in the road giggling derisively at him. Felix walked on alone, looking in the gutters and areas for his pencil case, until he encountered another friendly boy who took him to dig in a garden where they grew castor-oil plants. When he went home it was late; as he ran along under the high wall of the orphanage that occupied one end of his street its harsh peevish bell clanged out six notes. He scampered past the great gateway under the dismal arch that always filled him with uneasiness, he never passed it without feeling the sad trouble that a prison might give. He stepped into his own pleasant home, a little mute, and a little dirty in appearance; but at six years of age in a home so comfortable and kind the eve of the day that is to turn you into seven is an occasion great enough to yield an amnesty for peccadilloes. His father was already in from work, he could hear him singing. He gave his mother the sprigs he had picked from the castor-oil plant and told her about the pencil case. The meal was laid upon the table, and while mother was gone into the kitchen to boil the water for tea he sat down and tried to smooth out the stiff creases in the white table cloth. His father was singing gaily in the scullery as he washed and shaved:

High cockalorum,
Charlie ate the spinach....

He ceased for a moment to give the razor a vigorous stropping and then continued:

* * *

High cockalorum,
High cockalee....

Felix knew that was not the conclusion of the song. He listened, but for some moments all that followed was the loud crepitation of a razor searching a stubborn beard and the sigh of the kettle. Then a new vigour seized the singer:

But mother brought the pandy down
And bate the gree....

Again that rasping of chin briefly intervened, but the conclusion of the cropping was soon denoted by the strong rallentando of the singer:

...dy image,
High cockalorum,
High cock-a-lee.

Mrs. Tincler brought in the teapot and her husband followed her with his chin tightly shaven but blue, crying with mock horror:

"Faylix, my son! that is seven years old tomorrow! look at him, Mary, the face of him and the hands of him! I didn't know there was a bog in this parish; is it creeping in a bog you have been?"

The boy did not blench at his father's spurious austerity, he knew he was the soul of kindness and fun.

"Go wash yourself at the sink," interposed his mother. Kevin Tincler, taking his son by the hand, continued with mocking admonishment: "All the fine copybooks of the world that you've filled up with that blather about cleanliness and holiness, the up strokes very thin and the down strokes very thick! What was it, Mary, he has let it all out of his mind?"

"Go and wash, Felix, and come quickly and have your tea," laughed Mary Tincler.

"Ah, but what was it—in that grand book of yours?"

The boy stood, in his short buff tunic, regarding his father with shy amusement. The small round clear-skinned face was lovely with its blushes of faint rose; his eyes were big and blue, and his head was covered with thick curling locks of rich brown hair.

"Cleanliness comes next to godliness," he replied.

"Does it so, indeed?" exclaimed his father. "Then you're putting your godliness in a pretty low category!"

"What nonsense," said Mary Tincler as the boy left them.

The Irishman and his dark-eyed Saxon wife sat down at the table waiting for their son.

"There's a bit of a randy in the Town Gardens tonight, Mary—dancing on the green, fireworks! When the boy is put to bed we'll walk that way."

Mary expressed her pleasure but then declared she could not leave the boy alone in his bed.

"He'll not hurt, Mary, he has no fear in him. Give him the birthday gift before we go. Whisht, he's coming!"

The child, now clean and handsome, came to his chair and looked up at his father sitting opposite to him.

"Holy Mother!" exclaimed the admiring parent, "it's the neck of a swan he has. Faylix Tincler, may ye live to be the father of a bishop!"

After tea his father took him up on the down for an hour. As they left their doorway a group of the tidy but wretched orphans was marching back into their seminary, little girls moving in double columns behind a stiff-faced woman. They were all dressed alike in garments of charity exact as pilchards. Grey capes, worsted stockings, straw hats with blue bands round them, and hard boots. The boys were coming in from a different direction, but all of them, even the minutest, were clad in corduroy trousers and short jackets high throated like a gaoler's. This identity of garment was contrary to the will of God for he had certainly made their pinched bodies diverse enough. Some were short, some tall, dark, fair, some ugly, others handsome. The sight of them made Felix unhappy, he shrank into himself, until he and his father had slipped through a gap in a hedge and were going up the hill that stretched smoothly and easily almost from their very door. The top of the down here was quiet and lovely, but a great flank of it two miles away was scattered over with tiny white figures playing very deliberately at cricket. Pleasant it was up there in the calm evening, and still bright, but the intervening valley was full of grey ungracious houses, allotments, railway arches, churches, graveyards, and schools. Worst of all was the dull forbidding aspect of the Orphanage down beyond the roof of their own house.

They played with a ball and had some wrestling matches until the declining day began to grow dim even on the hill and the fat jumbo clouds over the town were turning pink. If those elephants fell on him—

what would they do? Why, they'd mix him up like ice-cream! So said his father.

"Do things ever fall out of the sky?"

"Rain," said Mr. Tincler.

"Yes, I know."

"Stars—maybe."

"Where do they go?"

"O they drop on the hills but ye can never find 'em."

"Don't Heaven ever?"

"What, drop down! no," said Mr. Tincler, "it don't. I have not heard of it doing that, but maybe it all just stoops down sometimes, Faylix, until it's no higher than the crown of your hat. Let us be going home now and ye'll see something this night."

"What is it?"

"Wait, Faylix, wait!"

As they crossed from the hill Mary drawing down the blinds signalled to them from the window.

"Come along, Felix," she cried, and the child ran into the darkened room. Upon the table was set a little church of purest whiteness. Kevin had bought it from an Italian hawker. It had a wonderful tall steeple and a cord that came through a hole and pulled a bell inside. And that was not all; the church was filled with light that was shining through a number of tiny arched windows, blue, purple, green, violet, the wonderful windows were everywhere. Felix was silent with wonder; how could you get a light in a church that hadn't got a door! then Mary lifted the hollow building from the table; it had no floor, and there was a night-light glowing in one of her patty-pans filled with water. The church was taken up to bed with him in the small chamber next his parents' room and set upon a bureau. Kevin and Mary then went off to the "bit of devilment" in the town gardens. Felix kept skipping from his bed, first to gaze at the church, and then to lean out of the window in his nightshirt, looking for the lamplighter who would come to the street lamp outside. The house was the very last, and the lamp was the very last lamp, on one of the roads that led from the town and thence went poking out into the steady furze-covered downs. And as the lamp was the very last to be lit darkness was always half-fallen by the time the old man arrived at his journey's end. He carried a pole with a brass tube at one end. There were holes in the brass tube showing gleams of light. The pole rested upon his shoulders as he trudged along humming huskily.

"Here he is," cried Felix, leaning from the window and waving a white arm. The dull road, empty of traffic and dim as his mother's pantry by day, curved slightly, and away at the other end of the curve a jet of light had sprung suddenly into the gloom like a bright flower bursting its sheath; a black figure moved along towards him under the Orphanage wall. Other lamps blossomed with light and the lamplighter, approaching the Tinclers' lamp, thrust the end of his pole into the lantern, his head meanwhile craning back like the head of a horse that has been pulled violently backwards. He deftly turned the tap; with a tiny dull explosion that sounded like a doormat being beaten against the wall in the next street the lamp was lit and the face of the old man sprang into vague brilliance, for it was not yet utterly dark. Vague as the light was, the neighbouring hills at once faded out of recognition and became black bulks of oblivion.

"Oi.... Oi...." cried the child, clapping his hands. The old man's features relaxed, he grunted in relief, the pole slid down in his palm. As the end of it struck the pavement a sharp knock he drew an old pipe from his pocket and lit it quite easily although one of his hands was deficient of a thumb and some fingers. He was about to travel back into the sparkling town when Felix called to him:

"Soloman! Soloman!"

"Goo an to yer bed, my little billycock, or you'll ketch a fever."

"No, but what's this?" Felix was pointing to the ground below him. The old man peered over the iron railings into the front garden that had just sufficient earth to cherish four deciduous bushes, two plants of marigold, and some indeterminate herbs. In the dimness of their shadows a glowworm beamed clearly.

"That?" exclaimed he. "O s'dripped off the moon, yas, right off, moon's wastin' away, you'll see later on if you'm watch out fer it, s'dripped off the moon, right off." Chuckling, he blew out the light at the end of his pole, and went away, but turned at intervals to wave his hand towards the sky, crying "Later on, right off!" and cackling genially until he came to a tavern.

The child stared at the glowworm and then surveyed the sky, but the tardy moon was deep behind the hills. He left the open window and climbed into bed again. The house was empty, but he did not mind, father and mother had gone to buy him another birthday gift. He did not mind, the church glowed in its corner on the bureau, the street lamp shined all over the ceiling and a little bit upon the wall where the splendid picture of Wexford Harbour was hanging. It was not gloomy at all although the Orphanage bell once sounded very piercingly. Sometimes people would stroll by, but not often, and he would hear them mumbling to each other. He would rather have a Chinese lantern first, and next to that a little bagpipe, and next to that a cockatoo with a yellow head, and then a Chinese lantern, and then.... He awoke; he thought he heard a heavy bang on the door as if somebody had thrown a big stone. But when he looked out of the window there was nobody to be seen. The little moon drip was still lying in the dirt, the sky was softly black, the stars were vivid, only the lamp dazzled his eyes and he could not see any moon. But as he yawned he saw just over the down a rich globe of light moving very gradually towards him, swaying and falling, falling in the still air. To the child's dazzled eyes the great globe, dropping towards him as if it would crush the house, was shaped like an elephant, a fat squat jumbo with a green trunk. Then to his relief it fell suddenly from the sky right on to the down where he and father had played. The light was extinguished and black night hid the deflated fire-balloon.

He scrambled back into bed again but how he wished it was morning so that he could go out and capture the old elephant—he knew he would find it! When at last he slept he sank into a world of white churches that waved their steeples like vast trunks, and danced with elephants that had bellies full of fire and hidden bells that clanged impetuously to a courageous pull of each tail. He did not wake again until morning was bright and birds were singing. It was early but it was his birthday. There were no noises in the street yet, and he could not hear his father or mother moving about. He crawled silently from his bed and dressed himself. The coloured windows in the little white fane gleamed still, but it looked a little dull now. He took the cake that mother always left at his bedside and crept down the stairs. There he put on his shoes and, munching the cake, tiptoed to the front door. It was not bolted but it was difficult for him to slip back the latch quietly, and when at last it was done and he stood outside upon the step he was doubly startled to hear a loud rapping on the knocker of a house a few doors away. He sidled quickly but warily to the corner of the street, crushing the cake into his pocket, and then peeped back. It was more terrible than he had anticipated! A tall policeman stood outside that house bawling to a woman with her hair in curl papers who was lifting the sash of an upper window. Felix turned and ran through the gap in the hedge and onwards up the hill. He did not wait; he thought he heard the policeman calling out "Tincler!" and he ran faster and faster, then slower and more slow as the down steepened, until he was able to sink down breathless behind a clump of the furze, out of sight and out of hearing. The policeman did not appear to be following him; he moved on up the hill and through the soft smooth alleys of the furze until he reached the top of the down, searching always for the white elephant which he knew must be hidden close there and nowhere else, although he had no clear idea in his mind of the appearance of his mysterious quarry. Vain search, the elephant was shy or cunning and eluded him. Hungry at last and tired he sat down and leaned against a large ant hill close beside the thick and perfumed furze. Here he ate his cake and then lolled, a little drowsy, looking at the few clouds in the sky and listening to birds. A flock of rooks was moving in straggling flight towards him, a wide flat changing skein, like a curtain of crape that was being pulled and stretched delicately by invisible fingers. One of the rooks flapped just over him; it had a small round hole right through the feathers of one wing—what was that for? Felix was just falling to sleep, it was so soft and comfortable there, when a tiny noise, very tiny but sharp and mysterious, went "Ping!" just by his ear, and something stung him lightly in the neck. He knelt up, a little startled, but he peered steadily under the furze. "Ping!" went something again and stung him in the ball of the eye. It made him blink. He drew back; after staring silently at the furze he said very softly "Come out!" Nothing came; he beckoned with his forefinger and called aloud with friendliness "Come on, come out!" At that moment his nose was almost touching a brown dry sheath of the furze bloom, and right before his eyes the dried flower burst with the faint noise of "Ping!" and he felt the shower of tiny black seeds shooting against his cheek. At once he comprehended the charming mystery of the furze's dispersal of its seeds, and he submitted himself to the fairylike bombardment with great glee, forgetting even the elephant until in one of the furze alleys he came in sight of a heap of paper that fluttered a little heavily. He went towards it; it was so large that he could not make out its shape or meaning. It was a great white bag made of paper, all crumpled and damp, with an arrangement of wire where the hole was and some burned tow fixed in it. But at last he was able to perceive the green trunk, and it also had pink eyes! He had found it and he was triumphant! There were words in large black letters painted upon it which he could not read, except one word which was CURE. It was an advertisement fire-balloon relating to a specific for catarrh. He rolled the elephant together carefully, and carrying the mass of it clasped in his two arms he ran back along the hill chuckling to himself, "I'm carrying the ole elephant." Advancing down the hill to his home he was precariously swathed in a drapery of balloon paper. The door stood open; he walked into the kitchen. No one was in the kitchen but there were sharp strange voices speaking in the room above. He thought he must have come into the wrong house but the strange noises frightened him into silence; he stood quite still listening to them. He had dropped the balloon and it unfolded upon the floor, partly revealing the astounding advertisement of

PEASEGOOD'S PODOPHYLLIN

The voices above were unravelling horror upon horror. He knew by some divining instinct that tragedy was happening to him, had indeed already enveloped and crushed him. A mortar had exploded at the fireworks display, killing and wounding people that he knew.

"She had a great hole of a wound in the soft part of her thigh as you could put a cokernut in...."

"God a mighty...!"

"Died in five minutes, poor thing."

"And the husband ... they couldn't...?"

"No, couldn't identify ... they could not identify him ... only by some papers in his pocket."

"And he'd got a little bagpipe done up in a package ... for their little boy...."

"Never spoke a word...."

"Never a word, poor creature."

"May Christ be good to 'em."

"Yes, yes," they all said softly.

The child walked quietly up the stairs to his mother's bedroom. Two policemen were there making notes in their pocket books, their helmets lying on the unused bed. There were also three or four friendly women neighbours. As he entered the room the gossip ceased abruptly. One of the women gasped "O Jesus!" and they seemed to huddle together eyeing him as if he had stricken them with terror. With his fingers still upon the handle of the door he looked up at the tallest policeman and said:

"What's the matter?"

The policeman did not reply immediately; he folded up his notebook, but the woman who had gasped came to him with a yearning cry and wrapped him in her protesting arms with a thousand kisses.

"Ye poor lamb, ye poor little orphan, whatever 'ull become of ye!"

At that moment the bell of the Orphanage burst into a peal of harsh impetuous clangour, and the policemen picked up their helmets from the bed.

THE ELIXIR OF YOUTH

THE ELIXIR OF YOUTH

Since the earth began its twisting, or since very soon after it began, there have been persons on it who perceived more or less early in life that it was seldom possible to get something in return for quite nothing, and that even if you did the delicate situation then arising was attended often with at least as much personal danger as delight, and generally with much more. Tom Toole knew all about it, so he was not going to sell his own little white soul to the devil, though he was sixty years of age and his soul, he expected, was shrivelled a bit now like a dried fig. He had no faith in Wishing Hats, or Magic Carpets, or Herbs of Longevity, and he had not heard of the Philosopher's Stone, but he had a belief in an Elixir, somewhere in the world, that would make you young again. He had heard, too, of the Transmutation of Metals; indeed, he had associated himself a great many years ago with a Belfast brassfounder in the production of certain sovereigns. The brassfounder perished under the rigours of his subsequent incarceration in gaol, but Tom Toole had been not at all uncomfortable in the lunatic asylum to which a compassionate retribution had assigned him. It was in the Asylum that he met the man from Kilsheelan who, if you could believe him, really had got a "touch" from the fairies and could turn things he had no wish for into the things he would be wanting. The man from Kilsheelan first discovered his gift, so he told Tom Toole, when he caught a turtle dove one day and changed it into a sheep. Then he turned the sheep into a lather-pot just to make sure, and it was sure. So he thought he would like to go to the land of the Ever Young which is in the western country, but he did not know how he could get there unless he went in a balloon. Sure, he sat down in his cabin and turned the shaving-pot into a fine balloon, but the balloon was so large it burst down his house and he was brought to the asylum. Well that was clear enough to Tom Toole, and after he had got good advice from the man from Kilsheelan it came into his mind one day to slip out of the big gates of the asylum, and, believe me, since then he had walked the roads of Munster singing his ballads and searching for something was difficult to find, and that was his youth. For Tom Toole was growing old, a little old creature he was growing, gay enough and a bit of a philanderer still, but age is certain and puts the black teeth in your mouth and the whiteness of water on your hair.

One time he met a strange little old quick-talking man who came to him; he seemed to just bob up in front of him from the road itself.

"Ah, good day t'ye, and phwat part are ye fram?"

"I'm from beyant," said Tom Toole, nodding back to the Knockmealdown Mountains where the good monks had lodged him for a night.

"Ah, God deliver ye and indeed I don't want to know your business at all but ... but ... where are ye going?"

Between his words he kept spitting, in six or seven little words there would be at least one spit. There was yellow dust in the flaps of his ears and neat bushes of hair in the holes. Cranks and wrinkles covered his nose, and the skull of him was bare but there was a good tuft on his chin. Tom Toole looked at him straight and queer for he did not admire the fierce expression of him, and there were smells of brimstone on him like a farmer had been dipping his ewes, and he almost expected to see a couple of horns growing out of his brow.

"It's not meself does be knowing at all, good little man," said Tom Toole to him, "and I might go to the fair of Cappoquin, or I might walk on to Dungarvan, in the harbour now, to see will I buy a couple of lobsters for me nice supper."

And he turned away to go off upon his road but the little old man followed and kept by his side, telling him of a misfortune he had endured; a chaise of his, a little pony chaise, had been almost destroyed, but the ruin was not so great for a kind lady of his acquaintance, a lady of his own denomination, had given him four pounds, one shilling and ninepence. "Ah, not that I'm needing your money, ma'am, says I, but damage is damage, I says, and it's not right, I says, that I should be at the harm of your coachman." And there he was spitting and going on like a clock spilling over its machinery when he unexpectedly grasped Tom Toole by the hand, wished him Good day, and Good luck, and that he might meet him again.

Tom Toole walked on for an hour and came to a cross roads, and there was the same old man sitting in a neat little pony chaise smoking his pipe.

"Where are ye going?" says he.

"Dungarvan," said Tom Toole.

"Jump in then," said the little old man, and they jogged along the road conversing together; he was sharp as an old goat.

"What is your aspiration?" he said, and Tom Toole told him.

"That's a good aspiration, indeed. I know what you're seeking, Tom Toole; let's get on now and there'll be tidings in it."

When Tom Toole and the little old man entered the public at Dungarvan there was a gang of strong young fellows, mechanics and people to drive the traction engines, for there was a circus in it. Getting their fill of porter, they were, and the nice little white loaves; very decent boys, but one of them a Scotchman with a large unrejoicing face. And he had a hooky nose with tussocks of hair in the nostrils and the two tails of hair to his moustache like an old Chinese man. Peter Mullane was telling a tale, and there was a sad bit of a man from Bristol, with a sickness in his breast and a cough that would heave out the side of a mountain. Peter Mullane waited while Tom Toole and his friend sat down and then he proceeded with his tale.

* * *

"Away with ye! said the devil to Neal Carlin, and away he was gone to the four corners of the world. And when he came to the first corner he saw a place where the rivers do be rushing, ..."

"... the only darn thing that does rush then in this country," interrupted the Scotchman with a sneer.

"Shut your ..." began the man from Bristol, but he was taken with the cough, until his cheeks were scarlet and his eyes, fixed angrily upon the Highland man, were strained to teardrops. "Shut your ..." he began it again, but he was rent by a large and vexing spasm that rocked him, while his friends looked at him and wondered would he be long for this world. He recovered quite suddenly and exclaimed "... dam face" to that Highland man. And then Peter Mullane went on:

"I am not given to thinking," said he, "that the Lord would put a country the like of Ireland in a wee corner of the world and he wanting the nook of it for thistles and the poor savages that devour them. Well, Neal Carlin came to a place where the rivers do be rushing ..." he paused invitingly—"and he saw a little fairy creature with fine tresses of hair sitting under a rowan tree."

"A rowan?" exclaimed the Highland man.

Peter nodded.

"A Scottish tree!" declared the other.

"O shut your ..." began the little coughing man, but again his conversation was broken, and by the time he had recovered from his spasms the company was mute.

* * *

"If," said Peter Mullane, "you'd wish to observe the rowan in its pride and beauty just clap your eye upon it in the Galtee Mountains. How would it thrive, I ask you, in a place was stiff with granite and sloppy with haggis? And what would ye do, my clever man, what would ye do if ye met a sweet fairy woman...?"

"I'd kiss the Judy," said the Highland man spitting a great splash.

Peter Mullane gazed at him for a minute or two as if he did not love him very much, but then he continued:

"Neal Carlin was attracted by her, she was a sweet creature. Warm! says she to him with a friendly tone. Begod, ma'am, it is a hot day, he said, and thinks he, she is a likely person to give me my aspiration. And sure enough when he sat down beside her she asked him What is your aspiration, Neal Carlin? and he said, saving your grace, ma'am, it is but to enjoy the world and to be easy in it. That is a good aspiration, she said, and she gave him some secret advice. He went home to his farm, Neal Carlin did, and he followed the advice, and in a month or two he had grown very wealthy and things were easy with him. But still he was not satisfied, he had a greedy mind, and his farm looked a drifty little place that was holding him down from big things. So he was not satisfied though things were easy with him, and one night before he went sleeping he made up his mind 'It's too small it is. I'll go away from it now and a farm twice as big I will have, three times as big, yes, I will have it ten times as big.' He went sleeping on the wildness of his avarice, and when he rolled off the settle in the morning and stood up to stretch his limbs he hit his head a wallop against the rafter. He cursed it and had a kind of thought that the place had got smaller. As he went from the door he struck his brow against the lintel hard enough to beat down the house. What is come to me, he roared in his pains; and looking into his field there were his five cows and his bullock no bigger than sheep—will ye believe that, then—and his score of ewes no bigger than rabbits, mind it now, and it was not all, for the very jackdaws were no bigger than chafers and the neat little wood was no more account than a grove of raspberry bushes. Away he goes to the surgeon's to have drops put in his eyes for he feared the blindness was coming on him, but on his return there was his bullock no bigger than an old boot, and his cabin had wasted to the size of a birdcage."

Peter leaned forward, for the boys were quiet, and consumed a deal of porter. And the Highland man asked him "Well, what happened?"

"O he just went up to his cabin and kicked it over the hedge as you might an old can, and then he strolled off to another corner of the world, Neal Carlin did, whistling 'The Lanty Girl.'"

Tom Toole's friend spoke to Peter Mullane. "Did ye say it was in the Galtee Mountains that the young fellow met the lady?"

"In the Galtee Mountains," said Peter.

"To the Galtee Mountains let us be going, Tom Toole," cried the little old man, "Come on now, there'll be tidings in it!"

So off they drove; and when they had driven a day and slept a couple of nights they were there, and they came to a place where the rivers do be rushing and there was a rowan tree but no lady in it.

"What will we do now, Tom Toole?" says the old man.

"We'll not stint it," says he, and they searched by night and by day looking for a person would give them their youth again. They sold the chaise for some guineas and the pony for a few more, and they were walking among the hills for a thousand days but never a dust of fortune did they discover. Whenever they asked a person to guide them they would be swearing at them or they would jeer.

"Well, may a good saint stretch your silly old skins for ye!" said one.

"Thinking of your graves and travelling to the priest ye should be!" said another.

"The nails of your boots will be rusty and rotted searching for the like of that," said a third.

"It's two quarts of black milk from a Kerry cow ye want," said one, "take a sup of that and you'll be young again!"

"Of black milk!" said Tom Toole's friend; "where would we get that?"

The person said he would get a pull of it in the Comeragh Mountains, fifty miles away.

"Tom Toole," said the little old-man, "it's what I'll do. I'll walk on to the Comeragh Mountains to see what I will see, and do you go on searching here, for to find that young girl would be better than forty guineas' worth of blather. And when I find the cow I'll take my fill of a cup and bring you to it."

So they agreed upon it and the old man went away saying, "I'll be a score of days, no more. Good day, Tom Toole, good day!" much as an old crow might shout it to a sweep.

When he was gone Tom Toole journeyed about the world and the day after he went walking to a fair. Along the road the little ass carts were dribbling into town from Fews and Carrigleena, when he saw a young girl in a field trying to secure an ass.

"Oi.... Oi...!" the girl was calling out to him and he went in the field and helped her with the ass, which was a devil to capture and it not wanting. She thanked him; she was a sweet slip of a colleen with a long fall of hair that the wind was easy with.

"'Tis warm!" she said to Tom Toole. "Begod, ma'am," says he to her quickly, taking his cue, "it is a hot day."

"Where are ye going, Tom Toole?" she asked him, and he said, "I am seeking a little contrivance, ma'am, that will let me enjoy the world and live easy in it. That is my aspiration."

"I'll give you what you are seeking," and she gave him a wee bottle with red juices in it.

"Indeed, ma'am, I'm obliged to ye," and he took her by the hand and wished her Good day and Good luck and that he might meet her again.

When he got the elixir of youth he gave over his searching. He hid the bottle in his breast and went up into the mountains as high as he could go to bide the coming of the little old man. It is a queer thing but Tom Toole had never heard the name of him—it would be some foreign place in the corners of the world like Portugal, that he had come from; no doubt. Up he went; first there was rough pasture for bullocks, then fern and burst furze, and then little but heather, and great rocks strewn about like shells, and sour brown streams coming from the bog. He wandered about for twenty days and the old man did not return, and for forty days he was still alone.

"The divil receive him but I'll die against his return!" And Tom Toole pulled the wee bottle from his breast. He was often minded to lift the cork and take a sup of the elixir of youth. "But," says he, "it would be an unfriendly deed. Sure if I got me youth sudden I'd be off to the wonders of the land and leave that old fool roaming till the day of Judgment." And he would put the bottle away and wait for scores of days until he was sick and sorry with grieving. A thousand days he was on his lonely wanderings, soft days as mellow as cream, and hard days when it is ribs of iron itself you would want to stiffen you against the crack of the blast. His skimpy hair grew down to the lappet of his coat, very ugly he was, but the little stranger sheep of the mountain were not daunted when he moved by, and even the flibeens had the soft call for him. A thousand days was in it and then he said:

"Good evening to me good luck. I've had my enough of this. Sure I'll despise myself for ever more if I wait the tide of another drifting day. It's tonight I'll sleep in a bed with a quilt of down over me heart, for I'm going to be young again."

He crept down the mountain to a neat little town and went in a room in the public to have a cup of porter. A little forlorn old man also came in from the road and sat down beside, and when they looked at each other they each let out a groan. "Glory be!" says he. "Glory be," cried Tom Toole, "it's the good little man in the heel of it. Where in hell are ye from?"

"From the mountains."

"And what fortune is in it, did ye find the farm?"

"Divil a clod."

"Nor the Kerry cow?"

"Divil a horn."

"Nor the good milk?"

"Divil a quart, and I that dry I could be drunk with the smell of it. Tom Toole, I have traipsed the high and the deep of this realm and believe you me it is not in it; the long and the wide of this realm ... not in it." He kept muttering sadly "not in it."

"Me good little man," cried Tom Toole, "don't be havering like an old goat. Here it is! the fortune of the world!"

He took the wee bottle from his breast and shook it before his eyes. "The drops that 'ull give ye your youth as easy as shifting a shirt. Come, now. I've waited the long days to share wid ye, for I couldn't bring myself to desart a comrade was ranging the back of the wild regions for the likes of me. Many's the time I've lifted that cork, and thinks I: He's gone, and soon I'll be going, so here goes. Divil a go was in it. I could not do it, not for silver and not for gold and not for all the mad raging mackerel that sleep in the sea."

The little old stranger took the wee bottle in his two hands. He was but a quavering stick of a man now; half dead he was, and his name it is Martin O'Moore.

"Is it the tale stuff, Tom Toole?"

"From herself I got it," he said, and he let on to him about that sweet-spoken young girl.

"Did she give you the directions on the head of it?"

"What directions is it?"

"The many drops is a man to drink!"

"No, but a good sup of it will do the little job."

"A good sup of it, Tom Toole, a good sup of it, ay?" says he unsqueezing the cork. "The elixir of youth, a good sup of it, says you, a good sup of it, a great good good sup of it!"

And sticking it into his mouth he drained the wee bottle of its every red drop. He stood there looking like a man in a fit, holding the empty bottle in his hand until Tom Toole took it from him with reproaches in his poor old eyes. But in a moment it was his very eyes he thought were deceiving him; not an inch of his skin but had the dew of fear on it, for the little old man began to change his appearance quick like the sand running through a glass, or as fast as the country changes down under a flying swan.

"Mother o' God!" screamed Martin O'Moore, "it's too fast backward I'm growing, dizzy I am."

And indeed his bald head suddenly got the fine black hair grown upon it, the whiskers flew away from him and his face was young. He began to wear a strange old suit that suddenly got new, and he had grown down through a handsome pair of trousers and into the little knickerbockers of a boy before you could count a score. And he had a bit of a cold just then, though he was out of it in a twink, and he let a sneeze that burst a button off his breeches, a little tin button, which was all that ever was found of him. Smaller and smaller he fell away, like the dust in an hour glass, till he was no bigger than an acorn and then devil a bit of him was left there at all.

Tom Toole was frightened at the quiet and the emptiness and he made to go away, but he turned in the doorway and stretching out his arms to the empty room he whispered "The greed! the avarice! May hell pour all its buckets on your bad little heart! May...." But just then he caught sight of the cup of porter that Martin O'Moore had forgotten to drink, so he went back to drink his enough and then went out into the great roaring world where he walked from here to there until one day he came right back to his old Asylum. He had been away for twenty years, he was an old man, very old indeed. And there was the man from Kilsheelan digging potatoes just inside the gates of the sunny garden.

"'Tis warm!" said the traveller staring at him through the railings, but the man from Kilsheelan only said "Come in, Tom Toole, is it staying or going ye are?"

THE CHERRY TREE

THE CHERRY TREE

There was uproar somewhere among the backyards of Australia Street. It was so alarming that people at their midday meal sat still and stared at one another. A fortnight before murder had been done in the street, in broad daylight with a chopper; people were nervous. An upper window was thrown open and a startled and startling head exposed.

"It's that young devil, Johnny Flynn, again! Killing rats!" shouted Mrs. Knatchbole, shaking her fist towards the Flynns' backyard. Mrs. Knatchbole was ugly; she had a goitred neck and a sharp skinny nose with an orb shining at its end, constant as grief.

"You wait, my boy, till your mother comes home, you just wait!" invited this apparition, but Johnny was gazing sickly at the body of a big rat slaughtered by the dogs of his friend George. The uproar was caused by the quarrelling of the dogs, possibly for honours, but more probably, as is the custom of victors, for loot.

"Bob down!" warned George, but Johnny bobbed up to catch the full anger of those baleful Knatchbole eyes. The urchin put his fingers promptly to his nose.

"Look at that for eight years old!" screamed the lady. "Eight years old 'e is! As true as God's my maker I'll...."

The impending vow was stayed and blasted for ever, Mrs. Knatchbole being taken with a fit of sneezing, whereupon the boys uttered some derisive "Haw haws!"

So Mrs. Knatchbole met Mrs. Flynn that night as she came from work, Mrs. Flynn being a widow who toiled daily and dreadfully at a laundry and perforce left her children, except for their school hours, to their own devices. The encounter was an emphatic one and the tired widow promised to admonish her boy.

"But it's all right, Mrs. Knatchbole, he's going from me in a week, to his uncle in London he is going, a person of wealth, and he'll be no annoyance to ye then. I'm ashamed that he misbehaves but he's no bad boy really."

At home his mother's remonstrances reduced Johnny to repentance and silence; he felt base indeed; he wanted to do something great and worthy at once to offset it all; he wished he had got some money, he'd have gone and bought her a bottle of stout—he knew she liked stout.

"Why do ye vex people so, Johnny?" asked Mrs. Flynn wearily. "I work my fingers to the bone for ye, week in and week out. Why can't ye behave like Pomony?"

His sister was a year younger than he; her name was Mona, which Johnny's elegant mind had disliked. One day he re-baptized her; Pomona she became and Pomona she remained. The Flynns sat down to supper. "Never mind, mum," said the boy, kissing her as he passed, "talk to us about the cherry tree!" The cherry tree, luxuriantly blooming, was the crown of the mother's memories of her youth and her father's farm; around the myth of its wonderful blossoms and fruit she could weave garlands of romance, and to her own mind as well as to the minds of her children it became a heavenly symbol of her old lost home, grand with acres and delightful with orchard and full pantry. What wonder that in her humorous narration the joys were multiplied and magnified until even Johnny was obliged to intervene. "Look here, how many horses *did* your father have, mum ... really, though?" Mrs. Flynn became vague, cast a furtive glance at this son of hers and then gulped with laughter until she recovered her ground with "Ah, but there *was* a cherry tree!" It was a grand supper—actually a polony and some potatoes. Johnny knew this was because he was going away. Ever since it was known that he was to go to London they had been having something special like this, or sheep's trotters or a pig's tail. Mother seemed to grow kinder and kinder to him. He wished he had some money, he would like to buy her a bottle of stout—he knew she liked stout.

Well, Johnny went away to live with his uncle, but alas he was only two months in London before he was returned to his mother and Pomony. Uncle was an engine-driver who disclosed to his astounded nephew a passion for gardening. This was incomprehensible to Johnny Flynn. A great roaring boiling locomotive was the grandest thing in the world. Johnny had rides on it, so he knew. And it was easy for him to imagine that every gardener cherished in the darkness of his disappointed soul an unavailing passion for a steam engine, but how an engine-driver could immerse himself in the mushiness of gardening was a baffling problem. However, before he returned home he discovered one important thing from his uncle's hobby, and he sent the information to his sister:

Dear Pomona—

Uncle Harry has got a alotment and grow veggutables. He says what makes the mold is worms. You know we pulled all the worms out off our garden and chukked them over Miss Natchbols wall. Well you better get some more quick a lot ask George to help you and I bring som seeds home when I comes next week by the xcursion on Moms birthday

Your sincerely brother
John Flynn

On mother's birthday Pomona met him at the station. She kissed him shyly and explained that mother was going to have a half holiday to celebrate the double occasion and would be home with them at dinner time.

"Pomony, did you get them worms?"

Pomona was inclined to evade the topic of worms for the garden, but fortunately her brother's enthusiasm for another gardening project tempered the wind of his indignation. When they reached home he unwrapped two parcels he had brought with him; he explained his scheme to his sister; he led her into the garden. The Flynns' backyard, mostly paved with bricks, was small and so the enclosing walls, truculently capped by chips of glass, although too low for privacy were yet too high for the growth of any cherishable plant. Johnny had certainly once reared a magnificent exhibit of two cowslips, but these had been mysteriously destroyed by the Knatchbole cat. The dank little enclosure was charged with sterility; nothing flourished there except a lot of beetles and a dauntless evergreen bush, as tall as Johnny, displaying a profusion of thick shiny leaves that you could split on your tongue and make squeakers with. Pomona showed him how to do this and they then busied themselves in the garden until the dinner siren warned them that Mother would be coming home. They hurried into the kitchen and Pomona quickly spread the cloth and the plates of food upon the table, while Johnny placed conspicuously in the centre, after laboriously extracting the stopper with a fork and a hair-pin, a bottle of stout brought from London. He had been much impressed by numberless advertisements upon the hoardings respecting this attractive beverage. The children then ran off to meet their mother and they all came home together with great hilarity. Mrs. Flynn's attention having been immediately drawn to the sinister decoration of her dining table, Pomona was requested to pour out a glass of the nectar. Johnny handed this gravely to his parent, saying:

"Many happy returns of the day, Mrs. Flynn!"

"O, dear, dear!" gasped his mother merrily, "you drink first!"

* * *

"Excuse me, no, Mrs. Flynn," rejoined her son, "many happy returns of the day!"

When the toast had been honoured Pomona and Johnny looked tremendously at each other.

"Shall we?" exclaimed Pomona.

"O yes," decided Johnny; "come on, mum, in the garden, something marvellous!"

She followed her children into that dull little den, and fortuitously the sun shone there for the occasion. Behold, the dauntless evergreen bush had been stripped of its leaves and upon its blossomless twigs the children had hung numerous couples of ripe cherries, white and red and black.

"What do you think of it, mum?" cried the children, snatching some of the fruit and pressing it into her hands, "what do you think of it?"

"Beautiful!" said the poor woman in a tremulous voice. They stared silently at their mother until she could bear it no longer. She turned and went sobbing into the kitchen.

CLORINDA WALKS IN HEAVEN

CLORINDA WALKS IN HEAVEN

Miss Smith, Clorinda Smith, desired not to die on a wet day. Her speculations upon the possibilities of one's demise were quite ingenuous and had their mirth, but she shrunk from that figure of her dim little soul—and it was only dimly that she could figure it at all—approaching the pathways of the Boundless in a damp, bedraggled condition.

"But the rain couldn't harm your spirit," declared her comforting friends.

"Why not?" asked Clorinda, "if there is a ghost of me, why not a ghost of the rain?"

There were other aspects, delectable and illusive, of this imagined apotheosis, but Clorinda always hoped—against hope be it said—that it wouldn't be wet. On three evenings there had been a bow in the sky, and on the day she died rain poured in fury. With a golden key she unlocked the life out of her bosom and moved away without fear, as if a great light had sprung suddenly under her feet in a little dark place, into a region where things became starkly real and one seemed to live like the beams rolling on the tasselled corn in windy acres. There was calmness in those translucent leagues and the undulation amid a vast implacable light until she drifted, like a feather fallen from an unguessed star, into a place which was extraordinarily like the noon-day world, so green and warm was its valley.

A little combe lay between some low hills of turf, and on a green bank beside a few large rocks was a man mending a ladder of white new-shaven willow studded with large brass nails, mending it with hard knocks that sounded clearly. The horizon was terraced only just beyond and above him, for the hills rolled steeply up. Thin pads of wool hung in the arch of the ultimate heavens, but towards the end of the valley the horizon was crowded with clouds torn and disbattled. Two cows, a cow of white and a cow of tan, squatted where one low hill held up, as it were, the sunken limits of the sky. There were larks—in such places the lark sings for ever—and thrushes—the wind vaguely active—seven white ducks—a farm. Each nook was a flounce of blooms and a bower for birds. Passing close to the man—he was sad and preoccupied, dressed in a little blue tunic—she touched his arm as if to enquire a direction, saying "Jacob!"

She did not know what she would have asked of him, but he gave her no heed and she again called to him "Jacob!" He did not seem even to see her, so she went to the large white gates at the end of the valley and approached a railway crossing. She had to wait a long time for trains of a vastness and grandeur were passing, passing without sound. Strange advertisements on the hoardings and curious direction posts gathered some of her attention. She observed that in every possible situation, on any available post or stone, people had carved initials, sometimes a whole name, often with a date, and Clorinda experienced a doubt of the genuineness of some of these so remote was the antiquity implied. At last, the trains were all gone by, and as the barriers swung back she crossed the permanent way.

There was neither ambiguity in her movements nor surprise in her apprehensions. She just crossed over to a group of twenty or thirty men who moved to welcome her. They were barelegged, sandal-footed, lightly clad in beautiful loose tunics of peacock and cinnamon, which bore not so much the significance of colour as the quality of light; one of them rushed eagerly forward, crying "Clorinda!" offering to her a long coloured scarf. Strangely, as he came closer, he grew less perceivable; Clorinda was aware in a flash that she was viewing him by some other mechanism than that of her two eyes. In a moment he utterly disappeared and she felt herself wrapt into his being, caressed with faint caresses, and troubled with dim faded ecstasies and recognitions not wholly agreeable. The other men stood grouped around them, glancing with half-closed cynical eyes. Those who stood farthest away were more clearly seen: in contiguity a presence could only be divined, resting only—but how admirably!—in the nurture of one's mind.

"What is it?" Clorinda asked: and all the voices replied, "Yes, we know you!"

* * *

She felt herself released, and the figure of the man rejoined the waiting group. "I was your husband Reuben," said the first man slowly, and Clorinda, who had been a virgin throughout her short life, exclaimed "Yes, yes, dear Reuben!" with momentary tremors and a queer fugitive drift of doubt. She stood there, a spook of comprehending being, and all the uncharted reefs in the map of her mind were anxiously engaging her. For a time she was absorbed by this new knowledge.

Then another voice spoke:

"I was your husband Raphael!"

"I know, I know," said Clorinda, turning to the speaker, "we lived in Judea."

"And we dwelt in the valley of the Nile," said another, "in the years that are gone."

"And I too ... and I too ... and I too," they all clamoured, turning angrily upon themselves.

Clorinda pulled the strange scarf from her shoulders where Reuben had left it, and, handling it so, she became aware of her many fugitive sojournings upon the earth. It seemed that all of her past had become knit in the scarf into a compact pattern of beauty and ugliness of which she was entirely aware; all its multiplexity being immediately resolved ... the habitations with cave men, and the lesser human unit of the lesser later day. Patagonian, Indian, Cossack, Polynesian, Jew ... of such stuff the pattern was intimately woven, and there were little plangent perfect moments of the past that fell into order in the web. Clorinda watching the great seabird with pink feet louting above the billows that roared upon Iceland, or Clorinda hanging her girdle upon the ebony hooks of the image of Tanteelee. She had taken voyaging drafts upon the whole world, cataract jungle and desert, ingle and pool and strand, ringing the changes upon a whole gamut of masculine endeavour ... from a prophet to a haberdasher. She could feel each little life lying now as in a sarsnet of cameos upon her visible breasts: thereby for these ... these *men* ... she was draped in an eternal wonder. But she could not recall any image of her past life in *these* realms, save only that her scarf was given back to her on every return by a man of these men.

She could remember with humility her transient passions for them all. None, not one, had ever given her the measure of her own desire, a strong harsh flame that fashioned and tempered its own body; nothing but a nebulous glow that was riven into embers before its beam had sweetened into pride. She had gone from them childless always and much as a little child.

From the crowd of quarrelling ghosts a new figure detached itself, and in its approach it subdued that vague vanishing which had been so perplexing to Clorinda. Out of the crowd it slipped, and loomed lovingly beside her, took up her thought and the interrogation that came into her mind.

"No," it said gravely, "there is none greater than these. The ultimate reaches of man's mind produce nothing but images of men."

"But," said Clorinda, "do you mean that our ideals, previsions of a vita-nuova...."

* * *

"Just so," it continued, "a mere intoxication. Even here you cannot escape the singular dower of dreams ... you can be drunk with dreams more easily and more permanently than with drugs."

The group of husbands had ceased their quarrelling to listen; Clorinda swept them with her glances thoughtfully and doubtfully.

"Could mankind be so poor," the angel resumed, "as poor as these, if it housed something greater than itself?"

With a groan the group of outworn husbands drew away. Clorinda turned to her companion with disappointment and some dismay.... "I hardly understand yet ... is this all then just...."

"Yes," it replies, "just the ghost of the world."

She turned unhappily and looked back across the gateway into the fair combe with its cattle, its fine grass, and the man working diligently therein. A sense of bleak loneliness began to possess her; here, then, was no difference save that there were no correlations, no consequences; nothing had any effect except to produce the ghost of a ghost. There was already in the hinterland of her apprehensions a ghost, a ghost of her new ghostship: she was to be followed by herself, pursued by figures of her own ceaseless being!

She looked at the one by her side: "Who are you?" she asked, and at the question the group of men drew again very close to them.

"I am your unrealized desires," it said: "Did you think that the dignity of virginhood, rarely and deliberately chosen, could be so brief and barren? Why, that pure idea was my own immaculate birth, and I was born, the living mate of you."

The hungry-eyed men shouted with laughter.

"Go away!" screamed Clorinda to them; "I do not want you."

Although they went she could hear the echoes of their sneering as she took the arm of her new lover "Let us go," she said, pointing to the man in the combe, "and speak to him." As they approached the man he lifted his ladder hugely in the air and dashed it to the ground so passionately that it broke.

"Angry man! angry man!" mocked Clorinda. He turned towards her fiercely. Clorinda began to fear him; the muscles and knots of his limbs were uncouth like the gnarl of old trees; she made a little pretence of no more observing him.

"Now what is it like," said she jocularly to the angel at her side, and speaking of her old home, "what is it like now at Weston-super-Mare?"

At that foolish question the man with the ladder reached forth an ugly hand and twitched the scarf from her shoulders.

It cannot now be told to what remoteness she had come, or on what roads her undirected feet had travelled there, but certain it is that in that moment she was gone.... Why, where, or how cannot be established: whether she was swung in a blast of annihilation into the uttermost gulfs, or withdrawn for her beauty into that mysterious Nox, into some passionate communion with the eternal husbands, or into some eternal combat with their passionate other wives ... from our scrutiny at least she passed for ever.

It is true there was a beautiful woman of this name who lay for a month in a deep trance in the West of England. On her recovery she was balladed about in the newspapers and upon the halls for quite a time, and indeed her notoriety brought requests for her autograph from all parts of the world, and an offer of marriage from a Quaker potato merchant. But she tenderly refused him and became one of those faded grey old maids who wear their virginity like antiquated armour.

CRAVEN ARMS

CRAVEN ARMS

I

The teacher of the sketching class at the evening school was a man who had no great capacity for enduring affection, but his handsome appearance often inspired in women those emotions which if not enduring are deep and disturbing. His own passions may have been deep but they were undeniably fickle.

The townspeople were proud of their new school for in addition to the daily curriculum evening instruction of an advanced modern kind was given. Of course all schools since the beginning of time have been modern at some period of their existence but this one was modern, so the vicar declared, because it was so blessedly hygienic. It was built upon a high tree-arboured slope overlooking the snug small town and on its western side stared ambiguously at a free upland country that was neither small nor snug. The seventeen young women and the nine young men were definitely, indeed articulately, inartistic, they were as unæsthetic as pork pies, all except Julia Tern, a golden-haired fine-complexioned fawn of a girl whose talent was already beyond the reach of any instruction the teacher could give. He could not understand why she continued to attend his classes.

One evening she brought for his criticism a portrait sketch of himself.

"This is extraordinarily beautiful," he murmured.

"Yes?" said Julia.

"I mean the execution, the presentation and so on."

Julia did not reply. He stared at her picture of him, a delicately modelled face with a suggestion of nobility, an air that was kind as it was grave. The gravity and nobility which so pleased him were perhaps the effect of a high brow from which the long brown hair flowed thinly back to curve in a tidy cluster at his neck. Kindness beamed in the eyes and played around the thin mouth, sharp nose, and positive chin. What could have inspired her to make this idealization of himself, for it was idealization in spite of its fidelity and likeness? He knew he had little enough nobility of character—too little to show so finely—and as for that calm gravity of aspect, why gravity simply was not in him. But there it was on paper, deliberate and authentic, inscribed with his name—*David Masterman 1910*.

"When, how did you come to do it?"

"I just wanted it, you were a nice piece, I watched you a good deal, and there you are!" She said it jauntily but there was a pink flush in her cheeks.

"It's delicious," he mused, "I envy you. I can't touch a decent head—not even yours. But why have you idealized me so?" He twitted her lightly about the gravity and nobility.

"But you are like that, you are. That's how I see you, at this moment."

She did not give him the drawing as he hoped she would. He did not care to ask her for it—there was delicious flattery in the thought that she treasured it so much. Masterman was a rather solitary man of about thirty, with a modest income which he supplemented with the fees from these classes. He lived alone in a wooden bungalow away out of the town and painted numbers of landscapes, rather lifeless imitations, as he knew, of other men's masterpieces. They were frequently sold.

Sometimes on summer afternoons he would go into woods or fields with a few of his pupils to sketch or paint farmhouses, trees, clouds, stacks, and other rural furniture. He was always hoping to sit alone with Julia Tern but there were other loyal pupils who never missed these occasions, among them the two Forrest girls, Ianthe the younger, and Katharine, daughters of a thriving contractor. Julia remained inscrutable, she gave him no opportunities at all; he could never divine her feelings or gather any response to his own, but there could be no doubt of the feelings of the Forrest girls—they quite certainly liked him enormously. Except for that, they too, could have no reason for continuing in his classes for both were as devoid of artistic grace as an inkstand. They brought fruit or chocolate to the classes and shared them with him. Their attentions, their mutual attentions, were manifested in many ways, small but significant and kind. On these occasions Julia's eyes seemed to rest upon him with an ironical gaze. It was absurd. He liked them well enough and sometimes from his shy wooing of the adorable but enigmatic Julia he would turn for solace to Ianthe. Yet strangely enough it was Kate, the least alluring to him of the three girls, who took him to her melancholy heart.

Ianthe was a little bud of womanhood, dark-haired but light-headed, dressed in cream coloured clothes. She was small and right and tight, without angularities or rhythms, just one dumpy solid roundness.

But she had an astonishing vulgarity of speech, if not of mind, that exacerbated him and in the dim corridors of his imagination she did not linger, she scurried as it were into doorways or upon twisting staircases or stood briefly where a loop of light fell upon her hair, her dusky face, her creamy clothes, and her delightful rotundities. She had eyes of indiscretion and a mind like a hive of bees, it had such a tiny opening and was so full of a cloying content.

One day he suddenly found himself alone with Ianthe in a glade of larch trees which they had all been sketching. They had loitered. He had been naming wild flowers which Ianthe had picked for the purpose and then thrown wantonly away. She spied a single plant of hellebore growing in the dimness under the closely planted saplings.

"Don't! don't!" he cried. He kept her from plucking it and they knelt down together to admire the white virginal flower.

* * *

His arm fell round Ianthe's waist in a light casual way. He scarcely realized its presumption. He had not intended to do it; as far as that went he did not particularly want to do it, but there his arm was. Ianthe took no notice of the embrace and he felt foolish, he could not retreat until they rose to walk on; then Ianthe pressed close to his side until his arm once more stole round her and they kissed.

"Heavens above!" she said, "you do get away with it quick."

"Life's short, there's no time to lose, I do as I'd be done by."

"And there are so many of us! But glory," said the jolly girl, taking him to her bosom, "in for a penny, in for a pound."

She did not pick any more flowers and soon they were out of the wood decorously joining the others. He imagined that Julia's gaze was full of irony, and the timid wonder in Kate's eyes moved him uncomfortably. There was something idiotic in the whole affair.

Until the end of the summer he met Ianthe often enough in the little town or the city three miles off. Her uncouthness still repelled him; sometimes he disliked her completely, but she was always happy to be with him, charmingly fond and gay with all the endearing alertness of a pert bird.

Her sister Kate was not just the mere female that Ianthe was; at once sterner and softer her passions were more strong but their defences stood solid as a rock. In spite of her reserve she was always on the brink of her emotions and they, unhappily for her, were often not transient, but enduring. She was nearly thirty, still unwed. Her dark beauty, for she, too, was fine, seemed to brood in melancholy over his attentions to the other two women. She was quiet, she had little to say, she seemed to stand and wait.

One autumn night at the school after the pupils had gone home he walked into the dim lobby for his hat and coat. Kate Forrest was there. She stood with her back to him adjusting her hat. She did not say a word nor did he address her. They were almost touching each other, there was a pleasant scent about her. In the classroom behind the caretaker was walking about the hollow-sounding floor, humming loudly as he clapped down windows and mounted the six chairs to turn out the six gas lamps. When the last light through the glazed door was gone and the lobby was completely dark Kate all at once turned to him, folded him in her arms and held him to her breast for one startling moment, then let him go, murmuring O ... O.... It made him strangely happy. He pulled her back in the gloom, whispering tender words. They walked out of the hall into the dark road and stopped to confront each other. The road was empty and dark except for a line of gas lamps that gleamed piercingly bright in the sharp air and on the polished surface of the road that led back from the hill down past her father's villa. There were no lamps in the opposite direction and the road groped its way out into the dark country where he lived, a mile beyond the town. It was windy and some unseen trees behind a wall near them swung and tossed with many pleasant sounds.

"I will come a little way with you," Kate said.

"Yes, come a little way," he whispered, pressing her arm, "I'll come back with you."

She took his arm and they turned towards the country. He could think of nothing to say, he was utterly subdued by his surprise; Kate was sad, even moody; but at last she said slowly: "I am unlucky, I always fall in love with men who can't love me."

"O but I can and do, dear Kate," he cried lightly. "Love me, Kate, go on loving me, I'm not, well, I'm not very wicked."

"No, no, you do not." She shook her head mournfully: after a few moments she added: "It's Julia Tern."

He was astounded. How could she have known this, how could any one have known—even Julia herself? It was queer that she did not refer to his friendship with Ianthe; he thought that was much more obvious than his love for Julia. In a mood that he only half understood he began to deny her reproachful charge.

"Why, you must think me very fickle indeed. I really love you, dear Kate, really you." His arm was around her neck, he smoothed her cheek fondly against his own. She returned his caresses but he could glimpse the melancholy doubt in her averted eyes.

"We often talk of you, we often talk of you at night, in bed, often."

* * *

"What do you say about me—in bed? Who?"

"Ianthe and me. She likes you."

"She likes me! What do you say about me—in bed?"

He hoped Ianthe had not been indiscreet but Kate only said: "She doesn't like you as I do—not like this."

Soon they began to walk back toward the town. He smiled once when, as their footsteps clattered unregularly upon the hard clean road, she skipped to adjust the fall of her steps to his.

"Do not come any further," she begged as they neared the street lamps. "It doesn't matter, not at all, what I've said to you. It will be all right. I shall see you again."

Once more she put her arms around his neck murmuring: "Goodnight, goodnight, goodnight."

He watched her tripping away. When he turned homewards his mind was full of thoughts that were only dubiously pleasant. It was all very sweet, surprisingly sweet, but it left him uneasy. He managed to light a cigarette, but the wind blew smoke into his eyes, tore the charred end into fiery rags and tossed the sparkles across his shoulder. If it had only been Julia Tern!—or even Ianthe!—he would have been wholly happy, but this was disturbing. Kate was good-looking but these quietly passionate advances amazed him. Why had he been so responsive to her? He excused himself, it was quite simple; you could not let a woman down, a loving woman like that, not at once, a man should be kind. But what did she mean when she spoke of always falling in love with men who did not like her? He tossed the cigarette away and turned up the collar of his coat for the faintest fall of warm rain blew against his face like a soft beautiful net. He thrust his hands into his pockets and walked sharply and forgettingly home.

II

Two miles away from the little town was the big city with tramways, electric light, factories, canals, and tens of thousands of people, where a few nights later he met Ianthe. Walking around and away from the happy lighted streets they came out upon the bank of a canal where darkness and loneliness were intensified by the silent passage of black water whose current they could divine but could not see. As they stepped warily along the unguarded bank he embraced her. Even as he did so he cursed himself for a fool to be so fond of this wretched imp of a girl. In his heart he believed he disliked her, but he was not sure. She was childish, artful, luscious, stupid—this was no gesture for a man with any standards. Silently clutching each other they approached an iron bridge with lamps upon it and a lighted factory beyond it. The softly-moving water could now be seen—the lamps on the bridge let down thick rods of light into its quiet depths and beyond the arch the windows of the factory, inverted in the stream, bloomed like baskets of fire with flaming fringes among the eddies caused by the black pillars. A boy shuffled across the bridge whistling a tune; there was the rumble and trot of a cab. Then all sounds melted into a quiet without one wave of air. The unseen couple had kissed, Ianthe was replying to him:

"No, no, I like it, I like you." She put her brow against his breast. "I like you, I like you."

His embracing hand could feel the emotion streaming within the girl.

"Do you like me better than her?"

"Than whom?" he asked.

Ianthe was coy. "You know, you know."

Masterman's feelings were a mixture of perturbation and delight, delight at this manifestation of jealousy of her sister which was an agreeable thing, anyway, for it implied a real depth of regard for him; but he was perturbed for he did not know what Kate had told this sister of their last strange meeting. He saluted her again exclaiming: "Never mind her. This is our outing, isn't it?"

"I don't like her," Ianthe added naïvely, "she is so awfully fond of you."

"O confound her," he cried, and then, "you mustn't mind me saying that so, so sharply, you don't mind, do you?"

Ianthe's lips were soft and sweet. Sisters were quite unscrupulous, Masterman had heard of such cases before, but he had tenderness and a reluctance to wound anybody's susceptibility, let alone the feelings of a woman who loved. He was an artist not only in paint, but in sentiment, and it is possible that he excelled in the less tangible medium.

"It's a little awkward," he ventured. Ianthe didn't understand, she didn't understand that at all.

"The difficulty, you see," he said with the air of one handling whimsically a question of perplexity that yet yielded its amusement, "is ... is Kate."

"Kate?" said Ianthe.

"She is so—so gone, so absolutely gone."

"Gone?"

"Well, she's really really in love, deeply, deeply," he said looking away anywhere but at her sister's eyes.

"With Chris Halton, do you mean?"

"Ho, ho!" he laughed, "Halton! Lord, no, with me, with me, isn't she?"

"With you!"

But Ianthe was quite positive even a little ironical about that. "She is not, she rather dislikes you, Mr. Prince Charming, so there. We speak of you sometimes at night in bed—we sleep together. She knows what *I* think of you but she's quite, well she doesn't like you at all—she acts the heavy sister."

"O," said Masterman, groping as it were for some light in his darkness.

"She—what do you think—she warns me against you," Ianthe continued.

"Against me?"

"As if I care. Do you?"

"No, no. I don't care."

They left the dark bank where they had been standing and walked along to the bridge. Halfway up its steps to the road he paused and asked: "Then who is it that is so fond of me?"

* * *

"O you know, you know." Ianthe nestled blissfully in his arm again.

"No, but who is it, I may be making another howler. I thought you meant Kate, what did she warn you of, I mean against me?"

They were now in the streets again, walking towards the tram centre. The shops were darkened and closed, but the cinemas lavished their unwanted illuminations on the street. There were no hurrying people, there was just strolling ease; the policemen at corners were chatting to other policemen now in private clothes. The brilliant trams rumbled and clanged and stopped, the saloons were full and musical.

"What did she warn you against?" he repeated.

"You," chuckled Ianthe.

"But what about? What has she got against me?"

"Everything. You know, you know you do." The archness of Ianthe was objectively baffling but under it all he read its significance, its invitation.

He waited beside her for a tram but when it came he pleaded a further engagement in the city. He had no other engagement, he only wanted to be alone, to sort out the things she had dangled before his mind, so he boarded the next car and walked from the Tutsan terminus to his cottage. Both girls were fond of him, then—Ianthe's candour left him no room for doubt—and they were both lying to each other about him. Well, he didn't mind that, lies were a kind of protective colouring, he lied himself whenever it was necessary, or suited him. Not often, but truth was not always possible to sensitive minded men. Why, after all, should sympathetic mendacity be a monopoly of polite society? "But it's also the trick of thieves and seducers, David Masterman," he muttered to himself. "I'm not a thief, no, I'm not a thief. As for the other thing, well, what is there against me—nothing, nothing at all." But a strange voiceless sigh seemed to echo from the trees along the dark road, "Not as yet, not as yet."

He walked on more rapidly.

Three women! There was no doubt about the third, Ianthe had thought of Julia, too, just as Kate had. What a fate for a misogamist! He felt like a mouse being taken for a ride in a bath chair. He had an invincible prejudice against marriage not as an institution but because he was perfectly aware of his incapacity for faithfulness. His emotions were deep but unprolonged. Love was love, but marriage turned love into the stone of Sisyphus. At the sound of the marriage bell—a passing bell—earth at his feet would burst into flame and the sky above would pour upon him an unquenching profusion of tears. Love was a fine and ennobling thing, but though he had the will to love he knew beyond the possibility of doubt that his own capacity for love was a meandering strengthless thing. Even his loyalty to Julia Tern—and that had the strongest flavour of any emotion that had ever beset him, no matter how brief its term—even that was a deviating zigzag loyalty. For he wanted to go on being jolly and friendly with Ianthe if only Julia did not get to know. With Kate, too, that tender melancholy woman; she would be vastly unhappy. Who was this Christopher whom Ianthe fondly imagined her sister to favour? Whoever he was, poor devil, he would not thank D. M. for his intervention. But he would drop all this; however had he, of all men, come to be plunged so suddenly into a state of things for which he had shown so little fancy in the past? Julia would despise him, she would be sure to despise him, sure to; and yet if he could only believe she would not it would be pleasant to go on being friendly with Ianthe pending ... pending what?

Masterman was a very pliant man, but as things shaped themselves for him he did not go a step further with Ianthe, and it was not to Julia at all that he made love.

III

The amour, if it may be described as such, of David Masterman and Kate Forrest took a course that was devoid of ecstasy, whatever other qualities may have illuminated their desires. It was an affair in which the human intentions, which are intellectual, were on both sides strong enough to subdue the efforts of passion, which are instinctive, to rid itself of the customary curbs; and to turn the clash of inhibitions wherein the man proposes and the woman rejects into a conflict not of ideal but of mere propriety. They were like two negative atoms swinging in a medium from which the positive flux was withdrawn; for them the nebulæ did not "cohere into an orb."

Kate's fine figure was not so fine as Julia Tern's; her dusky charms were excelled by those of Ianthe; but her melancholy immobility, superficial as it was, had a suggestive emotional appeal that won Masterman away from her rivals. Those sad eyes had but to rest on his and their depths submerged him. Her black hair had no special luxuriance, her stature no unusual grace; the eyes were almost blue and the thin oval face had always the flush of fine weather in it; but her strong hands, though not as white as snow, were paler than milk, their pallor was unnatural. Almost without an effort she drew him away from the entangling Ianthe, and even the image of Julia became but a fair cloud seen in moonlight, delicate and desirable but very far away; it would never return. Julia had observed the relations between them—no discerning eye could misread Kate's passion—and she gave up his class, a secession that had a deep significance for him, and a grief that he could not conceal from Kate though she was too wise to speak of it.

But in spite of her poignant aspect—for it was in that appearance she made such a powerful appeal to Masterman; the way she would wait silently for him on the outside of a crowd of the laughing chattering students was touching—she was an egotist of extraordinary type. She believed in herself and in her virtue more strongly than she believed in him or their mutual love. By midsummer, after months of wooing, she knew that the man who so passionately moved her and whose own love she no less powerfully engaged was a man who would never marry, who had a morbid preposterous horror of the domesticity and devotion that was her conception of living bliss. "The hand that rocks the cradle rocks the world," he said. He, too, knew that the adored woman, for her part, could not dream of a concession beyond the limits her virginal modesty prescribed. He had argued and stormed and swore that baffled love turns irrevocably to hatred. She did not believe him, she even smiled. But he had behaved grossly towards her, terrified her, and they had parted in anger.

He did not see her for many weeks. He was surprised and dismayed that his misery was so profound. He knew he had loved her, he had not doubted its sincerity but he had doubted its depth. Then one September evening she had come back to the class and afterwards she had walked along the road with him towards his home.

"Come to my house," he said, "you have never been to see it."

She shook her head, it was getting dark, and they walked on past his home further into the country. The eve was late but it had come suddenly without the deliberation of sunset or the tenuity of dusk. Each tree was a hatful of the arriving blackness. They stood by a white gate under an elm, but they had little to say to each other.

"Come to my house," he urged again and again; she shook her head. He was indignant at her distrust of him. Perhaps she was right but he would never forgive her. The sky was now darker than the road; the sighing air was warm, with drifting spots of rain.

"Tell me," she suddenly said taking his arm, "has anybody else ever loved you like that."

* * *

He prevaricated: "Like what?" He waited a long time for her answer. She gave it steadily.

"Like you want me to love you."

He, too, hesitated. He kissed her. He wanted to tell her that it was not wise to pry.

"Tell me," she urged, "tell me."

"Yes," he replied. He could not see her plainly in the darkness, but he knew of the tears that fell from her eyes.

"How unreasonable," he thought, "how stupid!" He tried to tell the truth to her—the truth as he conceived it—about his feelings towards her, and towards those others, and about themselves as he perceived it.

She was almost alarmed, certainly shocked.

"But you don't believe such things," she almost shivered, "I'm sure you don't, it isn't right, it is not true."

"It may not be true," he declared implacably, "but I believe it. The real warrant for holding a belief is not that it is true but that it satisfies you." She did not seem to understand that; she only answered irrelevantly. "I'll make it all up to you some day. I shall not change, David, toward you. We have got all our lives before us. I shan't alter—will you?"

"Not alter!" he began angrily but then subduedly added with a grim irony that she did not gather in: "No, I shall not alter."

She flung herself upon his breast murmuring: "I'll make it all up to you, some day."

He felt like a sick-minded man and was glad when they parted. He went back to his cottage grumbling audibly to himself. Why could he not take this woman with the loving and constant heart and wed her? He did not know why, but he knew he never would do that. She was fine to look upon but she had ideas (if you could call them ideas) which he disliked. Her instincts and propensities were all wrong, they were antagonistic to him, just, as he felt, his were antagonistic to her. What was true, though, was her sorrow at what she called their misunderstandings and what was profound, what was almost convincing, was her assumption (which but measured her own love for him) that he could not cease to love *her*. How vain that was. He had not loved any woman in the form she thought all love must take. These were not misunderstandings, they were just simply at opposite ends of a tilted beam; he the sophisticated, and she the innocent beyond the reach of his sophistries. But Good Lord, what did it all matter? what did anything matter? He would not see her again. He undressed, got into bed. He thought of Julia, of Ianthe, of Kate. He had a dream in which he lay in a shroud upon a white board and was interrogated by a saint who carried a reporter's notebook and a fountain pen.

"What is your desire, sick-minded man?" the saint interrogated him, "what consummation would exalt your languid eyes?"

"I want the present not to be. It is neither grave nor noble."

"Then that is your sickness. That mere negation is at once your hope and end."

* * *

"I do not know."

"If the present so derides the dignified past surely your desire lies in a future incarnating beautiful old historic dreams?"

"I do not know."

"Ideals are not in the past. They do not exist in any future. They rush on, and away, beyond your immediate activities, beyond the horizons that are for ever fixed, for ever charging down upon us."

"I do not know."

"What is it you do know?" asked the exasperated saint, jerking his fountain pen to loosen its flow, and Masterman replied like a lunatic:

"I know that sealing wax is a pure and beautiful material and you get such a lot of it for a penny."

He woke and slept no more. He cursed Kate, he sneered at Julia, he anathematized Ianthe, until the bright eye of morning began to gild once more their broken images.

IV

Between the sisters there grew a feud; Ianthe behaved evilly when she discovered their mutual infatuation for their one lover. The echoes of that feud, at first dim, but soon crashingly clear, reached him, touched him and moved him on Kate's behalf: all his loyalty belonged to her. What did it matter if he could not fathom his own desire, that Ianthe was still his for a word, that Kate's implacable virtue still offered its deprecatory hand, when Kate herself came back to him?

* * *

They were to spend a picnic day together and she went to him for breakfast. Her tremors of propriety were fully exercised as she cycled along to his home; she was too fond of him and he was more than fond of her; but all her qualms were lulled. He did not appear in any of the half-expected negligee, he was beautifully and amusingly at home.

"My dear!" he exclaimed in the enjoyment of her presence; she stood staring at him as she removed her wrap, the morn though bright being fresh and cool: "Why do I never do you justice! Why do I half forget! You are marvellously, irresistibly lovely. How do you do it—or how do I fail so?"

She could only answer him with blushes. His bungalow had but two rooms, both on the ground floor, one a studio and the other his living and sleeping room. It was new, built of bricks and unpainted boards. The interior walls were unplastered and undecorated except for three small saucepans hung on hooks, a shelf of dusty volumes, and nails, large rusty nails, projecting everywhere, one holding a discarded collar and a clothes brush. A tall flat cupboard contained a narrow bed to be lowered for sleeping, huge portmanteaus and holdalls reposed in a corner beside a bureau, there was a big brass candle-pan on a chair beside the round stove. While he prepared breakfast the girl walked about the room, making shy replies to his hilarious questions. It was warm in there but to her tidy comfort-loving heart the room was disordered and bare. She stood looking out of the window: the April air was bright but chilly, the grass in thin tufts fluttered and shivered.

"It is very nice," she said to him once, "but it's strange and I feel that I ought not to be here."

"O, never mind where you ought to be," he cried, pouring out her coffee, "that's where you are, you suit the place, you brighten and adorn it, it's your native setting, Kate. No—I know exactly what is running in your mind, you are going to ask if I suffer loneliness here. Well, I don't. A great art in life is the capacity to extract a flavour from something not obviously flavoured, but here it is all flavour. Come and look at things."

He rose and led her from egg and toast to the world outside. Long fields of pasture and thicket followed a stream that followed other meadows, soon hidden by the ambulating many folding valleys, and so on to the sea, a hundred miles away. Into his open door were blown, in their season, balls of thistledown, crisp leaves, twigs and dried grass, the reminder, the faint brush, of decay. The airs of wandering winds came in, odours of herb, the fragrance of viewless flowers. The land in some directions was now being furrowed where corn was greenly to thrive, to wave in glimmering gold, to lie in the stook, to pile on giant stack. Horses were trailing a harrow across an upland below the park, the wind was flapping the coats of the drivers, the tails and manes of the horses, and heaving gladly in trees. A boy fired the heaps of squitch whose smoke wore across the land in dense deliberate wreaths. Sportsmen's guns were sounding from the hollow park.

Kate followed Masterman around his cottage; he seemed to be fascinated by the smoke, the wind, the horses and men.

"Breakfast will be cold."

How queerly he looked at her before he said: "Yes, of course, breakfast will be getting cold," and then added, inconsequently: "Flowers are like men and women, they either stare brazenly at the sun or they bend humbly before it, but even the most modest desire the sun."

When he spoke like that she always felt that the words held a half-hidden, perhaps libidinous, meaning, which she could not understand but only guess at; and she was afraid of her guesses. Full of curious, not to say absurd superstitions about herself and about him, his strange oblique emotions startled her virginal understanding; her desire was to be good, very very good, but to be that she could not but suspect the impulses of most other people, especially the impulses of men. Well, perhaps she was right: the woman who hasn't any doubts must have many illusions.

He carried a bag of lunch and they walked out into the day. Soon the wind ceased, the brightness grew warm, the warmth was coloured; clouds lolled in the air like tufts of lilac. At the edge of a spinney they sat down under a tree. Boughs of wood blown down by the winter gales were now being hidden by the spring grass. A rabbit, twenty yards away, sat up and watched the couple, a fat grey creature. "Hoi," cried

Kate, and the rabbit hopped away. It could not run very fast, it did not seem much afraid.

"Is it wounded?" she asked.

"No, I think it is a tame one, escaped from a farm or a cottage near us, I expect."

Kate crept after it on hands and knees and it let her approach. She offered it the core of an apple she had just eaten. The rabbit took it and bit her finger. Then Kate caught it by the ears. It squealed but Kate held it to her bosom with delight, and the rabbit soon rested there if not with delight at least with ease. It was warm against her breast, it was delicious to feel it there, to pull its ears and caress its fat flanks, but as she was doing this she suddenly saw that its coat was infested with fleas. She dropped the rabbit with a scream of disgust and it rushed into the thicket.

"Come here," said Masterman to her, "let me search you, this is distressing."

She knelt down before him and in spite of her wriggling he reassured her.

"It's rather a nice blouse," he said.

"I don't care for it. I shall not wear it again. I shall sell it to someone or give it to them."

"I would love to take it from you stitch by stitch."

With an awkward movement of her arm she thrust at his face, crying loudly, "No, how dare you speak to me like that!"

"Is it very daring?" For a moment he saw her clenched hands, detestably bloodless, a symbol of roused virtue: but at once her anger was gone, Kate was contrite and tender. She touched his face with her white fingers softly as the settling of a moth. "O, why did we come here?"

He did not respond to her caresses, he was sullen, they left the spinney; but as they walked she took his arm murmuring: "Forgive me, I'll make it all up to you some day."

Coyness and cunning, passion and pride, were so much at odds that later on they quarrelled again. Kate knew that he would neither marry her nor let her go; she could neither let him go nor keep him. This figure of her distress amused him, he was callously provoking, and her resentment flowed out at the touch of his scorn. With Kate there seemed to be no intermediate stages between docility and fury, or even between love and hatred.

"Why are you like this?" she cried, beating her pallid hands together, "I have known you for so long."

"Ah, we have known each other for so long, but as for really knowing you—no! I'm not a tame rabbit to be fondled any more."

She stared for a moment, as if in recollection; then burst into ironical laughter. He caught her roughly in his arms but she beat him away.

"O, go to ... go to...."

"Hell?" he suggested.

"Yes," she burst out tempestuously, "and stop there."

He was stunned by her unexpected violence. She was coarse like Ianthe after all. But he said steadily:

"I'm willing to go there if you will only keep out of my way when I arrive."

Then he left her standing in a lane, he hurried and ran, clambering over stiles and brushing through hedges, anything to get away from the detestable creature. She did not follow him and they were soon out of sight of each other. Anger and commination swarmed to his lips, he branded her with frenzied opprobrium and all the beastliness that was in him. Nothing under heaven should ever persuade him to approach the filthy beast again, the damned intolerable pimp, never, never again, never.

But he came to a bridge. On it he rested. And in that bright air, that sylvan peace, his rancour fell away from him, like sand from a glass, leaving him dumb and blank at the meanness of his deed. He went back to the lane as fast as he could go. She was not there. Kate, Kate, my dove! But he could not find her.

He was lost in the fields until he came at last upon a road and a lonely tavern thereby. It had a painted sign; a very smudgy fox, in an inexplicable attitude, destroying a fowl that looked like a plum-pudding but was intended to depict a snipe. At the stable door the tiniest black kitten in the world was shaping with timid belligerency at a young and fluffy goose who, ignoring it, went on sipping ecstatically from a pan of water. On the door were nailed, in two semicircles of decoration, sixteen fox pads in various stages of decay, an entire spiral shaving from the hoof of a horse, and some chalk jottings:

2 pads
3 cruppers
1 Bellyband
2 Set britchin

* * *

The tavern was long and low and clean, its garden was bare but trim. There was comfort, he rested, had tea, and then in the bar his painful musings were broken by a ragged unfortunate old pedlar from Huddersfield.

"Born and bred in Slatterwick, it's no lie ah'm speaking, ah were born and bred Slatterwick, close to Arthur Brinkley's farm, his sister's in Canady, John Orkroyd took farm, Arthur's dead."

"Humph!"

"And buried. That iron bridge at Jackamon's belong to Daniel Cranmer. He's dead."

"Humph!"

"And buried. From th' iron bridge it's two miles and a quarter to Herbert Oddy's, that's the 'Bay Horse,' am ah right, at Shelmersdyke. Three miles and three-quarters from dyke to the 'Cock and Goat' at Shapley Fell, am ah right?"

Masterman, never having been within a hundred miles of Yorkshire, puffed at his cigarette and nodded moodily, "I suppose so" or "Yes, yes."

"From Arthur Brinkley's to th' iron bridge is one mile and a half and a bit, and from Arthur Brinkley's to Jury Cartright's is just four mile. He's dead, sir."

"Yes."

"And buried. Is that wrong? Am ah speaking wrong? No. It's long step from yon, rough tramp for an old man."

Masterman—after giving sixpence to the pedlar who, uttering a benediction, pressed upon him a card of shirt buttons—said "Good evening" and walked out to be alone upon the road with his once angry but now penitent mind. Kate, poor dear Kate!

The sun was low down lolling near the horizon but there was an astonishing light upon the land. Cottage windows were blocks of solid gold in this lateral brilliance, shafts of shapely shade lay across leagues of field, he could have counted every leaf among the rumpled boskage of the sycamores. A vast fan of indurated cloud, shell-like and pearly, was wavering over the western sky but in the east were snowy rounded masses like fabulous balloons. At a cross road he stood by an old sign post, its pillar plastered with the faded bill of a long-ago circus. He could read every word of it but when he turned away he found everything had grown dimmer. The wind arose, the forest began to roar like a heaving beast. All verdurous things leaned one way. A flock of starlings flew over him with one movement and settled in a rolling elm. How lonely it was. He took off his hat. His skull was fearfully tender—he had dabbed it too hard with his hair brush that morning. His hair was growing thin, like his youth and his desires.

What had become of Kate, where had she hidden? What *would* become of her? He would never see her again. He disliked everything about her, except her self. Her clothes, her speech, her walk, the way she carried her umbrella, her reticence that was nothing if not conspicuous, her melancholy, her angular concrete piety, her hands—in particular he disliked her pale hands. She had a mind that was cultivated as perfunctorily as a kitchen garden, with ideas like roots or beans, hostilities like briars, and a fence of prudery that was as tough as hoops of galvanized iron. And yet he loved her—or almost. He was ready to love her, he wanted to, he wanted her; her deep but guarded devotion—it was limited but it was devotion—compelled this return from him. It was a passionate return. He had tried to mould that devotion into a form that could delight him—he had failed. He knew her now, he could peer into her craven soul as one peers into an empty bottle, with one eye. For her the opportunities afforded by freedom were but the preludes to misadventure. What a fool she was!

When he reached home Kate stood in darkness at the doorway of his house. He exclaimed with delight, her surprising presence was the very centre of his desire, he wanted to embrace her, loving her deeply, inexplicably again; just in a moment.

"I want my bike," the girl said sullenly. "I left it inside this morning.

"Ah, your bicycle! Yes, you did." He unlocked the door. "Wait, there should be a candle, there should be."

She stood in the doorway until he had lit it.

"Come in, Kate," he said, "let me give you something. I think there is some milk, certainly I have some cake, come in, Kate, or do you drink beer, I have beer, come in, I'll make you something hot."

But Kate only took her bicycle. "I ought to have been home hours ago," she said darkly, wheeling it outside and lighting the lantern. He watched her silently as she dabbed the wick, the pallor of her hands had never appeared so marked.

"Let's be kind to each other," he said, detaining her, "don't go, dear Kate."

She pushed the bicycle out into the road.

"Won't you see me again?" he asked as she mounted it.

"I am always seeing you," she called back, but her meaning was dark to him.

"Faugh! The devil! The fool!" He gurgled anathemas as he returned to his cottage. "And me too! What am I?"

But no mortal man could ever love a woman of that kind. She did not love him at all, had never loved him. Then what was it she did love? Not her virtue—you might as well be proud of the sole of your foot; it was some sort of pride, perhaps the test of her virtue that the conflict between them provoked, the contest itself alone alluring her, not its aim and end. She was never happier than when having led him on she thwarted him. But she would find that his metal was as tough as her own.

Before going to bed he spent an hour in writing very slowly a letter to Kate, telling her that he felt they would not meet again, that their notions of love were so unrelated, their standards so different. "My morals are at least as high as yours though likely enough you regard me as a rip. Let us recognize then," he wrote concludingly, "that we have come to the end of the tether without once having put an ounce of strain upon its delightful but never tense cord. But the effort to keep the affair down to the level at which you seem satisfied has wearied me. The task of living down to that assured me that for you the effort of living up to mine would be consuming. I congratulate you, my dear, on coming through scatheless and that the only appropriate condolences are my own—for myself."

It was rather pompous, he thought, but then she wouldn't notice that, let alone understand it. She suffered not so much from an impediment of speech—how could she when she spoke so little?—as from an impediment of intellect, which was worse, much worse, but not so noticeable being so common a failing. She was, when all was said and done, just a fool. It was a pity, for bodily she must indeed be a treasure. What a pity! But she had never had any love for him at all, only compassion and pity for his bad thoughts about her; he had neither pity for her nor compunction—only love. Dear, dear, dear. Blow out the candle, lock the door, Good-night!

V

He did not see her again for a long time. He would have liked to have seen her, yes, just once more, but of course he was glad, quite glad, that she did not wish to risk it and drag from dim depths the old passion to break again in those idiotic bubbles of propriety. She did not answer his letter—he was amused. Then her long silence vexed him, until vexation was merged in alarm. She had gone away from Tutsan—of course—gone away on family affairs—oh, naturally!—she might be gone for ever. But a real grief came upon him. He had long mocked the girl, not only the girl but his own vision of her; now she was gone his mind elaborated her melancholy immobile figure into an image of beauty. Her absence, her silence, left him wretched. He heard of her from Ianthe who renewed her blandishments; he was not unwilling to receive them now—he hoped their intercourse might be reported to Kate.

After many months he did receive a letter from her. It was a tender letter though ill-expressed, not very wise or informative, but he could feel that the old affection for him was still there, and he wrote her a long reply in which penitence and passion and appeal were mingled.

"I know now, yes, I see it all now; solutions are so easy when the proof of them is passed. We were cold to each other, it was stupid, I should have *made* you love me and it would have been well. I see it now. How stupid, how unlucky; it turned me to anger and you to sorrow. Now I can think only of you."

She made no further sign, not immediately, and he grew dull again. His old disbelief in her returned. Bah! she loved him no more than a suicide loved the pond it dies in; she had used him for her senseless egoism, tempting him and fooling him, wantonly, he had not begun it, and she took a chaste pride in saving herself from him. What was it the old writer had said?

"Chastity, by nature the gentlest of all affections—give it but its head—'tis like a ramping and roaring lion." Saving herself! Yes, she would save herself for marriage.

He even began to contemplate that outcome.

Her delayed letter, when it came, announced that she was coming home at once; he was to meet her train in the morning after the morrow.

It was a dull autumnal morning when he met her. Her appearance was not less charming than he had imagined it, though the charm was almost inarticulate and there were one or two crude touches that momentarily distressed him. But he met with a flush of emotion all her glances of gaiety and love that were somehow, vaguely, different—perhaps there was a shade less reserve. They went to lunch in the city and at the end of the meal he asked her:

"Well, why have you come back again?"

She looked at him intently: "Guess!"

"I—well, no—perhaps—tell me, Kate, yourself."

"You are different now, you look different, David."

"Am I changed? Better or worse?"

She did not reply and he continued:

"You too, are changed. I can't tell how it is, or where, but you are."

"O, I am changed, much changed," murmured Kate.

"Have you been well?"

"Yes."

"And happy?"

"Yes."

"Then how unwise of you to come back."

"I have come back," said Kate, "to be happier. But somehow you are different."

* * *

"You are different, too. Shall we ever be happy again?"

"Why—why not!" said Kate.

"Come on!" he cried hilariously, "let us make a day of it, come along!"

Out in the streets they wandered until rain began to fall.

"Come in here for a while." They were passing a roomy dull building, the museum, and they went in together. It was a vast hollow-sounding flagstone place that had a central brightness fading into dim recesses and galleries of gloom. They examined a monster skeleton of something like an elephant, three stuffed apes, and a picture of the dodo. Kate stood before them without interest or amusement, she just contemplated them. What did she want with an elephant, an ape, or a dodo? The glass exhibit cases were leaned upon by them, the pieces of coal neatly arranged and labelled were stared at besides the pieces of granite or coloured rock with long names ending in *orite dorite* and *sorite* and so on to the precious gems including an imitation, as big as a bun, of a noted diamond. They leaned over them, repeating the names on the labels with the quintessence of vacuity. They hated it. There were beetles and worms of horror, butterflies of beauty, and birds that had been stuffed so long that they seemed to be intoxicated; their beaks fitted them as loosely as a drunkard's hat, their glassy eyes were pathetically vague. After ascending a flight of stone steps David and Kate stooped for a long time over a case of sea-anemones that had been reproduced in gelatine by a German with a fancy for such things. From the railed balcony they could peer down into the well of the fusty-smelling museum. No one else was visiting it, they were alone with all things dead, things that had died millions of years ago and were yet simulating life. A footfall sounded so harsh in the corridors, boomed with such clangour, that they took slow diffident steps, almost tiptoeing, while Kate scarcely spoke at all and he conversed in murmurs. Whenever he coughed the whole place seemed to shudder. In the recess, hidden from prying eyes, David clasped her willing body in his arms. For once she was unshrinking and returned his fervour. The vastness, the emptiness, the deadness, worked upon their feelings with intense magic.

"Love me, David," she murmured, and when they moved away from the gelatinous sea-urchins she kept both her arms clasped around him as they walked the length of the empty corridors. He could not understand her, he could not perceive her intimations, their meaning was dark to him. She was so altered, this was another Kate.

"I have come home to make it all up to you," she repeated, and he scarcely dared to understand her.

They approached a lecture-room; the door was open, the room was empty, they went in and stood near the platform. The place was arranged like a tiny theatre, tiers of desks rising in half-circles on three sides high up towards the ceiling. A small platform with a lecturer's desk confronted the rising tiers; on the wall behind it a large white sheet; a magic lantern on a pedestal was near and a blackboard on an easel. A pencil of white chalk lay broken on the floor. Behind the easel was a piano, a new piano with a duster on its lid. The room smelled of spilled acids. The lovers' steps upon the wooden floor echoed louder than ever after their peregrinations upon the flagstones; they were timid of the sound and stood still, close together, silent. He touched her bosom and pressed her to his heart, but all her surrender seemed strange and nerveless. She was almost violently different; he had liked her old rejections, they were fiery and passionate. He scarce knew what to do, he understood her less than ever now. Dressed as she was in thick winter clothes it was like embracing a tree, it tired him. She lay in his arms waiting, waiting, until he felt almost stifled. Something like the smell of the acids came from her fur necklet. He was glad when she stood up, but she was looking at him intently. To cover his uneasiness he went to the blackboard and picking up a piece of the chalk he wrote the first inconsequent words that came into his mind. Kate stood where he had left her, staring at the board as he traced the words upon it:

We are but little children weak

Laughing softly she strolled towards him.

"What do you write that for? I know what it is."

"What it is! Well, what is it?"

She took the chalk from his fingers.

"It's a hymn," she went on, "it goes...."

* * *

"A hymn!" he cried, "I did not know that."

Underneath the one he had written she was now writing another line on the board.

Nor born to any high estate.

"Of course," he whispered, "I remember it now. I sang it as a child—at school—go on, go on."

But she had thereupon suddenly turned away, silent, dropping her hands to her side. One of her old black moods had seized her. He let her go and picking up another fragment of chalk completed the verse.

What can we do for Jesu's sake
Who is so high and good and great?

She turned when he had finished and without a word walked loudly to the piano, fetched the duster and rubbed out the words they had written on the blackboard. She was glaring angrily at him.

"How absurd you are,"—he was annoyed—"let us go out and get some tea." He wandered off to the door, but she did not follow. He stood just outside gazing vacantly at a stuffed jay that had an indigo eye. He looked into the room again. She was there still, just as he had left her; her head bent, her hands hanging clasped before her, the dimness covering and caressing her—a figure full of sad thoughts. He ran to her and crushed her in his arms again.

"Kate, my lovely."

She was saying brokenly: "You know what I said. I've come to make it all up to you. I promised, didn't I?"

Something shuddered in his very soul—too late, too late, this was no love for him. The magic lantern looked a stupid childish toy, the smell of the acid was repulsive. Of all they had written upon the blackboard one word dimly remained: *Jesu*.

She stirred in his arms. "You are changed, David."

"Changed, yes, everything is changed."

"This is just like a theatre, like a play, as if we were acting."

"Yes, as if we were acting. But we are not acting. Let us go up and sit in the gallery."

They ascended the steps to the top ring of desks and looked down to the tiny platform and the white curtain. She sat fondling his hands, leaning against him.

"Have you ever acted—you would do it so well?"

"Why do you say that? Am I at all histrionic?"

"Does that mean insincere? O no. But you are the person one expects to be able to do anything."

"Nonsense! I've never acted. I suppose I could. It isn't difficult, you haven't to be clever, only courageous. I should think it very easy to be only an ordinary actor, but I'm wrong, no doubt. I thought it was easy to write—to write a play—until I tried. I once engaged myself to write a little play for some students to act. I had never done such a thing before and like other idiots I thought I hadn't ever done it simply because I hadn't ever wanted to. Heavens, how harassed I was and how ashamed! I could not do it, I got no further than the author's speech."

* * *

"Well that was something. Tell me it."

"It's nothing to do with the play. It's what the author says to the audience when the play is finished."

She insisted on hearing it whatever it was. "O well," he said at last, "let's do that properly, at least. I'll go down there and deliver it from the stage. You must pretend that you are the enthusiastic audience. Come and sit in the stalls."

They went down together.

"Now imagine that this curtain goes up and I suddenly appear."

Kate faintly clapped her hands. He stood upon the platform facing her and taking off his hat, began:

"Ladies and Gentlemen,

"I am so deeply touched by the warmth of this reception, this utterly undeserved appreciation, that—forgive me—I have forgotten the speech I had carefully prepared in anticipation of it. Let me meet my obligation by telling you a story; I think it is true, I made it up myself. Once upon a time there was a poor playwright—something like me—who wrote a play—something like this—and at the end of the performance the audience, a remarkably handsome well-fed intellectual audience—something like this—called him before the curtain and demanded a speech. He protested that he was unprepared and asked them to allow him to tell them a story—something like this. Well, that, too, was a remarkably handsome well-fed intellectual audience, so they didn't mind and he began again.—Once upon a time a poor playwright—and was just about to repeat the story I have already twice told you when suddenly, without a word of warning, without a sound, without a compunction, the curtain swooped down and chopped him clean in half."

Masterman made an elaborate obeisance and stepped off the platform.

"Is that all?" asked Kate.

"That's all."

At that moment a loud bell clanged throughout the building signifying that the museum was about to close.

"Come along!" he cried, but Kate did not move, she still sat in the stalls.

"Don't leave me, David, I want to hear the play?" she said archly.

"There *was* no play. There *is* no play. Come, or we shall be locked in for the night."

She still sat on. He went to her and seized her hands.

"What does it matter!" she whispered, embracing him. "I want to make it all up to you."

He was astoundingly moved. She was marvellously changed. If she hadn't the beauty of perfection she had some of the perfection of beauty. He adored her.

"But, no," he said, "it won't do, it really won't. Come, I have got to buy you something at once, a ring with a diamond in it, as big as a bun, an engagement ring, quickly, or the shops will be shut."

He dragged the stammering bewildered girl away, down the stairs and into the street. The rain had ceased, the sunset sky was bright and Masterman was intensely happy.

COTTON

COTTON

At the place where the road from Carnaby Down ends in the main western highway that goes towards Bath there stands, or once stood, a strongly built stone cottage confronting, on the opposite side of the highroad, a large barn and some cattle stalls. A man named Cotton lived with his wife lonely in this place, their whole horizon bounded by the hedges and fences of their farm. His Christian name, for some unchristian reason, was Janifex, people called him Jan, possibly because it rhymed with his wife's name, which was Ann. And Ann was a robust managing woman of five and thirty, childless, full of desolating cleanliness and kindly tyrannies, with no perceptions that were not determined by her domestic ambition, and no sympathies that could interfere with her diurnal energies whatever they might be. Jan was a mild husbandman, prematurely aged, with large teeth and, since "forty winters had besieged his brow," but little hair. Sometimes one of the large teeth would drop out, leaving terrible gaps when he opened his mouth and turning his patient smile to a hideous leer. These evacuations, which were never restored, began with the death of Queen Victoria; throughout the reign of her successor great events were punctuated by similar losses until at last Jan could masticate, in his staid old manner, only in one overworked corner of his mouth.

He would rise of a morning throughout the moving year at five of the clock; having eaten his bread and drunk a mug of cocoa he would don a long white jacket and cross the road diagonally to the gate at the eastern corner of the sheds; these were capped by the bright figure of a golden cockerel, voiceless but useful, flaunting always to meet the challenge of the wind. Sometimes in his deliberate way Jan would lift his forlorn eyes in the direction of the road coming from the east, but he never turned to the other direction as that would have cost him a physical effort and bodily flexion had ceased years and years ago. Do roads ever run backward—leaps not forward the eye? As he unloosed the gate of the yard his great dog would lift its chained head from some sacks under a cart, and a peacock would stalk from the belt of pines that partly encircled the buildings. The man would greet them, saying "O, ah!" In the rickyard he would pause to release the fowls from their hut and watch them run to the stubbles or spurn the chaff with their claws as they ranged between the stacks. If the day were windy the chaff would fall back in clouds upon their bustling feathers, and that delighted his simple mind. It is difficult to account for his joy in this thing for though his heart was empty of cruelty it seemed to be empty of everything else. Then he would pass into the stalls and with a rattle of can and churn the labour of the day was begun.

Thus he lived, with no temptations, and few desires except perhaps for milk puddings, which for some reason concealed in Ann's thrifty bosom he was only occasionally permitted to enjoy. Whenever his wife thought kindly of him she would give him a piece of silver and he would traipse a mile in the evening, a mile along to the *Huntsman's Cup*, and take a tankard of beer. On his return he would tell Ann of the things he had seen, the people he had met, and other events of his journey.

Once, in the time of spring, when buds were bursting along the hedge coverts and birds of harmony and swiftness had begun to roost in the wood, a blue-chinned Spaniard came to lodge at the farm for a few weeks. He was a labourer working at some particular contract upon the estate adjoining the Cottons' holding, and he was accommodated with a bed and an abundance of room in a clean loft behind the house. With curious shoes upon his feet, blazing check trousers fitting tightly upon his thighs, a wrapper of pink silk around his neck, he was an astonishing figure in that withdrawn corner of the world. When the season chilled him a long black cloak with a hood for his head added a further strangeness. Juan da Costa was his name. He was slightly round-shouldered with an uncongenial squint in his eyes; though he used but few words of English his ways were beguiling; he sang very blithely shrill Spanish songs, and had a pleasant courtesy of manner that presented a deal of attraction to the couple, particularly Ann, whose casual heart he reduced in a few hours to kindness, and in a few days, inexplicably perhaps, to a still warmer emotion—yes, even in the dull blankness of that mind some ghostly star could glimmer. From the hour of his arrival she was an altered woman although, with primitive subtlety the transition from passivity to passion was revealed only by one curious sign, and that was the spirit of her kindness evoked for the amiable Jan, who now fared mightily upon his favourite dishes.

Sometimes the Spaniard would follow Jan about the farm. "Grande!" he would say, gesturing with his arm to indicate the wide-rolling hills.

"O, ah!" Jan would reply, "there's a heap o' land in the open air."

The Spaniard does not understand. He asks: "What?"

"O, ah!" Jan would echo.

But it was the cleanly buxom Ann to whom da Costa devoted himself. He brought home daily, though not ostensibly to her, a bunch of the primroses, a stick of snowbudded sallow, or a sprig of hazel hung with catkins, soft caressable things. He would hold the hazel up before Ann's uncomprehending gaze and strike the lemon-coloured powder from the catkins on to the expectant adjacent buds, minute things with stiff female prongs, red like the eyes of the white rabbit which Ann kept in the orchard hutch.

One day Juan came home unexpectedly in mid-afternoon. It was a cold dry day and he wore his black cloak and hood.

"See," he cried, walking up to Ann, who greeted him with a smile; he held out to her a posy of white violets tied up with some blades of thick grass. She smelt them but said nothing. He pressed the violets to his lips and again held them out, this time to her lips. She took them from him and touched them with the front of her bodice while he watched her with delighted eyes.

"You ... give ... me ... something ... for ... los flores?"

"Piece a cake!" said Ann, moving towards the pantry door.

"Ah ... cake...!"

As she pulled open the door, still keeping a demure eye upon him, the violets fell out and down upon the floor, unseen by her. He rushed towards them with a cry of pain and a torrent of his strange language; picking them up he followed her into the pantry, a narrow place almost surrounded by shelves with pots of pickles and jam, plates, cups and jugs, a scrap of meat upon a trencher, a white bowl with cob nuts and a pair of iron crackers.

"See ... lost!" he cried shrilly as she turned to him. She was about to take them again when he stayed her with a whimsical gesture.

"Me ... me," he said, and brushing her eyes with their soft perfume he unfastened the top button of her bodice while the woman stood motionless; then the second button, then the third. He turned the corners inwards and tucked the flowers between her flesh and underlinen. They stood eyeing one another, breathing uneasily, but with a pretence of nonchalance. "Ah!" he said suddenly; before she could stop him he had seized a few nuts from the white bowl and holding open her bodice where the flowers rested he dropped the nuts into her warm bosom. "One ... two ... three!"

"Oh...!" screamed Ann mirthfully, shrinking from their tickling, but immediately she checked her laughter—she heard footsteps. Beating down the grasping arms of the Spaniard she darted out of the doorway and shut him in the pantry, just in time to meet Jan coming into the kitchen howling for a chain he required.

"What d'ye want?" said Ann.

"That chain for the well-head, gal, it's hanging in the pantry." He moved to the door.

"Tain't," said Ann barring his way. "It's in the barn. I took it there yesterday, on the oats it is, you'll find it, clear off with your dirty boots." She "hooshed" him off much as she "hooshed" the hens out of the garden. Immediately he was gone she pulled open the pantry door and was confronted by the Spaniard holding a long clasp knife in his raised hand. On seeing her he just smiled, threw down the knife and took the bewildered woman into his arms.

"Wait, wait," she whispered, and breaking from him she seized a chain from a hook and ran out after her husband with it, holding up a finger of warning to the Spaniard as she brushed past him. She came back panting, having made some sort of explanation to Jan; entering the kitchen quietly she found the Spaniard's cloak lying upon the table; the door of the pantry was shut and he had apparently gone back there to await her. Ann moved on tiptoe round the table; picking up the cloak she enveloped herself in it and pulled the hood over her head. Having glanced with caution through the front window to the farmyard, she coughed and shuffled her feet on the flags. The door of the pantry moved slowly open; the piercing ardour of his glance did not abash her, but her curious appearance in his cloak moved his shrill laughter. As he approached her she seized his wrists and drew him to the door that led into the orchard at the back of the house; she opened it and pushed him out, saying, "Go on, go on." She then locked the door against him. He walked up and down outside the window making lewd signs to her. He dared not call out for fear of attracting attention from the farmyard in front of the house. He stood still, shivered, pretended in dumb show that he was frozen. She stood at the window in front of him and nestled provocatively in his cloak. But when he put his lips against the pane he drew the gleam of her languishing eyes closer and closer to meet his kiss through the glass. Then she stood up, took off the black cloak, and putting her hand into her bosom brought out the three nuts, which she held up to him. She stood there fronting the Spaniard enticingly, dropped the nuts back into her bosom one ... two ... three ... and then went and opened the door.

In a few weeks the contract was finished, and one bright morning the Spaniard bade them each farewell. Neither of them knew, so much was their intercourse restricted, that he was about to depart, and Ann watched him with perplexity and unhappiness in her eyes.

"Ah, you Cotton, good-bye I say, and you señora, I say good-bye."

With a deep bow he kissed the rough hand of the blushing country woman. "Bueno." He turned with his kit bag upon his shoulder, waved them an airy hand and was gone.

On the following Sunday Jan returned from a visit in the evening and found the house empty; Ann was out, an unusual thing, for their habits were fixed and deliberate as the stars in the sky. The sunsetting light was lying in meek patches on the kitchen wall, turning the polished iron pans to the brightness of silver, reddening the string of onions, and filling glass jars with solid crystal. He had just sat down to remove his heavy boots when Ann came in, not at all the workaday Ann but dressed in her best clothes smelling of scent and swishing her stiff linen.

"Hullo," said Jan, surprised at his wife's pink face and sparkling eyes, "bin church?"

"Yes, church," she replied, and sat down in her finery. Her husband ambled about the room for various purposes and did not notice her furtive dabbing of her eyes with her handkerchief. Tears from Ann were inconceivable.

The year moved through its seasons, the lattermath hay was duly mown, the corn stooked in rows; Ann was with child and the ridge of her stays was no longer visible behind her plump shoulders. Fruit dropped from the orchard boughs, the quince was gathered from the wall, the hunt swept over the field. Christmas came and went, and then a child was born to the Cottons, a dusky boy, who was shortly christened Juan.

"He was a kind chap, that man," said Ann, "and we've no relations to please, and it's like your name—and your name *is* outlandish!"

Jan's delight was now to sit and muse upon the child as he had ever mused upon chickens, lambs and calves. "O, ah!" he would say, popping a great finger into the babe's mouth, "O, ah!" But when, as occasionally happened, the babe squinted at him, a singular fancy would stir in his mind, only to slide away before it could congeal into the likeness of suspicion.

Snow, when it falls near spring upon those Cotswold hills, falls deeply and the lot of the husbandmen is hard. Sickness, when it comes, comes with a flail and in its hobnailed boots. Contagious and baffling, disease had stricken the district; in mid March great numbers of the country folk were sick abed, hospitals were full, and doctors were harried from one dawn to another. Jan would come in of an evening and recite the calendar of the day's dooms gathered from men of the adjacent fields.

"Amos Green 'ave gone then, pore o' chap."

"Pore Amos," the pitying Ann would say, wrapping her babe more warmly.

"And Buttifant's coachman."

"Dear, dear, what 'ull us all come to!"

* * *

"Mrs. Jocelyn was worse 'en bad this morning."

"Never, Jan! Us'll miss 'er."

"Ah, and they do say Parson Rudwent won't last out the night."

"And whom's to bury us then?" asked Ann.

The invincible sickness came to the farm. Ann one morning was weary, sickly, and could not rise from her bed. Jan attended her in his clumsy way and kept coming in from the snow to give her comforts and food, but at eve she was in fever and lay helpless in the bed with the child at her breast. Jan went off for the doctor, not to the nearest village for he knew that quest to be hopeless, but to a tiny town high on the wolds two miles away. The moon, large, sharp and round, blazed in the sky and its light sparkled upon the rolling fields of snow; his boots were covered at every muffled step; the wind sighed in the hedges and he shook himself for warmth. He came to the hill at last; halfway up was a church, its windows glowing with warm-looking light and its bells pealing cheerfully. He passed on and higher up met a priest trotting downwards in black cassock and saintly hat, his hands tucked into his wide sleeves, trotting to keep himself warm and humming as he went. Jan asked a direction of the priest, who gave it with many circumstances of detail, and after he had parted he could hear the priest's voice call still further instructions after him as long as he was in sight. "O, ah!" said Jan each time, turning and waving his hand. But after all his mission was a vain one; the doctor was out and away, it was improbable that he would be able to come, and the simple man turned home with a dull heart. When he reached the farm Ann was delirious but still clung to the dusky child, sleeping snugly at her bosom. The man sat up all night before the fire waiting vainly for the doctor, and the next day he himself became ill. And strangely enough as he worked among his beasts the crude suspicion in his mind about the child took shape and worked without resistance until he came to suspect and by easy degrees to apprehend fully the time and occasion of Ann's duplicity.

"Nasty dirty filthy thing!" he murmured from his sick mind. He was brushing the dried mud from the hocks of an old bay horse, but it was not of his horse he was thinking. Later he stood in the rickyard and stared across the road at the light in their bedroom. Throwing down the fork with which he had been tossing beds of straw he shook his fist at the window and cried out: "I hate 'er, I does, nasty dirty filthy thing!"

When he went into the house he replenished the fire but found he could take no further care for himself or the sick woman; he just stupidly doffed his clothes and in utter misery and recklessness stretched himself in the bed with Ann. He lay for a long while with aching brows, a snake-strangled feeling in every limb, an unquenchable drouth in his throat, and his wife's body burning beside him. Outside the night was bright, beautiful and still sparkling with frost; quiet, as if the wind had been wedged tightly in some far corner of the sky, except for a cracked insulator on the telegraph pole just near the window, that rattled and hummed with monstrous uncare. That, and the ticking of the clock! The lighted candle fell from its sconce on the mantelpiece; he let it remain and it flickered out. The glow from the coals was thick upon the ceiling and whitened the brown ware of the teapot on the untidy hearth. Falling asleep at last he began dreaming at once, so it seemed, of the shrill cry of lambs hailing him out of wild snow-covered valleys, so wild and prolonged were the cries that they woke him, and he knew himself to be ill, very ill indeed. The child was wailing piteously, the room was in darkness, the fire out, but the man did not stir, he could not care, what could he do with that flame behind his eyes and the misery of death consuming him? But the child's cries were unceasing and moved even his numbed mind to some effort. "Ann!" he gasped. The poor wife did not reply. "Ann!" He put his hand out to nudge her; in one instant the blood froze in his veins and then boiled again. Ann was cold, her body hard as a wall, dead ... dead. Stupor returned upon him; the child, unhelped, cried on, clasped to that frozen breast until the man again roused himself to effort. Putting his great hands across the dead wife he dragged the child from her arms into the warmth beside him, gasping as he did so, "Nasty ... dirty ... thing." It exhausted him but the child was still unpacified and again he roused himself and felt for a biscuit on the table beside the bed. He crushed a piece in his mouth and putting the soft pap upon his finger fed thus the hungry child until it was stilled. By now the white counterpane spread vast like a sea, heaving and rocking with a million waves, the framework of the bedstead moving like the tackle of tossed ships. He knew there was only one way to stem that sickening movement. "I hate 'er, I does," rose again upon his lips, and drawing up his legs that were at once chilly and streaming with sweat, full of his new hatred he urged with all his might his wife's cold body to the edge of the bed and withdrew the bedclothes. Dead Ann toppled and slid from him and her body clumped upon the floor with a fall that shook the room; the candle fell from the mantelpiece, bounced from the teapot and rolled stupidly along the bare boards under the bed. "Hate 'er!" groaned the man; he hung swaying above the woman and tried to spit upon her. He sank back again to the pillow and the child, murmuring "O, ah!" and gathering it clumsily to his breast. He became tranquil then, and the hollow-sounding clock beat a dull rhythm into his mind, until that sound faded out with all light and sound, and Jan fell into sleep and died, with the dusky child clasped in his hard dead arms.

A BROADSHEET BALLAD

A BROADSHEET BALLAD

At noon the tiler and the mason stepped down from the roof of the village church which they were repairing and crossed over the road to the tavern to eat their dinner. It had been a nice little morning, but there were clouds massing in the south; Sam the tiler remarked that it looked like thunder. The two men sat in the dim little taproom eating, Bob the mason at the same time reading from a newspaper an account of a trial for murder.

"I dunno what thunder looks like," Bob said, "but I reckon this chap is going to be hung, though I can't rightly say for why. To my thinking he didn't do it at all: but murder's a bloody thing and someone ought to suffer for it."

"I don't think," spluttered Sam as he impaled a flat piece of beetroot on the point of a pocket-knife and prepared to contemplate it with patience until his stuffed mouth was ready to receive it, "he ought to be hung."

"There can be no other end for him though, with a mob of lawyers like that, and a judge like that, and a jury too ... why the rope's half round his neck this minute; he'll be in glory within a month, they only have three Sundays, you know, between the sentence and the execution. Well, hark at that rain then!"

A shower that began as a playful sprinkle grew to a powerful steady summer downpour. It splashed in the open window and the dim room grew more dim and cool.

"Hanging's a dreadful thing, continued Sam, and 'tis often unjust I've no doubt, I've no doubt at all."

"Unjust! I tell you ... at the majority of trials those who give their evidence mostly knows nothing at all about the matter; them as knows a lot—they stays at home and don't budge, not likely!"

"No? But why?"

"Why? They has their reasons. I know that, I knows it for truth ... hark at that rain, it's made the room feel cold."

They watched the downfall in complete silence for some moments.

"Hanging's a dreadful thing," Sam at length repeated, with almost a sigh.

"I can tell you a tale about that, Sam, in a minute," said the other. He began to fill his pipe from Sam's brass box which was labelled cough lozenges and smelled of paregoric.

"Just about ten years ago I was working over in Cotswold country. I remember I'd been in to Gloucester one Saturday afternoon and it rained. I was jogging along home in a carrier's van; I never seen it rain like that afore, no, nor ever afterwards, not like that. B-r-r-r-r! it came down ... bashing! And we come to a cross roads where there's a public house called *The Wheel of Fortune*, very lonely and onsheltered it is just there. I see'd a young woman standing in the porch awaiting us, but the carrier was wet and tired and angry or something and wouldn't stop. 'No room'—he bawled out to her—'full up, can't take you!' and he drove on. 'For the love o' God. Mate,'—I says—'pull up and take that young creature! She's ... she's ... can't you see!' 'But I'm all behind as 'tis'—he shouts to me—'you know your gospel, don't you: time and tide wait for no man?' 'Ah, but dammit all, they always call for a feller'—I says. With that he turned round and we drove back for the girl. She clumb in and sat on my knees; I squat on a tub of vinegar, there was nowhere else and I was right and all, she was going on for a birth. Well, the old van rattled away for six or seven miles; whenever it stopped you could hear the rain clattering on the tarpaulin, or sounding outside on the grass as if it was breathing hard, and the old horse steamed and shivered with it. I had knowed the girl once in a friendly way, a pretty young creature, but now she was white and sorrowful and wouldn't say much. By and bye we came to another cross roads near a village, and she got out there. 'Good day, my gal'—I says, affable like, and 'Thank you, sir,'—says she, and off she popped in the rain with her umbrella up. A rare pretty girl, quite young, I'd met her before, a girl you could get uncommon fond of, you know, but I didn't meet her afterwards, she was mixed up in a bad business. It all happened in the next six months while I was working round these parts. Everybody knew of it. This girl's name was Edith and she had a younger sister Agnes. Their father was old Harry Mallerton, kept *The British Oak* at North Quainy; he stuttered. Well, this Edith had a love affair with a young chap William, and having a very loving nature she behaved foolish. Then she couldn't bring the chap up to the scratch nohow by herself, and of course she was afraid to tell her mother or father: you know how girls are after being so pesky natural, they fear, O they do fear! But soon it couldn't be hidden any longer as she was living at home with them all, so she wrote a letter to her mother. 'Dear Mother,' she wrote, and told her all about her trouble.

"By all accounts the mother was angry as an old lion, but Harry took it calm like and sent for young William, who'd not come at first. He lived close by in the village so they went down at last and fetched him.

"'All right, yes,' he said, 'I'll do what's lawful to be done. There you are, I can't say no fairer, that I can't.'

"'No,' they said, 'you can't.'

"So he kissed the girl and off he went, promising to call in and settle affairs in a day or two. The next day Agnes, which was the younger girl, she also wrote a note to her mother telling her some more strange news:

"'God above!' the mother cried out, 'can it be true, both of you girls, my own daughters, and by the same man! whatever were you thinking on, both of ye! Whatever can be done now!'"

"What!" ejaculated Sam, "both on 'em, both on 'em!"

* * *

"As true as God's my mercy—both on 'em—same chap. Ah! Mrs. Mallerton was afraid to tell her husband at first, for old Harry was the devil born again when he were roused up, so she sent for young William herself, who'd not come again, of course, not likely. But they made him come, O yes, when they told the girls' father.

"'Well, may I go to my d ... d ... d ... damnation at once!' roared old Harry—he stuttered, you know—'at once, if that ain't a good one!' So he took off his coat, he took up a stick, he walked down the street to William and cut him off his legs. Then he beat him until he howled for his mercy, and you couldn't stop old Harry once he were roused up—he was the devil born again. They do say as he beat him for a solid hour; I can't say as to that, but then old Harry picked him up and carried him off to *The British Oak* on his own back, and threw him down in his own kitchen between his own two girls like a dead dog. They do say that the little one Agnes flew at her father like a raging cat until he knocked her senseless with a clout over head; rough man he was."

"Well, a' called for it, sure," commented Sam.

"Her did," agreed Bob, "but she was the quietest known girl for miles round those parts, very shy and quiet."

"A shady lane breeds mud," said Sam.

"What do you say?—O ah!—mud, yes. But pretty girls both, girls you could get very fond of, skin like apple bloom, and as like as two pinks they were. They had to decide which of them William was to marry."

* * *

"Of course, ah!"

"'I'll marry Agnes'—says he.

"'You'll not'—says the old man—'You'll marry Edie.'

"'No, I won't,'—William says—'it's Agnes I love and I'll be married to her or I won't be married to e'er of 'em.' All the time Edith sat quiet, dumb as a shovel, never a word, crying a bit; but they do say the young one went on like a ... a young ... Jew."

"The jezebel!" commented Sam.

"You may say it; but wait, my man, just wait. Another cup of beer. We can't go back to church until this humbugging rain have stopped."

"No, that we can't."

"Its my belief the 'bugging rain won't stop this side of four o'clock."

"And if the roof don't hold it off it 'ull spoil they Lord's commandments that's just done up on the chancel front."

"O, they be dry by now." Bob spoke reassuringly and then continued his tale. "'I'll marry Agnes or I won't marry nobody'—William says—and they couldn't budge him. No, old Harry cracked on but he wouldn't have it, and at last Harry says: 'It's like this.' He pulls a half crown out of his pocket and 'Heads it's Agnes,' he says, 'or tails it's Edith,' he says."

"Never! Ha! Ha!" cried Sam.

"'Heads it's Agnes, tails it's Edie,' so help me God. And it come down Agnes, yes, heads it was—Agnes—and so there they were."

"And they lived happy ever after?"

* * *

"Happy! You don't know your human nature, Sam; wherever was you brought up? 'Heads it's Agnes,' said old Harry, and at that Agnes flung her arms round William's neck and was for going off with him then and there, ha! But this is how it happened about that. William hadn't any kindred, he was a lodger in the village, and his landlady wouldn't have him in her house one mortal hour when she heard of it; give him the rightabout there and then. He couldn't get lodgings anywhere else, nobody would have anything to do with him, so of course, for safety's sake, old Harry had to take him, and there they all lived together at *The British Oak*—all in one happy family. But they girls couldn't bide the sight of each other, so their father cleaned up an old outhouse in his yard that was used for carts and hens and put William and his Agnes out in it. And there they had to bide. They had a couple of chairs, a sofa, and a bed and that kind of thing, and the young one made it quite snug."

"'Twas a hard thing for that other, that Edie, Bob."

"It was hard, Sam, in a way, and all this was happening just afore I met her in the carrier's van. She was very sad and solemn then; a pretty girl, one you could like. Ah, you may choke me, but there they lived together. Edie never opened her lips to either of them again, and her father sided with her, too. What was worse, it came out after the marriage that Agnes was quite free of trouble—it was only a trumped-up game between her and this William because he fancied her better than the other one. And they never had no child, them two, though when poor Edie's mischance came along I be damned if Agnes weren't fonder of it than its own mother, a jolly sight more fonder, and William—he fair worshipped it."

"You don't say!"

"I do. 'Twas a rum go, that, and Agnes worshipped it, a fact, can prove it by scores o' people to this day, scores, in them parts. William and Agnes worshipped it, and Edie—she just looked on, 'long of it all, in the same house with them, though she never opened her lips again to her young sister to the day of her death."

"Ah, she died? Well, it's the only way out of such a tangle, poor woman."

"You're sympathizing with the wrong party." Bob filled his pipe again from the brass box; he ignited it with deliberation; going to the open window he spat into a puddle in the road. "The wrong party, Sam; 'twas Agnes that died. She was found on the sofa one morning stone dead, dead as a adder."

"God bless me!" murmured Sam.

"Poisoned!" added Bob, puffing serenely.

"Poisoned!"

Bob repeated the word poisoned. "This was the way of it," he continued: "One morning the mother went out in the yard to collect her eggs, and she began calling out 'Edie, Edie, here a minute, come and look where that hen have laid her egg; I would never have believed it,'—she says. And when Edie went out her mother led her round the back of the outhouse, and there on the top of a wall this hen had laid an egg. 'I would never have believed it, Edie'—she says—'scooped out a nest there beautiful, ain't she? I wondered where her was laying. T'other morning the dog brought an egg round in his mouth and laid it on the doormat. There now Aggie, Aggie, here a minute, come and look where the hen have laid that egg.' And as Aggie didn't answer the mother went in and found her on the sofa in the outhouse, stone dead."

"How'd they account for it?" asked Sam, after a brief interval.

"That's what brings me to the point about that young feller that's going to be hung," said Bob, tapping the newspaper that lay upon the bench. "I don't know what would lie between two young women in a wrangle of that sort; some would get over it quick, but some would never sleep soundly any more not for a minute of their mortal lives. Edie must have been one of that sort. There's people living there now as could tell a lot if they'd a mind to it. Some knowed all about it, could tell you the very shop where Edie managed to get hold of the poison, and could describe to me or to you just how she administrated it in a glass of barley water. Old Harry knew all about it, he knew all about everything, but he favoured Edith and he never budged a word. Clever old chap was Harry, and nothing came out against Edie at the inquest—nor the trial neither."

"Was there a trial then?"

"There was a kind of a trial. Naturally. A beautiful trial. The police came and fetched poor William. They took him away and in due course he was hanged."

"William! But what had he got to do with it?"

"Nothing. It was rough on him, but he hadn't played straight and so nobody struck up for him. They made out a case against him—there was some onlucky bit of evidence which I'll take my oath old Harry knew something about—and William was done for. Ah, when things take a turn against you it's as certain as twelve o'clock, when they take a turn; you get no more chance than a rabbit from a weasel. It's like dropping your matches into a stream, you needn't waste the bending of your back to pick them out—they're no good on, they'll never strike again. And Edith, she sat in court through it all, very white and trembling and sorrowful, but when the judge put his black cap on they do say she blushed and looked across at William and gave a bit of a smile. Well, she had to suffer for his doings, so why shouldn't he suffer for hers. That's how I look at it...."

"But God-a-mighty...!"

"Yes, God-a-mighty knows. Pretty girls they were, both, and as like as two pinks."

There was quiet for some moments while the tiler and the mason emptied their cups of beer. "I think," said Sam then, "the rain's give over now."

"Ah, that it has," cried Bob. "Let's go and do a bid more on this 'bugging church or she won't be done afore Christmas."

POMONA'S BABE

POMONA'S BABE

Johnny Flynn was then seventeen years old. At that age you could not call him boy without vexing him, or man without causing him to blush—his teasing, ruddy and uproarious mother delighted to produce either or both of these manifestations for her offspring was a pale mild creature—but he had given a deal of thought to many manly questions. Marriage, for instance, was one of these. That was an institution he admired but whose joys, whatever they were, he was not anxious to experience; its difficulties and disasters as ironically outlined by the widow Flynn were the subject of his grossest scepticism, scepticism in general being not the least prominent characteristic of Johnny Flynn.

Certainly his sister Pomona was not married; she was only sixteen, an age too early for such bliss, but all the same she was going to have a baby; he had quarrelled with his mother about that. He quarrelled with his mother about most things, she delighted in quarrels, they amused her very much; but on this occasion she was really very angry, or she pretended to be so—which was worse, much worse than the real thing.

* * *

The Flynns were poor people, quite poor, living in two top-floor rooms at the house of a shoemaker, also moderately poor, whose pelting and hammering of soles at evening were a durable grievance to Johnny. He was fond of the shoemaker, a kind bulky tall man of fifty, though he did not like the shoemaker's wife, as bulky as her husband and as tall but not kind to him or to anything except Johnny himself; nor did he like any of the other lodgers, of whom there were several, all without exception beyond the reach of affluence. The Flynn apartments afforded a bedroom in front for Mrs. Flynn and Pomona, a room where Johnny seldom intruded, never without a strained sense of sanctity similar to the feeling he experienced when entering an empty church as he sometimes did. He slept in the other room, the living room, an arrangement that also annoyed him. He was easily annoyed, but he could never go to bed until mother and sister had retired, and for the same reason he had always to rise before they got up, an exasperating abuse of domestic privilege.

One night he had just slipped happily into his bed and begun to read a book called "Rasselas," which the odd-eyed man at the public library had commended to him, when his mother returned to the room, first tapping at the door, for Johnny was a prude as she knew not only from instinct and observation but from protests which had occasionally been addressed to her by the indignant boy. She came in now only half clad, in petticoat and stockinged feet, her arms quite bare. They were powerful arms as they had need to be, for she was an ironer of linen at a laundry, but they were nice to look at and sometimes Johnny liked looking at them, though he did not care for her to run about like that very often. Mrs. Flynn sat down at the foot of his couch and stared at her son.

"Johnny," she began steadily, but paused to rub her forehead with her thick white shiny fingers. "I don't know how to tell you, I'm sure, or what you'll say...." Johnny shook "Rasselas" rather impatiently and heaved a protesting sigh. "I can't think," continued his mother, "no, I can't think that it's our Pomony, but there she is and it's got to be done, I must tell you; besides you're the only man in our family now, so it's only right for you, you see, and she's going to have a baby. Our Pomony!"

The boy turned his face to the wall, although his mother was not looking at him—she was staring at that hole in the carpet near the fender. At last he said, "Humph ... well?" And as his mother did not say anything, he added, "What about it, I don't mind?" Mrs. Flynn was horrified at his unconcern, or she pretended to be so; Johnny was never sure about the genuineness of her moods. It was most unfilial, but he was like that—so was Mrs. Flynn. Now she cried out, "You'll have to mind, there, you must. I can't take everything on my own shoulders. You're the only man left in our family now, you must, Johnny. What are we to do?"

He glared at the wallpaper a foot from his eyes. It had an unbearable pattern of blue but otherwise indescribable flowers; he had it in his mind to have some other pattern there—some day.

"Eh?" asked his mother sharply, striking the foot of the bed with her fist.

"Why ... there's nothing to be done ... now ... I suppose." He was blushing furiously. "How did it happen, when will it be?"

"It's a man she knows, he got hold of her, his name is Stringer. Another two months about. Stringer. Hadn't you noticed anything? Everybody else has. You are a funny boy, I can't make you out at all, Johnny, I can't make you out. Stringer his name is, but I'll make him pay dearly for it, and that's what I want you—to talk to you about. Of course he denies of everything, they always do."

Mrs. Flynn sighed at this disgusting perfidy, brightening however when her son began to discuss the problem. But she talked so long and he got so sleepy at last that he was very glad when she went to bed again. Secretly she was both delighted and disappointed at his easy acceptance of her dreadful revelation; fearing a terrible outburst of anger she had kept the knowledge from him for a long time. She was glad to escape that, it is true, but she rather hungered for some flashing reprobation of this unknown beast, this Stringer. She swore she would bring him to book, but she felt old and lonely, and Johnny was a strange son, not very virile. The mother had told Pomona terrifying prophetic tales of what Johnny would do, what he would be certain to do; he would, for instance, murder that Stringer and drive Pomony into the street; of course he would. Yet here he was, quite calm about it, as if he almost liked it. Well, she had told him, she could do no more, she would leave it to him.

In the morning Johnny greeted his sister with tender affection and at evening, having sent her to bed, he and his mother resumed their discussion.

"Do you know, mother," he said, "she is quite handsome, I never noticed it before."

Mrs. Flynn regarded him with desperation and then informed him that his sister was an ugly disgusting little trollop who ought to be birched.

"No, no, you are wrong, mother, it's bad, but it's all right."

"You think you know more about such things than your own mother, I suppose." Mrs. Flynn sniffed and glared.

He said it to her gently: "Yes."

She produced a packet of notepaper and envelopes "*The Monster Packet for a Penny*," all complete with a wisp of pink blotting paper and a penholder without a nib, which she had bought at the Chandler's on her way home that evening, along with some sago and some hair oil for Johnny whose stiff unruly hair provoked such spasms of rage in her bosom that she declared that she was "sick to death of it." On the supper table lay also a platter, a loaf, a basin of mustard pickle, and a plate with round lengths of cheese shaped like small candles.

"Devil blast him!" muttered Mrs. Flynn as she fetched from a cupboard shelf a sour-looking bottle labelled *Writing Fluid*, a dissolute pen, and requested Johnny to compose a letter to Stringer—devil blast him!—telling him of the plight of her daughter Pomona Flynn, about whom she desired him to know that she had already consulted her lawyers and the chief of police and intimating that unless she heard from him satisfactory by the day after tomorrow the matter would pass out of her hands.

"That's no good, it's not the way," declared her son thoughtfully; Mrs. Flynn therefore sat humbly confronting him and awaited the result of his cogitations. Johnny was not a very robust youth, but he was growing fast now, since he had taken up with running; he was very fleet, so Mrs. Flynn understood, and had already won a silver-plated hot water jug, which they used for the milk. But still he was thin and not tall, his dark hair was scattered; his white face was a nice face, thought Mrs. Flynn, very nice, only there was always something strange about his clothes. She couldn't help that now, but he had such queer fancies, there was no other boy in the street whose trousers were so baggy or of such a colour. His starched collars were all right of course, beautifully white and shiny, she got them up herself, and they set his neck off nicely.

"All we need do," her son broke in, "is just tell him."

"Tell him?"

"Yes, just tell him about it—it's very unfortunate—and ask him to come and see you. I hope, though," he paused, "I hope they won't want to go and get married."

"He ought to be made to, devil blast him," cried Mrs. Flynn, "only she's frightened, she is; afraid of her mortal life of him! We don't want him here, neither, she says he's a nasty horrible man."

Johnny sat dumb for some moments. Pomona was a day girl in service at a restaurant. Stringer was a clerk to an auctioneer. The figure of his pale little sister shrinking before a ruffian (whom he figured as a fat man with a red beard) startled and stung him.

"Besides," continued Mrs. Flynn, "he's just going to be married to some woman, some pretty judy, God help her ... in fact, as like as not he's married to her already by now. No, I gave up that idea long ago, I did, before I told you, long ago."

"We can only tell him about Pomony then, and ask him what he would like to do."

"What he would *like* to do, well, certainly!" protested the widow.

"And if he's a decent chap," continued Johnny serenely, "it will be all right, there won't be any difficulty. If he ain't, then we can do something else."

His mother was reluctant to concur but the boy had his way. He sat with his elbows on the table, his head pressed in his hands, but he could not think out the things he wanted to say to this man. He would look up and stare around the room as if he were in a strange place, though it was not strange to him at all for he had lived in it many years. There was not much furniture in the apartment, yet there was but little space in it. The big table was covered with American cloth, mottled and shiny. Two or three chairs full of age and discomfort stood upon a carpet that was full of holes and stains. There were some shelves in a recess, an engraving framed in maple of the player scene from "Hamlet," and near by on the wall hung a gridiron whose prongs were woven round with coloured wools and decorated with satin bows. Mrs. Flynn had a passion for vases, and two of these florid objects bought at a fair companioned a clock whose once snowy face had long since turned sallow because of the oil Mrs. Flynn had administered "to make it go properly."

But he could by no means think out this letter; his mother sat so patiently watching him that he asked her to go and sit in the other room. Then he sat on, sniffing, as if thinking with his nose, while the room began to smell of the smoking lamp. He was remembering how years ago, when they were little children, he had seen Pomony in her nightgown and, angered with her for some petty reason, he had punched her on the side. Pomony had turned white, she could not speak, she could not breathe. He had been momentarily proud of that blow, it was a good blow, he had never hit another boy like that. But Pomony had fallen into a chair, her face tortured with pain, her eyes filled with tears that somehow would not fall. Then a fear seized him, horrible, piercing, frantic: she was dying, she would die, and there was nothing he could do to stop her! In passionate remorse and pity he had flung himself before her, kissing her feet—they were small and beautiful though not very clean,—until at last he had felt Pomony's arms droop caressingly around him and heard Pomony's voice speaking lovingly and forgivingly to him.

After a decent interval his mother returned to him.

"What are we going to do about *her*?" she asked, "she'll have to go away."

"Away! Do you mean go to a home? No, but why go away? I'm not ashamed; what is there to be ashamed of?"

"Who the deuce is going to look after her? You talk like a tom-fool—yes, you are," insisted Mrs. Flynn passionately. "I'm out all day from one week's end to the other. She can't be left alone, and the people downstairs are none too civil about it as it is. She'll have to go to the workhouse, that's all."

Johnny was aghast, indignant, and really angry. He would never never consent to such a thing! Pomony! Into a workhouse! She should not, she should stop at home, here, like always, and have a nurse.

"Fool!" muttered his mother, with castigating scorn. "Where's the money for nurses and doctors to come from? I've got no money for such things!"

"I'll get some!" declared Johnny hotly.

"Where?"

"I'll sell something."

"What?"

"I'll save up."

"How?"

* * *

"And I'll borrow some."

"You'd better shut up now or I'll knock your head off," cried his mother. "Fidding and fadding about—you're daft!"

"She shan't go to any workhouse!"

"Fool!" repeated his mother, revealing her disgust at his hopeless imbecility.

"I tell you she shall not go there," shouted the boy, stung into angry resentment by her contempt.

"She shall, she must."

"I say she shan't!"

"O don't be such a blasted fool," cried the distracted woman, rising from her chair.

Johnny sprang to his feet almost screaming, "You are the blasted fool, you, you!"

Mrs. Flynn seized a table knife and struck at her son's face with it. He leaped away in terror, his startled appearance, glaring eyes and strained figure so affecting Mrs. Flynn that she dropped the knife, and, sinking into her chair, burst into peals of hysterical laughter. Recovering himself the boy hastened to the laughing woman. The maddening peals continued and increased, shocking him, unnerving him again; she was dying, she would die. His mother's laughter had always been harsh but delicious to him, it was so infectious, but this was demoniacal, it was horror.

"O, don't, don't, mother, don't," he cried, fondling her and pressing her yelling face to his breast. But she pushed him fiercely away and the terrifying laughter continued to sear his very soul until he could bear it no longer. He struck at her shoulders with clenched fist and shook her frenziedly, frantically, crying:

"Stop it, stop, O stop it, she'll go mad, stop it, stop."

He was almost exhausted, when suddenly Pomona rushed into the room in her nightgown. Her long black hair tumbled in lovely locks about her pale face and her shoulder; her feet were bare.

"O Johnny, what are you doing?" gasped his little pale sister Pomony, who seemed so suddenly, so unbelievably, turned into a woman. "Let her alone."

She pulled the boy away, fondling and soothing their distracted mother until Mrs. Flynn partially recovered.

"Come to bed now," commanded Pomona, and Mrs. Flynn thereupon, still giggling, followed her child. When he was alone trembling Johnny turned down the lamp flame which had filled the room with smoky fumes. His glance rested upon the table knife; the room was silent and oppressive now. He glared at the picture of Hamlet, at the clock with the oily face, at the notepaper lying white upon the table. They had all turned into quivering semblances of the things they were; he was crying.

II

A letter, indited in the way he desired, was posted by Johnny on his way to work next morning. He was clerk in the warehouse of a wholesale provision merchant and he kept tally, in some underground cellars carpeted with sawdust, of hundreds of sacks of sugar and cereals, tubs of butter, of lard, of treacle, chests of tea, a regular promontory of cheeses, cases of candles, jam, starch, and knife polish, many of them stamped with the mysterious words "Factory Bulked." He did not like those words, they sounded ugly and their meaning was obscure. Sometimes he took the cheese-tasting implement from the foreman's bench and, when no one was looking, pierced it into a fine Cheddar or Stilton, withdrawing it with a little cylinder of cheese lying like a small candle in the curved blade. Then he would bite off the piece of rind, restore it neatly to the body of the cheese, and drop the other candle-like piece into his pocket. Sometimes his pocket was so full of cheese that he was reluctant to approach the foreman fearing he would smell it. He was very fond of cheese. All of them liked cheese.

The Flynns waited several days for a reply to the letter, but none came. Stringer did not seem to think it called for any reply. At the end of a week Johnny wrote again to his sister's seducer. Pomona had given up her situation at the restaurant; her brother was conspicuously and unfailingly tender to her. He saved what money he could, spent none upon himself, and brought home daily an orange or an egg for the girl. He wrote a third letter to the odious Stringer, not at all threateningly, but just invitingly, persuasively. And he waited, but waited in vain. Then in that underground cheese tunnel where he worked he began to plot an alternate course of action, and as time passed bringing no recognition from Stringer his plot began to crystallize and determine itself. It was nothing else than to murder the man; he would kill him, he had thought it out, it could be done. He would wait for him near Stringer's lodgings one dark night and beat out his brains with a club. All that was necessary then would be to establish an alibi. For some days Johnny dwelt so gloatingly upon the details of this retribution that he forgot about the alibi. By this time he had accumulated from his mother—for he could never once bring himself to interrogate Pomona personally about her misfortune—sufficient description of Stringer to recognize him among a thousand, so he thought. It appeared that he was not a large man with a red beard, but a small man with glasses, spats, and a slight limp, who always attended a certain club of which he was the secretary at a certain hour on certain nights in each week. To Johnny's mind, the alibi was not merely important in itself, it was a romantic necessity. And it was so easy; it would be quite sufficient for Johnny to present himself at the public library where he was fairly well known. The library was quite close to Stringer's lodgings and they, fortunately, were in a dark quiet little street. He would borrow a book from the odd-eyed man in the reference department, retire to one of the inner study rooms, and at half past seven creep out unseen, creep out, creep out with his thick stick and wait by the house in that dark quiet little street; it was very quiet, and it would be very dark; wait there for him all in the dark, just creep quietly out—and wait. But in order to get that alibi quite perfect he would have to take a friend with him to the library room, so that the friend could swear that he had really been there all the time, because it was just possible the odd-eyed man wouldn't be prepared to swear to it; he did not seem able to see very much, but it was hard to tell with people like that.

Johnny Flynn had not told any of his friends about his sister's misfortune; in time, time enough, they were bound to hear of it. Of all his friends he rejected the close ones, those of whom he was very fond, and chose a stupid lump of a fellow, massive and nasal, named Donald. Though awkward and fat he had joined Johnny's running club; Johnny had trained him for his first race. But he had subjected Donald to such exhausting exercise, what with skipping, gymnastics, and tiring jaunts, that though his bulk disappeared his strength went with it; to Johnny's great chagrin he grew weak, and failed ignominiously in the race. Donald thereafter wisely rejected all offers of assistance and projected a training system of his own. For weeks he tramped miles into hilly country, in the heaviest of boots to the soles of which he had nailed some thick pads of lead. When he donned his light running shoes for his second race he displayed an agility and suppleness, a god-like ease, that won not only the race, but the admiration and envy of all the competitors. It was this dull lumpish Donald that Johnny fixed upon to assist him. He was a great tool and it would not matter if he did get himself into trouble. Even if he did Johnny could get him out again, by confessing to the police; so that was all right. He asked Donald to go to the library with him on a certain evening to read a book called "Rasselas"—it was a grand book, very exciting—and Donald said he would go. He did not propose to tell Donald of his homicidal intention; he would just sit him down in the library with "Rasselas" while he himself sat at another table behind Donald, yes, behind him; even if Donald noticed him creeping out he would say he was only going to the counter to get another book. It was all quite clear, and safe. He would be able to creep out, creep out, rush up to the dark little street—yes, he would ask Donald for a piece of that lead and wrap it round the head of the stick—he would creep out, and in ten minutes or twenty he would be back in the library again asking for another book or sitting down by Donald as if he had not been outside the place, as if nothing had happened as far as he was concerned, nothing at all!

The few intervening days passed with vexing deliberation. Each night seemed the best of all possible nights for the deed, each hour that Stringer survived seemed a bad hour for the world. They were bad slow hours for Johnny, but at last the day dawned, passed, darkness came, and the hour rushed upon him.

He took his stick and called for Donald.

"Can't come," said Donald, limping to the door in answer to Johnny's knock. "I been and hurt my leg."

For a moment Johnny was full of an inward silent blasphemy that flashed from a sudden tremendous hatred, but he said calmly:

"But still ... no, you haven't ... what have you hurt it for?"

* * *

Donald was not able to deal with such locution. He ignored it and said:

"My knee-cap, my shin, Oo, come and have a look. We was mending a flue ... it was the old man's wheelbarrow.... Didn't I tell him of it neither!"

"O, you told him of it?"

Johnny listened to his friend's narration very abstractedly and at last went off to the library by himself. As he walked away he was conscious of a great feeling of relief welling up in him. He could not get an alibi without Donald, not a sure one, so he would not be able to do anything tonight. He felt relieved, he whistled as he walked, he was happy again, but he went on to the library. He was going to rehearse the alibi by himself, that was the wise thing to do, of course, rehearse it, practise it; it would be perfect next week when Donald was better. So he did this. He got out a book from the odd-eyed man, who strangely enough was preoccupied and did not seem to recognize him. It was disconcerting, that; he specially wanted the man to notice him. He went into the study room rather uneasily. Ten minutes later he crept out unseen, carrying his stick—he had forgotten to ask Donald for the piece of lead—and was soon lurking in the shadow of the dark quiet little street.

It was a perfect spot, there could not be a better place, not in the middle of a town. The house had an area entry through an iron gate; at the end of a brick pathway, over a coalplate, five or six stone steps led steeply up to a narrow front door with a brass letter box, a brass knocker, and a glazed fanlight painted 29. The windows too were narrow and the whole house had a squeezed appearance. A church clock chimed eight strokes. Johnny began to wonder what he would do, what would happen, if Stringer were suddenly to come out of that gateway. Should he—would he—could he...? And then the door at the top of the steps did open wide and framed there in the lighted space young Flynn saw the figure of his own mother.

She came down the steps alone and he followed her short jerky footsteps secretly until she reached the well-lit part of the town, where he joined her. It was quite simple, she explained to him with an air of superior understanding: she had just paid Mr. Stringer a visit, waiting for letters from that humbug had made her "popped." Had he thought she would creep on her stomach and beg for a fourpenny piece when she could put him in jail if all were known, as she would too, if it hadn't been for her children, poor little fatherless things? No, middling boxer, not that! So she had left off work early, had gone and caught him at his lodgings and taxed him with it. He denied of it; he was that cocky, it so mortified her, that she had snatched up the clock and thrown it at him. Yes, his own clock.

"But it was only a little one, though. He was frightened out of his life and run upstairs. Then his landlady came rushing in. I told her all about it, everything, and she was that 'popped' with him she give me the name and address of his feons—their banns is been put up. She made him come downstairs and face me, and his face was as white as the driven snow. Johnny, it was. He was obliged to own up. The lady said to him 'Whatever have you been at, Mr. Stringer,' she said to him. 'I can't believe it, knowing you for ten years, you must have forgot yourself.' O, a proper understanding it was," declared Mrs. Flynn finally; "his lawyers are going to write to us and put everything in order; Duckle & Hoole, they are."

Again a great feeling of relief welled up in the boy's breast, as if, having been dragged into a horrible vortex he had been marvellously cast free again.

The days that followed were blessedly tranquil, though Johnny was often smitten with awe at the thought of what he had contemplated. That fool, Donald, too, one evening insisted on accompanying him to the library where he spent an hour of baffled understanding over the pages of "Rasselas." But the lawyers Duckle & Hoole aroused a tumult of hatred in Mrs. Flynn. They pared down her fond anticipations to the minimum; they put so much slight upon her family, and such a gentlemanly decorum and generous forbearance upon the behaviour of their client, Mr. Stringer, that she became inarticulate. When informed that that gentleman desired no intercourse whatsoever with any Flynn or the offspring thereof she became speechless. Shortly, Messrs. Duckle & Hoole begged to submit for her approval a draft agreement embodying their client's terms, one provision of which was that if the said Flynns violated the agreement by taking any proceedings against the said Stringer they should thereupon *ipso facto* willy nilly or whatever forfeit and pay unto him the said Stringer not by way of penalty but as damages the sum of £100. Whereupon Mrs. Flynn recovered her speech and suffered a little tender irony to emerge.

The shoemaker, whose opinion upon this draft agreement was solicited, confessed himself as much baffled by its phraseology as he was indignant at its tenor and terms.

"That man," he declared solemnly to Johnny, "ought to have his brain knocked out"; and he conveyed by subtle intimations to the boy that that was the course he would favour were he himself standing in Johnny's shoes. "One dark night," he had roared with a dreadful glare in his eyes, "with a neat heavy stick!"

The Flynns also consulted a cabman who lodged in the house. His legal qualifications appeared to lie in the fact that he had driven the private coach of a major general whose son, now a fruit farmer in British Columbia, had once been entered for the bar. The cabman was a very positive and informative cabman. "List and learn," he would say, "list and learn": and he would regale Johnny, or any one else, with an oration to which you might listen as hard as you liked but from which you could not learn. He was husky, with a thick red neck and the cheek bones of a horse. Having perused the agreement with one eye judicially cocked, the other being screened by a drooping lid adorned with a glowing nodule, he carefully refolded the folios and returned them to the boy:

"Any judge—who was up to snuff—would impound that dockyment."

* * *

"What's that?"

"They would impound it," repeated the cabman smiling wryly.

"But what's impound it? What for?"

"I tell you it would be impounded, that dockyment would," asseverated the cabman. Once more he took the papers from Johnny, opened them out, reflected upon them and returned them again without a word. Catechism notwithstanding, the oracle remained impregnably mystifying.

The boy continued to save his pocket money. His mother went about her work with a grim air, having returned the draft agreement to the lawyers with an ungracious acceptance of the terms.

One April evening Johnny went home to an empty room; Pomona was out. He prepared his tea and afterwards sat reading "Tales of a Grandfather." That was a book if anybody wanted a book! When darkness came he descended the stairs to enquire of the shoemaker's wife about Pomony, he was anxious. The shoemaker's wife was absent too and it was late when she returned accompanied by his mother.

Pomona's hour had come—they had taken her to the workhouse—only just in time—a little boy—they were both all right—he was an uncle.

His mother's deceit stupified him, he felt shamed, deeply shamed, but after a while that same recognizable feeling of relief welled up in his breast and drenched him with satisfactions. After all what could it matter where a person was born, or where one died, as long as you had your chance of growing up at all, and, if lucky, of growing up all right. But this babe had got to bear the whole burden of its father's misdeed, though; it had got to behave itself or it would have to pay its father a hundred pounds as damages. Perhaps that was what that queer bit of poetry meant, "The child is father of the man."

His mother swore that they were very good and clean and kind at the workhouse, everything of the best and most expensive; there was nothing she would have liked better than to have gone there herself when Johnny and Pomony were born.

"And if ever I have any more," Mrs. Flynn sighed, but with profound conviction, "I will certainly go there."

Johnny gave her half the packet of peppermints he had bought for Pomona. With some of his saved money he bought her a bottle of stout—she looked tired and sad—she was very fond of stout. The rest of the money he gave her for to buy Pomony something when she visited her. He would not go himself to visit her, not there. He spent the long intervening evenings at the library—the odd-eyed man had shown him a lovely book about birds. He was studying it. On Sundays, in the spring, he was going out to catch birds himself, out in the country, with a catapult. The cuckoo was a marvellous bird. So was a titlark. Donald Gower found a goatsucker's nest last year.

Then one day he ran from work all the way home, knowing Pomony would at last be there. He walked slowly up the street to recover his breath. He stepped up the stairs, humming quite casually, and tapped at the door of their room—he did not know why he tapped. He heard Pomony's voice calling him. A thinner paler Pomony stood by the hearth, nursing a white-clothed bundle, the fat pink babe.

"O, my dear!" cried her ecstatic brother, "the beauty he is! what larks we'll have with him!"

He took Pomona into his arms, crushing the infant against her breast and his own. But she did not mind. She did not rebuke him, she even let him dandle her precious babe.

"Look, what is his name to be, Pomony? Let's call him Rasselas."

Pomona looked at him very doubtfully.

"Or would you like William Wallace then, or Robert Bruce?"

"I shall call him Johnny," said Pomona.

"O, that's silly!" protested her brother. But Pomona was quite positive about this. He fancied there were tears in her eyes, she was always tender-hearted.

"I shall call him Johnny, Johnny Flynn."

THE HURLY-BURLY

THE HURLY-BURLY

The Weetmans, mother, son, and daughter, lived on a thriving farm. It was small enough, God knows, but it had always been a turbulent place of abode. For the servant it was: "Phemy, do this," or "Phemy, have you done that?" from dawn to dark, and even from dark to dawn there was a hovering of unrest. The widow Weetman, a partial invalid, was the only figure that manifested any semblance of tranquillity, and it was a misleading one for she sat day after day on her large hams knitting and nodding and lifting her grey face only to grumble, her spectacled eyes transfixing the culprit with a basilisk glare. And her daughter Alice, the housekeeper, who had a large face, a dominating face, in some respects she was all face, was like a blast in a corridor with her "Maize for the hens, Phemy!—More firewood, Phemy!—Who has set the trap in the harness room?—Come along!—Have you scoured the skimming pans?—Why not!—Where are you idling?—Come along, Phemy, I have no time to waste this morning, you really must help me." It was not only in the house that this cataract of industry flowed; outside there was activity enough for a regiment. A master-farmer's work consists largely of a series of conversations with other master-farmers, a long-winded way of doing long-headed things, but Glastonbury Weetman, the son, was not like that at all; he was the incarnation of energy, always doing and doing, chock-full of orders, adjurations, objurgatives, blame, and blasphemy, That was the kind of place Phemy Madigan worked at. No one could rest on laurels there. The farm and the home possessed everybody, lock, stock, and barrel; work was like a tiger, it ate you up implacably. The Weetmans did not mind—they liked being eaten by such a tiger.

After six or seven years of this Alice went back to marry an old sweetheart in Canada, where the Weetmans had originally come from, but Phemy's burden was in no way lessened thereby. There were as many things to wash and sew and darn; there was always a cart of churns about to dash for a train it could not possibly catch, or a horse to shoe that could not possibly be spared. Weetman hated to see his people merely walking: "Run over to the barn for that hay-fork," or "Slip across to the ricks, quick now," he would cry, and if ever an unwary hen hampered his own path it did so only once—and no more. His labourers were mere things of flesh and blood, but they occasionally resented his ceaseless flagellations. Glas Weetman did not like to be impeded or controverted; one day in a rage he had smashed that lumbering loon of a carter called Gathercole. For this he was sent to jail for a month.

The day after he had been sentenced Phemy Madigan, alone in the house with Mrs. Weetman, had waked at the usual early hour. It was a foggy September morning; Sampson and his boy Daniel were clattering pails in the dairy shed. The girl felt sick and gloomy as she dressed; it was a wretched house to work in, crickets in the kitchen, cockroaches in the garret, spiders and mice everywhere. It was an old long low house; she knew that when she descended the stairs the walls would be stained with autumnal dampness, the banisters and rails oozing with moisture. She wished she was a lady and married and living in a palace fifteen stories high.

It was fortunate that she was big and strong, though she had been only a charity girl taken from the workhouse by the Weetmans when she was fourteen years old. That was seven years ago. It was fortunate that she was fed well at the farm, very well indeed; it was the one virtue of the place. But her meals did not counterbalance things; that farm ate up the body and blood of people. And at times the pressure was charged with a special excitation, as if a taut elastic thong had been plucked and released with a reverberating ping.

It was so on this morning. Mrs. Weetman was dead in her bed.

At that crisis a new sense descended upon the girl, a sense of responsibility. She was not in fear, she felt no grief or surprise. It concerned her in some way, but she herself was unconcerned, and she slid without effort into the position of mistress of the farm. She opened a window and looked out of doors. A little way off a boy with a red scarf stood by an open gate.

"Oi ... oi, kup, kup, kup!" he cried to the cows in that field. Some of the cows having got up stared amiably at him, others sat on ignoring his hail, while one or two plodded deliberately towards him. "Oi ... oi, kup, kup, kup!"

"Lazy rascal, that boy," remarked Phemy, "we shall have to get rid of him. Dan'l! Come here, Dan'l!" she screamed, waving her arm wildly. "Quick!"

She sent him away for police and doctor. At the inquest there were no relatives in England who could be called upon, no witnesses other than Phemy. After the funeral she wrote a letter to Glastonbury Weetman in jail informing him of his bereavement, but to this he made no reply. Meanwhile the work of the farm was pressed forward under her control, for though she was revelling in her personal release from the torment she would not permit others to share her intermission. She had got Mrs. Weetman's keys and her box of money. She paid the two men and the boy their wages week by week. The last of the barley was reaped, the oats stacked, the roots hoed, the churns sent daily under her supervision. And always she was bustling the men.

"O dear me, these lazy rogues!" she would complain to the empty rooms, "they waste time, so it's robbery, it *is* robbery. You may wear yourself to the bone and what does it signify to such as them? All the responsibility, too!—They would take your skin if they could get it off you—and they can't!"

She kept such a sharp eye on the corn and meal and eggs that Sampson got surly. She placated him by handing him Mr. Weetman's gun and a few cartridges, saying: "Just shoot me a couple of rabbits over in the warren when you got time." At the end of the day Mr. Sampson had not succeeded in killing a rabbit so he kept the gun and the cartridges many more days. Phemy was really happy. The gloom of the farm had disappeared. The farmhouse and everything about it looked beautiful, beautiful indeed with its yard full of ricks, the pond full of ducks, the fields full of sheep and cattle, and the trees still full of leaves and birds. She flung maize about the yard; the hens scampered towards it and the young pigs galloped, quarrelling over the grains which they groped and snuffed for, grinding each one separately in their iron jaws, while the white pullets stalked delicately among them, picked up the maize seeds, One, Two, Three, and swallowed them like ladies. Sometimes on cold mornings she would go outside and give an apple to the fat bay pony when he galloped back from the station. He would stand puffing with a kind of rapture, the wind from his nostrils discharging in the frosty air vague shapes like smoky trumpets. Presently upon his hide a little ball of liquid mysteriously suspired, grew, slid, dropped from his flanks into the road. And then drops would begin to come from all parts of him until the road beneath was dabbled by a shower from his dew-distilling outline. Phemy would say:

"The wretches! They were so late they drove him near distracted, poor thing. Lazy rogues, but wait till master comes back, they'd better be careful!"

And if any friendly person in the village asked her: "How are you getting on up there, Phemy?" she would reply, "Oh, as well as you can expect with so much to be done—and such men." The interlocutor might hint that there was no occasion in the circumstances to distress oneself, but then Phemy would be vexed. To her, honesty was as holy as the sabbath to a little child. Behind her back they jested about her foolishness; but, after all, wisdom isn't a process, it's a result, it's the fruit of the tree. One can't be wise, one can only be fortunate.

On the last day of her Elysium the workhouse master and the chaplain had stalked over the farm shooting partridges. In the afternoon she met them and asked for a couple of birds for Weetman's return on the morrow. The workhouse was not far away, it was on a hill facing west, and at sunset time its windows would often catch the glare so powerfully that the whole building seemed to burn like a box of contained and smokeless fire. Very beautiful it looked to Phemy.

II

The men had come to work punctually and Phemy herself found so much to do that she had no time to give the pony an apple. She cleared the kitchen once and for all of the pails, guns, harness, and implements that so hampered its domestic intention, and there were abundant signs elsewhere of a new impulse at work in the establishment. She did not know at what hour to expect the prisoner so she often went to the garden gate and glanced up the road. The night had been wild with windy rain, but the morn was sparklingly clear though breezy still. Crisp leaves rustled about the road where the polished chestnuts beside the parted husks lay in numbers, mixed with coral buds of the yews. The sycamore leaves were black rags, but the delicate elm foliage fluttered down like yellow stars. There was a brown field neatly adorned with white coned heaps of turnips, behind it a small upland of deeply green lucerne, behind that nothing but blue sky and rolling cloud. The turnips, washed by the rain, were creamy polished globes.

When at last he appeared she scarcely knew him. Glas Weetman was a big, though not fleshy, man of thirty with a large boyish face and a flat bald head. Now he had a thick dark beard. He was hungry, but his first desire was to be shaved. He stood before the kitchen mirror, first clipping the beard away with scissors, and as he lathered the remainder he said:

"Well, it's a bad state of things this, my sister dead and my mother gone to America. What shall us do?"

He perceived in the glass that she was smiling.

"There's naught funny in it, my comic gal," he bawled indignantly, "what are you laughing at?"

"I wer'n't laughing. It's your mother that's dead."

"My mother that's dead. I know."

"And Miss Alice that's gone to America."

"To America, I know, I know, so you can stop making your bullock's eyes and get me something to eat. What's been going on here?"

She gave him an outline of affairs. He looked at her sternly when he asked her about his sweetheart.

"Has Rosa Beauchamp been along here?"

"No," said Phemy, and he was silent. She was surprised at the question. The Beauchamps were such respectable high-up people that to Phemy's simple mind they could not possibly favour an alliance, now, with a man that had been in prison: it was absurd, but she did not say so to him. And she was bewildered to find that her conviction was wrong, for Rosa came along later in the day and everything between her master and his sweetheart was just as before; Phemy had not divined so much love and forgiveness in high-up people.

It was the same with everything else. The old harsh rushing life was resumed, Weetman turned to his farm with an accelerated vigour to make up for the lost time and the girl's golden week or two of ease became an unforgotten dream. The pails, the guns, the harness, crept back into the kitchen. Spiders, cockroaches, and mice were more noticeable than ever before, and Weetman himself seemed embittered, harsher. Time alone could never still him, there was a force in his frame, a buzzing in his blood. But there was a difference between them now; Phemy no longer feared him. She obeyed him, it is true, with eagerness, she worked in the house like a woman and in the fields like a man. They ate their meals together, and from this dissonant comradeship the girl in a dumb kind of way began to love him.

One April evening on coming in from the fields he found her lying on the couch beneath the window, dead plumb fast asleep, with no meal ready at all. He flung his bundle of harness to the flags and bawled angrily to her. To his surprise she did not stir. He was somewhat abashed, he stepped over to look at her. She was lying on her side. There was a large rent in her bodice between sleeve and shoulder; her flesh looked soft and agreeable to him. Her shoes had slipped off to the floor; her lips were folded in a sleepy pout.

"Why, she's quite a pretty cob," he murmured. "She's all right, she's just tired, the Lord above knows what for."

But he could not rouse the sluggard. Then a fancy moved him to lift her in his arms; he carried her from the kitchen and staggering up the stairs laid the sleeping girl on her own bed. He then went downstairs and ate pie and drank beer in the candle-light, guffawing once or twice, "A pretty cob, rather." As he stretched himself after the meal a new notion amused him: he put a plateful of food upon a tray together with a mug of beer and the candle. Doffing his heavy boots and leggings he carried the tray into Phemy's room. And he stopped there.

III

The new circumstance that thus slipped into her life did not effect any noticeable alteration of its general contour and progress, Weetman did not change towards her. Phemy accepted his mastership not alone because she loved him but because her powerful sense of loyalty covered all the possible opprobrium. She did not seem to mind his continued relations with Rosa.

Towards midsummer one evening Glastonbury came in in the late dusk. Phemy was there in the darkened kitchen. "Master," she said immediately he entered. He stopped before her. She continued: "Something's happened."

"Huh, while the world goes popping round something shall always happen."

"It's me—I'm took—a baby, master," she said. He stood stock-still. His face was to the light, she could not see the expression on his face, perhaps he wanted to embrace her.

"Let's have a light, sharp," he said in his brusque way. "The supper smells good but I can't see what I'm smelling, and I can only fancy what I be looking at."

She lit the candles and they ate supper in silence. Afterwards he sat away from the table with his legs outstretched and crossed, hands sunk into pockets, pondering while the girl cleared the table. Soon he put his powerful arm around her waist and drew her to sit on his knees.

"Are ye sure o' that?" he demanded.

She was sure.

"Quite?"

She was quite sure.

"Ah, well then," he sighed conclusively, "we'll be married."

The girl sprang to her feet. "No, no, no—how can you be married—you don't mean that—not married—there's Miss Beauchamp!" She paused and added, a little unsteadily: "She's your true love, master."

"Ay, but I'll not wed her," he cried sternly. "If there's no gainsaying this that's come on you, I'll stand to my guns. It's right and proper for we to have a marriage."

His great thick-fingered hands rested upon his knees; the candles threw a wash of light upon his polished leggings; he stared into the fireless grate.

"But we do not want to do that," said the girl, dully and doubtfully. "You have given your ring to her, you've given her your word. I don't want you to do this for me. It's all right, master, it's all right."

"Are ye daft?" he cried. "I tell you we'll wed. Don't keep clacking about Rosa.... I'll stand to my guns." He paused before adding: "She'd gimme the rightabout, fine now—don't you see, stupid—but I'll not give her the chance."

Her eyes were lowered. "She's your true love, master."

"What would become of you and your child? Ye couldn't bide here!"

"No," said the trembling girl.

"I'm telling you what we must do, modest and proper; there's naught else to be done, and I'm middling glad of it, I am. Life's a see-saw affair. I'm middling glad of this."

So, soon, without a warning to any one, least of all to Rosa Beauchamp, they were married by the registrar. The change in her domestic status produced no other change; in marrying Weetman she had married all his ardour, she was swept into its current. She helped to milk cows, she boiled nauseating messes for pigs, chopped mangolds, mixed meal, and sometimes drove a harrow in his windy fields. Though they slept together she was still his servant. Sometimes he called her his "pretty little cob" and then she knew he was fond of her. But in general his custom was disillusioning. His way with her was his way with his beasts; he knew what he wanted, it was easy to get. If for a brief space a little romantic flower began to bud in her breast it was frozen as a bud, and the vague longing disappeared at length from her eyes. And she became aware that Rosa Beauchamp was not yet done with; somewhere in the darkness of the fields Glastonbury still met her. Phemy did not mind.

In the new year she bore him a son that died as it came to life. Glas was angry at that, as angry as if he had lost a horse. He felt that he had been duped, that the marriage had been a stupid sacrifice, and in this he was savagely supported by Rosa. And yet Phemy did not mind; the farm had got its grip upon her, it was consuming her body and blood.

Weetman was just going to drive into town; he sat fuming in the trap behind the fat bay pony.

"Bring me that whip from the passage," he shouted; "there's never a damn thing handy!"

Phemy appeared with the whip. "Take me with you," she said.

"God-a-mighty! What for? I be comin' back in an hour. They ducks want looking over and you've all the taties to grade."

She stared at him irresolutely.

"And who's to look after the house? You know it won't lock up—the key's lost. Get up there!"

* * *

He cracked his whip in the air as the pony dashed away.

In the summer Phemy fell sick, her arm swelled enormously. The doctor came again and again. It was blood-poisoning, caught from a diseased cow that she had milked with a cut finger. A nurse arrived but Phemy knew she was doomed, and though tortured with pain she was for once vexed and protestant. For it was a June night, soft and nubile, with a marvellous moon; a nightingale threw its impetuous garland into the air. She lay listening to it, and thinking with sad pleasure of the time when Glastonbury was in prison, how grand she was in her solitude, ordering everything for the best and working superbly. She wanted to go on and on for evermore, though she knew she had never known peace in maidenhood or marriage. The troubled waters of the world never ceased to flow; in the night there was no rest—only darkness. Nothing could emerge now. She was leaving it all to Rosa Beauchamp. Glastonbury was gone out somewhere—perhaps to meet Rosa in the fields. There was the nightingale, and it was very bright outside.

"Nurse," moaned the dying girl, "what was I born into the world at all for?"